Eventyr

Book One

by Ellias Quinn

ISBN 978-1-944755-01-0

Published by Second March, LLC
www.elliasquinn.com

For my readers.

Table of Contents

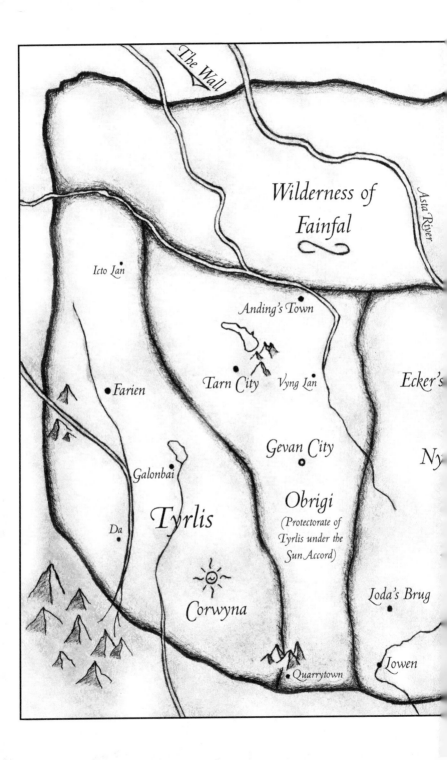

Velana dri alva,	Awaken the fairies,
drimesk ermoli.	the forest is young.
Dri dyri ajarten,	The animals await,
driskur erusi.	the sun is new.
Velana dri alva,	Awaken the fairies,
kothym ervanoss.	their home is alive.
Den hjardan erglir,	Its heart is clear,
den valdri erveross.	its guardians are true.
Velana dri alva,	Awaken the fairies,
olakot, kodu.	all of them, rise.
Eletsol	Life
Ranycht	Night
Nervoda	Water
Brandur	Fire
Sangriga	Light
Obrigi	Earth
Kyndelin	Animal
Skorgon	Crawler
Velana.	Awaken.

Prologue

Lyria was jolted out of her dreams by loud pounding on the front door. She rubbed the sleep from her eyes and threw off the bedcover. Her shimmering wings dimly lit up the room. She pulled a robe around herself, cursing the persistent knocking. Out of instinct, she grabbed her sturdy staff of office, a branch topped with a thick metal triangle. One could never be too careful.

She half-flew, half-jumped down the stairs and zoomed through the entrance hall. Staff at the ready, she opened the tall door. Outside stood a city guard, as indicated by his armor and tassels. He looked worried and out of breath, his wings shining behind him with intensity.

"Councilwoman!" he said, dipping his head. "The Book of Myrkhar has been stolen."

"*What?* That's impossible!" Lyria put a hand over her eyes, and then looked at the guard fiercely. "Do you know who stole it?"

"An unidentified Ranycht. We are currently pursuing the thief."

"Good."

"Guard Captain Dyfith and Commander Dalen have called together the core Council members at the Amber-meet. You are to report there immediately."

Lyria nodded and then scowled. "Councilman Nider will be present?"

"Think about it. A dark-skinned alva this close to Nycht-fal has to be a Ranycht."

"And what're you doing in Obrigi?"

"That's none of your business."

"*Why, you dung-lurkin', answer-avoiding*—oh hey, shush, she's waking up."

The woman lying on the ground squinted as she lifted her arm off her face and sunlight flooded her vision. She propped herself up and looked at the two figures who had been talking. They looked back at her.

She saw a tall blonde woman. Solidly built and very, very tall. The woman stood nearly twice as tall as the man hovering next to her. His black feathery wings flapped agitatedly in an attempt to stay at the same height as the tall woman's head. Both had pointy ears, though the woman's ears were short and the man's ears were large and bat-like.

Towering blades of grass bordered the little clearing they were all currently occupying. The woman on the ground blinked and opened her eyes wide, taking in the strange new sights. She could hear birds chirping, and animals scampering nearby.

The tall woman stomped over and sat down gently. "I'm Khelya," she said. "What's your name? What are you?"

The woman on the ground was confused. And her head *hurt*.

The man glided over to them and landed, shooting Khelya a dirty look. "Yeah, what's your name?" he said. "Mine is Dask."

"I…" There was something missing. "I don't know my name." She looked at them, afraid that she had answered incorrectly.

"You don't know your own name?" Khelya said. She scratched under the brown strip of cloth that was tied around her head. Underneath the cloth, her hair was pulled back in a tight ponytail.

Dask frowned. He had wavy black hair, brown skin, bright green eyes, and a long nose. "Do you even have a name?"

The woman's eyes widened, worried. Khelya and Dask exchanged looks.

Khelya gave her a reassuring smile. "That's not important right now. But, uh, it's easier to talk to someone when you know their name." She paused. "Can I call you Matil? You look like a Matil."

"Okay."

"So, Matil, what are you?"

"Huh?"

"What kind of alva are you?"

"I'm a…" Matil wilted miserably and shook her head.

"You don't know what you are," Dask said flatly.

Matil shook her head again. She looked down at herself. Her skin was brown like Dask's, but she was almost completely certain she didn't have wings. She looked back just in case. Nothing. The black, side-tied tunic she wore was open in the back, however. Maybe the opening was for wings. Why was she wearing the tunic, then?

Khelya didn't have wings either, but she was so big and thick-limbed. Matil thought that she herself was around Dask's size. She reached up and felt her ears. They were cupped like Dask's ears. She was a lot like Dask and a little like Khelya. What *was* she?

She inspected the rest of what she was wearing. Brown trousers tucked into boots of lightweight black leather.

On a belt around her waist, she found a dagger. She pulled it from its sheathe. It was thin and sharp, made for stabbing. Soft leather had been wrapped around the grip. A word came to mind. Stiletto. This was a stiletto dagger. Why wear a weapon? Perhaps she traveled in dangerous places. She sheathed the dagger.

Matil remembered something that Khelya had said. She looked up at her two new acquaintances. "What's an alva?"

They seemed taken aback.

"Um, it's us," Dask said.

"Yeah. *We're* alva. I mean, we don't look alike but we're all alva. Unless you're not an alva." Khelya gasped. "You could be a human!"

"Hah!" Dask paused and looked at Khelya. "Oh, you weren't joking? *Ahahaha!*"

"What? Why're you laughing?"

"You *would* believe in humans."

"What do you mean?"

"You're a boulderhead Obrigi."

"And you're a dirty mudskin!"

"Be careful," Dask said. He drew his knife and twirled it around in his hand, stopping the blade near Khelya's arm. "My hand might slip."

Khelya turned bright red and she shuffled away from Dask. "Even if she's no human, she could've come from outside Eventyr. Maybe they have alva like her there. Wouldn't that be something?"

"How would she get into Eventyr in the first place?"

"I don't know. Magic?"

Dask scratched his ear. "A bunch of alva have tried getting out with magic and it never works. You'd know that if you actually had magic."

Khelya pulled back her fist.

"Wait!" Matil shouted. Khelya and Dask looked at her. "I don't want you getting in a fight. Why are you fighting, anyway?"

"Because the Obrigi – *her* kind of alva – are tree-brained lumps." Dask folded his arms.

Khelya scowled. "Because the Ranycht – *his* idiot race – are slimy centipedes."

"I…meant, what's the specific reason? Why are you here and why are you fighting?"

"Oh," said Dask, looking embarrassed. "I found you—"

Khelya cleared her throat violently.

Dask rolled his eyes. "*We* found you lying here and, well, the Obrigi and the Ranycht border each other. We're very close to this border right now and we want to know whose side you're on. If you're a Ranycht, you should get back to Nychtfal before the Obrigi discover you, they tell the Sangriga, and a war gets started. If you're an Obrigi, which I highly doubt, the Obrigi can recruit you to build or fight or farm or whatever it is they do. In case a war does happen, I'd rather we had more alva on our side than the Sangriga and Obrigi do."

"You're fighting over me?" Matil said.

"Basically."

"Okay. I'm not an Obrigi *or* a Ranycht. At least until I find out what I really am."

Khelya turned to Dask. "What if she's a Kyndelin or a Nervoda?"

Dask tapped his chin and looked at Matil. "Hm. Can you turn into an animal?"

"How do I know that?"

"Try it out."

Matil opened her mouth, then closed it again. Might as well. She closed her eyes and focused on turning into an animal. Any kind of animal. Nothing happened. "I don't think so."

"Can you control water?"

Matil looked around. The grass was still dotted with morning dew. She stared very hard at a particular dewdrop, willing it to move. She had no success, so she tried a different one. "No."

Dask spread out his hands. "There's your answer, tree-legs."

"So you'll stop fighting over me now?" Matil said.

"Fine, fine," Dask said.

Khelya pushed up her sweatband. "If you're sure."

"I'm sure." Matil studied her hands and then looked shyly up at Khelya and Dask. "Could one of you help me find out who I am?"

"Sorry, no," Dask said. "I've got work to do."

Khelya tilted her head. "…Me too. Planting season. You seem nice and all, but my farm should come first."

Matil had hoped that at least one of them could help her. Now she didn't know where to start. "That's okay," she said.

Khelya brightened. "I can give you some stuff, though. My house is—"

"Do you hear something?" Dask said.

A buzzing sound made Matil sit up straight. It was very faint, as if it came from a distance. "Yes…"

"What is it?" Khelya asked. "I don't hear anything."

Matil listened. "There's something buzzing. It's coming closer."

They were all silent, then Dask relaxed.

"It went away," he said. "Is a buzzing noise normal in this part of the forest?"

"There are a couple bee hives nearby," Khelya said.

"That was probably it."

"Where was I? Oh, yeah. My house is a few steps over that way. I can get you a map and some camping gear, maybe. I wonder if I still have that tent."

"I'm outta here." Dask nodded to Matil. "Nice to meet

you, good luck, goodbye. Ruined my day to meet *you*," he said to Khelya. She frowned. He grinned and jumped into the air, his wings unfurled.

Matil waved. "Thank you."

"For what?"

"For explaining things to me."

"Oh. Um. Okay. No problem." He rose up, but soon stopped. His wings flapped quietly.

The buzzing had come back.

Khelya squinted. "I can hear it. Sounds like the whole hive decided to visit."

Dask peered through the thick grass. "I don't think it's bees."

A dark green blur shot out at Dask.

"Agh!" He dropped to the ground to avoid the thing and drew his knife.

It was some kind of insect. Or was it an alva wearing shiny green armor? Its face and head looked normal except for the gray skin and slimy mandibles. Transparent wings buzzed furiously. As it rushed at Dask again, Matil noticed that it had an extra pair of arms.

Khelya stared, wide-eyed, at the thing wrestling with Dask. She nearly fell over as another one came up from behind and attached itself around her neck.

Matil jumped up and unsheathed her dagger. Her body turned out to be very stiff, causing her to falter. Which one should she help first? Dask separated from the creature and was circling it, knife out. Khelya had pulled off her opponent, a purplish bug-alva with huge black eyes, and was trying to keep it away from her face.

Matil stepped toward Khelya, but was jerked back. Arms scooped her up and lifted her high above the ground. Turning her head, she got a good look at her captor, who had a long, green face with wide-set black eyes, no nose, and small, chomping mandibles. She screamed and stabbed the underside of one of its arms. The creature let out a high-pitched whine, but its flight was unaffected. She sliced and stabbed blindly, the creature's plated skin turning her dagger aside.

The bug-alva was yanked downward and its whining turned into unbearable screaming. Matil cringed and looked down. Dask had grabbed onto its legs and was chopping off bits of it. He had severed an entire misshapen foot.

The arms around Matil suddenly let go. As she plummeted, she closed her eyes and thought about how very short this day had been.

Something caught her in its arms and Matil cried out. She wriggled wildly to escape.

"Stop squirming!" Khelya said. "Aah!"

Matil hit the ground and groaned. Khelya's face came into view.

"I told you to stop," she said, bending over. She held out her large hand, which was covered with green goo, and pulled Matil up.

Matil groaned again, rubbing her back. The purple bug-alva lay dead nearby. "Thanks."

"You're welcome."

Dask landed next to Matil. "It got away," he said to her. "Are you all right?"

"I'm doing fine, kinda sickish," Khelya said. "Thanks for asking."

He waved his hand dismissively at her. "Matil?"

"I'm just a little sore. What happened to the one you were fighting earlier?"

He frowned. "It flew off before I could finish it."

Matil looked at the purple creature's corpse and shuddered. "What *were* those?"

"Skorgon," Dask said.

Khelya breathed out. "I didn't think they were real."

"We trade with them sometimes. You wouldn't believe how much spider Skorgon silk goes for."

"Of course, a Ranycht *would* deal with the Skorgon."

"They're not nearly as vicious as the legends make them out to be."

"Really? Reeaaally?"

"Listen, I don't know what just happened. The Skorgon shouldn't even be this far from Deep Valdingfal."

"I think they were looking for me," Matil said quietly. "I wasn't being attacked. I was being carried." She put her arms around herself and eyed the grass. She didn't hear anything but birds. "We should go."

Khelya nodded resolutely. "Follow me."

Dask kicked at the ground. "Can I come with you? I don't want to run into those Skorgon without backup. If I could just lay low for a bit—"

"Go lay low in one of those pits you call cities."

"Gee, maybe I will."

"Can he come?" Matil looked up at Khelya with pleading eyes. "He's been nice so far. Or," she bit her lip, "to me, at least."

"To you." Khelya turned to go.

Dask gritted his teeth. "All right, sorry. I promise I'll be civil if you let me go with you."

"You'd best be more than civil, blowfly," Khelya said, crossing her arms.

"*I'll be*—" Dask caught sight of Matil shaking her head. "—very polite."

Khelya walked away and pushed aside two blades of grass. "Come on."

Dask zoomed over and Matil went after them unsteadily. Her whole body ached. Stepping into the cool shade of the grass, she glanced around, nervous. What if the Skorgon knew who she was? It was too bad they hadn't been friendlier.

2

The Giant's Farm

Matil couldn't stop staring at the forest of grass surrounding them and the huge, knotty tree roots they occasionally passed. Animals and insects passed them, sometimes buzzing right overhead and scaring them all, sometimes only stirring a few swishing blades of grass. The group walked through bearable dimness and into patches of bright sunlight. During the latter, Matil and Dask had to cover their eyes while Khelya hardly reacted.

"What is it you two do? For a living?" Matil said, trying to break up the awkward silence in which they had been traveling.

"I'm a—" Khelya said.

"I do—" Dask said at the exact same time.

Dask cleared his throat. "You go ahead."

Khelya looked sharply at Dask. "Why?"

"Why not?" he said irritably.

"Seems awful…nice of you." Khelya narrowed her eyes.

"Is it so crazy to think that maybe I'm just a nice guy?"

"Yes."

"Khelya, Dask?"

They turned to Matil.

She put on a hesitant smile. "Khelya, why don't you accept Dask's generous offer and go first?"

"Okay. I'm a farmer. I farm. Uh…right now I'm planting and finishing up construction. I moved out here and started workin' last Thrual."

"Threw-all?"

"Nadyl's *apron*, you don't remember?" Khelya scratched underneath her headband. "The season of Thrual starts with the harvest. So we pick our plants, store 'em up, and snow and ice comes. We're in Briden now, when the forest thaws and everything's growin'. Vana happens next."

"Oh. I see."

"Anyway. Farming. Yep."

"That sounds good."

"I s'pose it is." Khelya put her hands on her hips. "Now go on, birdface, what were you stalling for? Oh, sorry, being nice for?"

"I wasn't—shut up!"

"I'm not sayin' anything. I'm letting you talk. So talk."

Dask made a disgusted noise. "I do a lot of different things."

"What kind of things?" Matil said.

"Picking things up, dropping things off, traveling places to get news, stuff like that."

"So you're an errand boy?" Khelya said mockingly.

"Khelya…" Matil said worriedly.

"Yeah, and you lick dirt," Dask said.

"You *have* to so you know if it's good for the seed!"

"Still, slugs lick dirt."

Matil wrung her hands. "Dask…"

"You comparing me to a slug?"

"I don't know if I even have to. There's already quite a resemblance."

"Yeah? Want me to compare my fist to your face?"

"Like you'd be able to catch me—*whoa!*" Dask hopped backward to avoid a punch from Khelya.

"*Khelya! Dask!* Stop it! Are you children?" Matil gasped and covered her mouth, hoping she hadn't gone too far. What if they left her?

They looked completely shocked. They were definitely going to leave her. She decided to try patching things up. "I'm sorry, I—"

"No, you're right," Khelya said. She turned forward. "Sorry. Let's go."

Dask appeared chastened. "Yeah. Um. Sorry." He followed Khelya and began walking.

Matil hesitated and then hurried to catch up. "Are you… mad at me?"

He laughed. "*I'm* not mad."

"Neither am I!" Khelya said angrily.

"Of course not," he said in a soothing voice. "You sound the opposite of mad."

"Dask," Matil warned.

"Riiight. I'll stop."

* * *

Khelya's house was a sturdy building with a shingle roof and sloping walls made of wood and stone. It loomed large over Matil and Dask, but was a perfect fit for Khelya. Stretches of cleared land surrounded it on three sides and grass butted up against the back of the house. The trees had thinned out in this part of the forest, allowing sunlight to reach the cleared land. Out in front of the house was a well, and a half-built barn stood nearby.

"Isn't this place nice?" Khelya said. She looked around with pride.

Matil nodded. "I like it."

"I built the house myself. It's a scaled-down replica of my telvogir's – that's what I call my ma's grandpa – my telvogir's house. I always loved it when we visited. And my parents bought this land for me."

"Good for you," Dask said under his breath, rolling his eyes.

Khelya continued obliviously. "Someday, when the farm is big enough, I'll use my own money to buy the land west of my property." She stopped them at the well and brought up the water bucket, and they all washed.

Matil brushed strands of hair from her sweaty forehead. Most of her hair was pulled back in a very messy braid. She untied the string that bound it, and then brushed it out with her fingers. That was better. She'd braid it again later.

After washing, they reached the front of the house and Khelya held the heavy door open for them.

They entered a room crowded by its furnishings. Two Obrigi-sized chairs were arranged around the empty fireplace opposite the door. The only decorations were a single potted tulip in the corner and an unrolled scroll on the wall. It bore several lines of writing, but what stood out most was the word '*Chivishi*', in large letters. Khelya briefly lowered her head toward it.

Matil murmured appreciatively as Khelya led them through the first room and into a larger room. New-looking counters and cabinets lined the walls. Dirty pots and cooking utensils sat piled in a washbasin and the stone oven took up a large portion of one wall. A thick wooden table and more chairs stood in the center. The table was so big that it couldn't have fit through the door. It must have been built right there in the kitchen.

Matil felt like a child in Khelya's house. Everything was taller and wider than it should have been.

Khelya gestured at the chairs and opened a few cupboards. "I've got some bread and squirrel," she said. "Want any?"

The thought of food made Matil's stomach feel empty. "Yes, please." When had she last eaten? Too bad she couldn't remember.

Dask fluttered up onto a chair while Matil climbed into the chair closest to her. She only took up half of the seat and her feet dangled above the floor.

"Do you have a looking glass?" she asked hesitantly. "Maybe I'll remember everything if I see myself."

"Uh, sure." Khelya searched through her cabinets until she found a small, polished metal pan and handed it to Matil, who thanked her.

Matil looked closely at herself in the reflection. Her appearance was familiar, but it didn't bring back her memory. She had dark brown hair, most of it tucked behind her large ears. Her eyes were a rich purple. At the sight of her pointy nose, she scrunched it up in dislike. Oh, well. It was a suitable face. She put aside the pan.

Khelya had set a big loaf of bread, a few large cups, a jug of water, and strips of dried, salted meat on the table. Now she was slicing the bread with a frighteningly large knife. "So, Matil, do you know anything about the Skorgon? Such as why they would want to kill us and capture you?"

"No. I don't know *anything*." Matil's ears drooped slightly and she took a strip of squirrel meat.

The kitchen was quiet except for Dask chewing noisily on the tough food.

"That's why you're going to learn," Khelya said.

"You're right. Where do you think I should start?"

"I dunno." Khelya pushed a tray with crumbly slices of bread into the middle of the table. She stared at Dask as he immediately grabbed two.

"Maybe you should go to Deep Valdingfal," he said around a mouthful of bread. "That's where the Skorgon live."

"I don't think that's a good idea." Matil washed down her food with a refreshing draft of water. It felt like she'd never eaten before. The meat was so flavorful and the bread incredibly hearty, with just a hint of sweetness.

"Why not?"

"Why not?" she repeated incredulously. "The Skorgon tried to kill you!"

"But you said they only wanted to carry *you* off. You'd probably be safe enough by yourself."

"Yes, but would I really want to go with creepy Skorgon who didn't say a word before trying to kill my friends?"

Khelya and Dask looked at Matil in surprise.

"Hey, wait," Dask said. "I'm not…I mean, we just met and we're not…"

"Oh, shut up." Khelya tore off a chunk of meat. "You're probably right. *I* wouldn't go with those nasty critters if they just up and tried to carry *me* off. If they could even get me off the ground."

"I'm ruling out Deep Valdingfal, then. What else is there?" Matil said.

Dask tapped his chin. "You could wander around Eventyr until something jogs your memory."

"Unless she got lucky, that would take until she was well and old," Khelya said dismissively.

"So what do you suggest?"

She looked uncomfortable.

Dask nodded. "Exactly."

"It does sound kinda…exciting," Khelya admitted.

"And it might be the only way. It's the best idea I have, anyway, and Khelno here won't be any help."

Khelya glowered at Dask but didn't contradict him.

"What does he mean?" Matil said.

"It's like this," Khelya said. "Obrigi can build or make anything. But the plans have to be given to us. We're not so good with ideas. Okay? Okay." Khelya made a sour face and stood up. "I'll get supplies for you." She went through the doorway at the back of the kitchen.

Dask raised his eyebrows and cleared his throat. "So, what do you think of the 'going around Eventyr' thing?"

"What is Eventyr?" Matil asked.

"You don't know?"

"I wish I did."

"Oh, yeah. Sorry. Eventyr is the world, the entire forest."

Matil rubbed her nose. "Would it really take as long as Khelya said?"

"I don't think so. You should be able to see all the important parts of Eventyr in less than a year if you go quickly. You'll have to travel *very* carefully, though, and I suggest staying away from western Eventyr altogether. I don't think the Obrigi or Sangriga would like seeing you running around. I hear the Sangriga execute Ranycht they catch across the borders."

"What does that leave?"

"No Deep Valdingfal, no Obrigi, no Tyrlis. That cuts down on half of the entire forest. Fainfal, Nychtfal, and Vangara are left. It's still a lot of traveling. Do you really want to go to all this trouble to find out who you are?"

"What if I have a family out there? What if they miss me? It would be the saddest thing in the world if they were wondering what happened to me while I didn't even know they existed. Even if that's not true, there's so much that *could* be true. I need to find the place where I used to belong. I need to."

"If you say so."

They ate without speaking for a moment.

"Did you mean actual friends?" Dask said.

Matil finished chewing and swallowed. "Well, I like you two. But after I leave, we'll probably never see each other again."

"Oh. Um, yeah. You know, I've been thinking. I said I had work to do – that's true – but it might be able to wait, so I could help you out." Dask frowned speculatively. "I could even…quit."

"No, don't quit your job!"

"I've wanted to quit for a while now, but it never seemed like the right time. Especially since I'm going solo."

"Why not?"

"It's—"

Khelya leaned out from the doorway. "Do you smell something weird?"

Matil sniffed the air. It didn't smell weird, it smelled like a newly built house. She and Dask shook their heads.

"Huh." Khelya went back through.

Dask lifted an eyebrow. "Anyway. There are alva who wouldn't like it if I quit. Besides, I always have to consider the usual things. They wouldn't give me the same job if I decided to go back and I won't have a steady income."

"I see," Matil said.

He swallowed another bite. "Yeah. That said, my pay hasn't been that great lately, and I could do odd jobs wherever if I were traveling."

She felt her hopes rise. Maybe she wouldn't have to go alone. She coughed. Now she *did* smell something weird. Something thick and tingly and horribly familiar.

Dask leaped up. "Smoke."

"Yes, but…" As far as she could tell, the stove was not on. Did that mean the house was on fire? "Oh, no. *Khelya!*" She slid off the chair and ran to the doorway. "*Khelya, are you—*"

Khelya appeared in the doorway. She was carrying a bundle of cloth and a bag. "I'm okay, but I think the roof is on fire," she said grimly. "I'm gonna have to replace it. Don't know how it caught. Weather's been wet enough."

A loud crash came from somewhere in the back rooms. Khelya looked behind her, alarmed.

"We'd better get out," Dask said.

"My house…"

"Come on, Khelya," Matil said. She grabbed Khelya's hand and pulled on it anxiously.

They hurried out of the house. Khelya ran to the well and pulled up the bucket. She turned to look at the house and her shoulders slumped.

The roof was covered in flames and part of it had already collapsed. Matil suspected that even with their help, Khelya wouldn't be able to put out the fire in time.

Wiry arms closed around Matil tightly. She yelped as she was yanked off the ground. With effort, she twisted her head around to see a gray-skinned face and eerily normal dark eyes staring back at her. It was the Skorgon that Dask had fought earlier.

Matil instinctively reached for her dagger, but the Skorgon was pinning her arms to her sides. She struggled to move. Its grip only became stronger and its spiny armor dug into her skin. She swung her legs uselessly. Even being able to move her neck didn't help; she couldn't manage a proper headbutt. Feeling like a failure, she stopped and looked up. The Skorgon was buzzing onward past tree trunks and branches.

"Matil..."

Someone was calling her name. It sounded like Dask.

"Dask!" she screamed as loudly as she could. "I'm over here! I'm—mmf!" The Skorgon clamped an oily, four-fingered hand over her mouth.

"Matil!"

Was it louder this time?

The whole world flipped again and again as somebody – it was Dask! – barreled into the Skorgon from behind, and they all went tumbling through the air. The Skorgon righted itself and punched Dask with one of its fists, keeping Matil locked in the other three arms.

Wind whipped her long hair back, striking her with an idea. She shook her hair in the Skorgon's face to obscure its vision. They swerved and skidded across the side of a tree, knocking the breath out of Matil and causing the Skorgon to let go of her.

Her stomach dropped and she heard both Dask's yelling and her own panicked cries as she fell. Again.

Dask caught her and flapped his wings desperately. Their descent slowed until they landed on the ground in a heap. Dask immediately sprang up and Matil heard him joining battle with the Skorgon. She pushed herself off the ground and looked around. Dask and the Skorgon were wrestling. Both had lost their weapons. Scrambling to her feet, she tore her dagger out of its sheath. A distant, calculating calm took over as she watched and waited for the right opening.

The Skorgon swiped at Dask and crawled for his sword, which lay a few steps away. He hadn't seen Matil yet. With as much strength as she could muster, she sprinted and leaped at the Skorgon's winged back, stabbing hard. The Skorgon screeched as the dagger pierced his chest. She pulled it out and ran it through his neck, to make sure he couldn't ever hurt her and take her stuff. She blinked. Take her stuff?

The calm lifted, leaving her in disarray. She yanked the dagger out and hopped backward as the Skorgon twitched and crumpled to the ground. Shivers ran across her skin.

"You really do know how to use that thing," Dask said.

Matil turned around. He was wiping his knife on a blade of grass, and she went to do the same. "Yeah," she said shakily. "Are you all right?"

Dask nodded, rubbing his cheek where the Skorgon punched him. "We're lucky there aren't too many of them. They're not very hard to handle when there's only one. But I've seen a street fight between some Ranycht and a bee Skorgon gang before. It wasn't, uh…" he grimaced, "pleasant."

"Were *you* in the fight?"

"No, no, my ga—um, my group wasn't involved in the disagreement."

"Oh, okay. Let's go find Khelya."

Dask stuck his tongue out.

"Don't be like that. Come on!"

As Matil ran and Dask flew back to the farm, Khelya, carrying the bag over her shoulder, nearly ran past them. She pushed them in the direction she was going. Matil stumbled and Khelya yanked her up by her arm.

"The fire's gonna spread!" she said. "We've gotta get well away!"

"How fast will it spread?" Dask yelled.

"Slow enough that the neighbors will spot it before it gets to them. Fast enough that we don't want to be near."

"Where are we going?" Matil gasped. She tripped over a pebble, but caught herself before she fell. It was difficult to keep up with Khelya's long strides.

"I don't know! Ask the Ranycht!"

"Dask?"

"Maybe…Lowen!"

"What?"

"Why Lowen?" Khelya said.

"I know someone there who might be able to help!"

Matil struggled to draw breath. "When can we…stop?"

Khelya stopped abruptly and knelt down. "Hurry, get on my back."

Matil scrambled up.

"Ow! Watch where you put your feet!"

"Sorry!"

Khelya stood up and continued running. Matil bounced up and down uncomfortably.

Many lengths passed beneath them before Khelya slowed down. "I think we'll be safe from the fire now. Here, I'll let you down."

Dask was breathing hard and dragging his wings, but Khelya didn't even look like she'd just been in a mad dash.

* * *

"Is Lowen a city?" Matil said.

"As city as the south gets."

Khelya squinted down at Dask. "And who's this friend of yours?"

"A good man," he said indignantly. "He doesn't ask questions and won't pass on our conversation to interested parties."

"What *interested parties?*"

"Like the, uh, Skorgon who were after us."

"Uh-huh…" Khelya glared.

"*What?* Stop looking at me like that!"

"Matil, can I talk to you in private?"

"Sure," Matil said, confused. Khelya and Dask were very strange sometimes.

Dask narrowed his eyes at Khelya and flew away in a rush of air.

Khelya knelt down and leaned toward Matil. "I don't trust that Ranycht," she said in a low voice.

"What, Dask? Why not?"

"He keeps saying things all shady-like as if he's lying."

"He's nice, though. Why would he lie?"

"Matil, not every nice alva is good. Sometimes they're nice to cover up something about themselves. Something bad."

Matil looked up at Khelya in dismay. "But…but why is he helping me if he's bad?"

"I don't know. I just think we should ditch him. He's no good. If we're really quiet, we could leave right now, him being none the wiser." Khelya turned to go.

"No."

"Huh?"

Matil crossed her arms. "He wants to help, I can tell. And I'd like him to help. He's my friend."

"You don't just make friends with someone in a day!"

"You mean you're not my friend?"

"I mean you have to be careful about who you trust."

"Then how can I make friends with Dask if I go on without him?"

Khelya made a frustrated noise. "Fine! Fine. But I'm watching him close. One wrong step and…even if you won't leave him, I will. It'll be me or him, okay?"

Matil's eyes widened. "Do you really mean that?"

"Yes. Don't make that face at me, don't—are you going to cry? Don't cry, I wasn't—oh, thiffen, really?"

Matil wiped her face. "I'm sorry, it's…you and Dask are the first friends I've ever had. I don't want to leave *either* of you."

"Well, for now it looks like we're both stayin'. Just don't let that get in the way of seeing him for what he is."

Matil frowned.

Khelya rolled her eyes. "Or might be."

"Okay…I know you and Dask don't like each other, so thanks for staying. I'd be completely lost if you two hadn't found me."

"No problem. I s'pose that's it, then." She stood and cupped her hands around her mouth. "*Daaask!*"

A few moments went by. Matil was suddenly worried that Dask had ditched *them*. Then the leaves rustled in a nearby bush and Dask shot through. He landed next to them and cleared his throat.

"Let's get going, then?" he said. He glanced furtively at Matil.

"Yeah," Khelya said, raising her chin defiantly at Dask.

Matil followed as Dask began to walk. Watching him, she wondered if there was truth to what Khelya said.

3

Fade Away

Matil watched her feet as she walked. Right, left, right, left, right. She looked up. "Khelya, is it dangerous for you to be in Miktfal?"

"Nychtfal," Dask corrected. "And it's not exactly smart for her to be here. In southern Nychtfal, though, the only rule is not to get caught. Alva keep to themselves down here. Not to mention, we won't run into too many Ranycht during the day."

"We won't?"

"We'll probably see plenty in Lowen, but the giant's not going in there. See, most Ranycht like sleeping in the daytime and going around at night. Much nicer."

Matil nodded, squinched up her eyes at the daylight shining through the tree canopy, and immediately looked away. "I agree. Why are you awake, then?"

"I have to – had to – switch my schedule around for my job, because I was the fastest flyer and could get things done when alva were asleep. They call alva like me 'dayflyers'."

"And *why'd* you need to do *that*, hmm? Got secrets to keep?" Khelya said.

"Hey, I don't need to tell you my life story, okay?"

"Maybe you should."

"If he wants to tell us, he can," Matil said. "But we shouldn't force him to."

Khelya stared hard at Dask. "Maybe later."

They had been walking for a little while when Dask turned to Matil uncertainly and said, "Thanks."

"Oh, uh, you're welcome."

The monolithic trees grew closer together and the grass gave way to just dirt and sometimes springy, hard-to-walk-on moss. After a particularly dire experience where the moss seemed to grab at Matil and drag her under, Khelya carried her across those parts.

Though it was still daytime, the leaves blocked the direct sunlight. It felt good not to squint. The shade was refreshing, but Matil found herself wishing that it was fully night. Then it would be dark and she could fly up through the ceiling of leaves and as high into the starry sky as she dared. The moon would seem so close and she'd try to touch it…

Matil blinked. She couldn't fly.

There were times when Matil knew they were being watched, and she even saw a few faces peek at them around plants, toadstools, and rocks. Usually they were brown faces with colorful eyes, but she once saw a furry, alva-like creature with a bushy tail. Beetles, woodlice, and other insects occasionally lumbered across the group's path, startling Matil. She didn't care much for bugs after the run-in with the Skorgon.

At first, she tried to get Dask and Khelya involved in a conversation. She soon had to put the conversation to a stop. Afterward, she addressed them separately and could only have peace if the other one agreed to stay quiet.

"Dask," she said, "do Ranycht have magic? Do *you* have magic?"

"Mm-hm. We can hide ourselves and see in the dark. Some Ranycht can even make alva blind for a little while or summon clouds of darkness. I always wished I could do that. Sometimes I think—well, never mind."

"Do you think I'd be able to do any of that?"

"Now wait a mo'," Khelya said indignantly. "You're *not* a Ranycht. Why would you think you'd be able to—"

"And how do you know she's not?" Dask crossed his arms and raised his eyebrows. "By now, I'm certain her wings just came off or something. She looks like a Ranycht. And she doesn't seem to like the sun much, *like a Ranycht*."

Matil bit her lip. "Khelya, I think I must be a Ranycht."

"No, you ain't." Khelya said, frowning. "At least not to me. Ranycht are filthy and underhanded, and you're a...a *nice* alva. I mean, that's what you seem like. There."

"Oh! Thank you."

"Anyway," Dask said, "I don't know if you could use magic. You're not exactly…" he looked at her sideways, "… normal. I'm not saying that's bad or anything. Or, hm, it could be." After a moment he said, "You could try."

"I'd like to. How does it work?"

"When we hide, it's called fading. Fading is sort of like covering yourself with the darkness. And you can't do it when you're moving unless you move really slowly."

"Can we stop and try? Please?"

Khelya sighed loudly.

"I think that's a yes," Dask said. They all came to a halt. "See, what you do is you find somewhere dark." He walked over to a large rock and crouched down in the shadow that it cast.

Matil copied him, pressing her hands against the cool rock behind her.

"And now, in your head, you pull the dark closer and closer." His gaze lost focus and he quickly disappeared, though Matil could see a slight disturbance.

"Whoa," she whispered. She closed her eyes. In her mind, she wrapped the shadow around herself and quieted her breathing. It was like slipping on a comfortable shoe.

"You did it!"

Matil was startled out of her peace and looked down to see if it really did work. She was still visible.

"Not anymore," Dask said. "It's something you have to concentrate on." He stood and helped her back up. "Good job, though."

Khelya gave them a disgruntled look. "That's eerie."

"You're eerie."

"What were you saying earlier about clouds of darkness?" Matil said.

"Oh, yeah, that. It's pretty crazy, seeing it happen. I wonder if you could do it. Someone told me that using the more powerful kind of magic feels like you have a rope in your back or something and you pull threads out of the rope."

"I don't feel a rope in my back."

Dask smiled. "That's all right. You're like me, then."

"Didn't I just go over this?" Khelya said. "She's not like you."

"Hey, I don't see you using any magic!"

Matil sighed and covered her face with her hands.

* * *

Eventually they came upon a thin dirt trail. Khelya wondered why flying alva would need a trail, but Dask explained that it was easy to get lost in what was called Valdingfal, this thick part of the forest. They followed the trail until they reached a rotten wood sign. Written sloppily on it was *'Lowen, half a greatlength ahead.'*

"This is where you go and hide, Khelduh," Dask said.

Khelya glared at him. "Where?"

"There'll be someplace. These woods have hidden more outlaws than most alva realize. Let's see if you can hide, too."

Matil shivered. She followed them off the trail and helped search. Shortly, she spotted a dark hole partially covered by brambles. "There!"

"Let's hope nobody else – or no*thing* else – is hiding there." Dask grinned.

"Stop it," Matil said.

"Oh, don't worry, we'll be fine. Besides, we've got a giant who's ten times scarier than anything that could fit in that hole."

"So, you're paying me compliments now?" Khelya said.

"When I said scary, I didn't mean tough."

Matil and Dask could see through the darkness, so they investigated the hole. It led into an extensive tunnel network, part of which was occupied by mice tending their babies, but the opening they had found was empty.

Khelya squeezed herself into the tunnel entrance, making a sullen face at Dask the entire time. They covered the hole with some more branches and said a quick goodbye to Khelya.

When they were back on the trail, Dask cleared his throat. "Khelya's a little hard to drag around, isn't she?"

"We're not dragging her around," Matil said, hurt. "So far she's carried more than her own weight. She has maps and camping gear and food—"

"Hey, that's easy enough to get. I have some money. We're about to be in town."

"Still, we're not *dragging* her."

"But she's so big and easy to see. How are we supposed to avoid notice when you don't have wings and she's, well, an Obrigi in Ranycht territory?"

"Then maybe we should teach her how to be sneakier."

"Sure, that'll *definitely* work."

Matil smiled. "Good." Maybe it would help Khelya and Dask learn how to work together.

Dask looked askance at her, and then shook his head. "She's not very pleasant to be around."

"If you're nice to her, she's nice back. She's outspoken, but that isn't necessarily a bad thing."

"You haven't been on the receiving end of her bad mood all day long."

"Dask, what if she thinks exactly the same thing about you? I think you're nice, too, but Khelya doesn't get to see that because you two keep arguing."

"A guy can't just take the kind of insults she's been throwing out. I've gotta give 'em back so she knows she shouldn't mess with me."

Matil made an exasperated noise. "What does insulting alva prove?"

"It…shows them you're smarter than they are. And it feels good!"

Matil closed her eyes. "Just don't insult *Khelya. Please.* She's been a big help—"

"Big is right."

"—and I *don't* want us to split up because you two can't get along."

Birdsong echoed through the dusky forest. "I'll see what I can do," Dask finally said. "But you'd better give her this talk. One alva can't make up for two."

4

Going To Town

After a little while of walking, they arrived. Stretching above them, at least as tall as Khelya, was a wall made of rotting, mossy wood.

"This is Lowen," Dask said. "Look familiar?"

"I don't think so."

"Tell me if anything does."

"I will."

Tired-looking guards wearing mismatched uniforms flanked the city's gate. They watched curiously as Matil and Dask approached. One of the guards dragged open the gate while the other narrowed his eyes at them.

"Why don't she have wings?" he said.

Dask looked at Matil. "She got sick once. Her wings fell right off."

The guard leaned away from Matil. "It in't contiguous, is it? No one'll catch it?"

"No, it was a long time ago."

"Awright," he said cautiously. "Go on in."

Matil squirmed uncomfortably. He had just lied to cover for her. Somewhere in the back of her mind was a quiet voice that said, *It's wrong to lie.*

They stepped through the gate and went down the wide main street, which was lined with rickety buildings piled up to three stories tall: a butchers' shop, a tanner, an herbalist, some taverns, and other stores. Many of the doors were shut tight and bore padlocks. The Ranycht that were out gawked at Matil and gave the two a wide berth. Twisting through the air was a screen of smoke and the smell of roasting meat. The ground was dirt for the first several lengths, and then they were walking on scuffed plank decking.

Matil took in as much as she could. She glimpsed winged forms high above that darted over the rooftops. Stall merchants – some of whom were packing up for the day – asked Matil to browse their wares, and then cut themselves off as they noticed her lack of wings. The clutter of buildings soon ended and the city opened up before them.

At first, Matil had thought that the city sprawled out along level ground. Instead, it was built from where they were standing down into a ravine, and was split into two parts by a wide creek running through the center. The city was a jumble, with buildings built on other buildings and wooden walkways that threaded haphazardly in and out of the chaos.

Wooden cranes lifted crates from tied-up barges and lowered goods onto rafts that were preparing to go further down the creek. Ranycht walked and flew through the city. There were brown wings, gray wings, and black. Speckled and solid-colored, large and small.

Matil found herself wishing she could fly up and join them.

"Lowen *is* sort of nice, in a beat-up kind of way," Dask said, looking at Matil's expression. "Nothing compared to the Brug, though. That place is huge. Alva all over, whether it's night or day."

"The Brug? Where is that?"

"Ecker's Brug is up in the north. It's where I'm from." He walked to the edge of their platform to look out over the ravine. "Come on. I think I can find Kerl in this mess."

They wended their way through the city, up and down the ramshackle walkways that doubled back on themselves and followed roundabout paths. Matil suspected that the city hadn't been designed for walking.

Dask seemed frustrated as he tried to find their destination, and Matil was close to telling him he could go ahead and fly, when he said, "There it is!"

Matil looked where he was pointing, at a rusty sign hanging over the entrance of a damp, dark corridor. The paint on the sign was faded and some letters had completely vanished under a layer of grime. It read, *'Cob le and Shew Re are'*.

She reluctantly followed Dask into the narrow corridor. It was short, a dead end. The soft light of a single candle shone through a large, dingy shop window, and a doorway with no door opened into the shop. Another sign was nailed above the doorway, this one saying, '*obbler nd ~~Shu Sho~~ Shew Repare*'. Through the window, Matil could see that the store was tiny. Strange tools and pairs of boots and shoes hung all over the walls. The store was cramped, even with only three men looking through the footwear. Their murmurs of, "'Scuse me," and, "Jus' gotta squeeze over there…thanks," drifted through the doorway.

Dask walked over to a scruffy old man hunched on the ground outside of the shop. The man was sewing up a leather shoe, his hands moving quickly and steadily.

"Hey, Kerl," Dask said. "How are things?"

Kerl looked up and blinked his filmy red eyes. He had a mane of white hair, in sharp contrast with his dark eyebrows and brown, wrinkly skin. "Hm. Soaking up splinters, as usual," he grunted. His gaze snapped over to Matil and then back to Dask. He gave them a smile full of holes. "I haven't seen you in weeks, Dask. How've *you* been?"

"I was really busy all that time and, uh, today's been interesting. Listen—"

"Hey, aren'tcha gonna introduce us?" Kerl said, tilting his head toward Matil. He set down the needle, thread, and shoe, and stood up, extending his hand.

"Um, yeah, Matil, this is my friend Kerl. Kerl, this is my friend Matil. Now you know each other." He leaned forward. "Listen, I need to know the latest. Got any big news?"

Kerl rubbed his hands together. "Big news, okay."

Matil listened closely in anticipation.

"Some Ranycht smugglers were rounded up in Obrigi territory yesterday, Anding's Town up near Fainfal. Lotsa Sangriga guards swarmin' the place. I'd suggest not going there if you can help it. And Dwell is going crazy about the Sangriga. Alva fightin' in the streets. The Assembly don't want a war with the Sun Accord, but everybody else does. You should prob'ly avoid Dwell, too. You know what? Just stay in town for a week, keep your ears outta the wind. I hear there's trouble spreadin' through the forest, *deep* trouble. Smart alva won't have none to do with it. You're a smart fella, Dask."

Dask gave Kerl a half-smile, which slipped off his face as he looked down contemplatively. He turned to Matil. "Did any of that sound familiar?"

Matil shook her head.

"Hm. Have you heard anything about a wingless Ranycht, Kerl?"

"Can't say that I have, other'n what I see before me."

"All right. Is that everything?"

Kerl pushed his mouth to the side. "Is that it…? Oh, yeah! I was savin' best for last. A bunch of Ranycht soldiers are camping at the border, keeping some Sangriga and Obrigi from gettin' in. They won't say none about it, but I 'spect it has to do with the rumor that's been going around."

"Rumor?"

"Alva been saying that the very Book of Myrkhar was *stolen*, right out from under the Sangriga's sparkly wings!"

Matil shuddered. Myrkhar.

She knew that name.

"No, no," Dask said. "The Sangriga might be full of themselves, but they're right about the Vault. Nobody gets in."

"I'd think the same myself, but I heard the Sangriga are *very* eager to get into Nychtfal."

"Whatever. So—"

"What's the Book of Myrkhar?" Matil said.

"You don't know?"

"No."

"It's this artifact thing that the Sangriga have. All the stories say that it was made by Myrkhar the Evil Elder Guy. It's a spell book or something. Does it sound familiar?"

"I think so."

"Really? Then you've heard of it somewhere before?"

"No, no, I haven't *heard* it."

"Have you read it? Seen it somewhere?"

"I just know it. It's…" Matil frowned in concentration. "It's giving me a headache."

"Still, that's a lead. Where are the camps?"

"Directly west a' Loda's Brug."

"Thanks for the help, Kerl."

Kerl dipped his head. "Glad I could."

"And uh, it would be best if no one knew I'd been here. Or, better yet, *redirect* them. They might come looking."

"Got yourself in trouble?"

"Not exactly. That thing I mentioned a while back might be happening."

"*Oh*...Good luck, then."

"What thing?" Matil said, looking from Kerl to Dask.

"I'll tell you later." Dask nodded briskly at Kerl. "We're going to the border, then. See you around."

"Colthal, boy." Kerl held up a hand. "Colthal."

Dask raised an eyebrow. "Bye, Kerl. Colthal." He strolled away, arms crossed.

Matil smiled at Kerl. "Thank you for your help."

"My pleasure. You take care of him, missy."

She chuckled, but the old Ranycht looked very serious. "All right," she said. "Goodbye." She hurried away to catch up with Dask. "Dask?"

Dask looked up. "Hm?"

"What does 'colthal' mean?"

He laughed. "It's a really old and formal way of saying goodbye. These days alva use it when, say, someone's about to move out from their parent's house or go on a long journey. Or when someone goes off to war."

"But we didn't tell Kerl we're going on a long journey."

"Kerl knows much more than he lets on." Dask ran a hand through his hair. "Colthal means a lot, especially coming from him. It worries me."

Matil looked at him with concern. "Well, um...what was

'that thing' you and Kerl were talking about?"

"Right. That was just me quitting my job, like I told you before."

"You said someone might look for you."

"They want me to give notice, of course, but they're not the kind of alva who'll take that news well. I'm probably safer not telling them face-to-face."

"Are they dangerous?"

"Not as long as we keep moving. Don't worry about it, Matil."

"Are you sure?"

"Absolutely."

"…Okay."

* * *

When they got back to Khelya's hiding place, it was surrounded by little Ranycht children. The children called out to each other and watched the hole carefully.

Matil looked at Dask with wide eyes. "What do we do?" she whispered.

A crafty look was growing on his face. "It doesn't look like they've seen her yet." He tapped his chin, then nodded decisively. "Stand next to me and look scared." He strolled forward. "What're ya kids doin' out here?" he said, adopting a thick version of the accent that the alva in Lowen had.

A few of the children turned around, and a boy with a mop of curly dark hair answered. "We heard somein' tibsing around in dat hole."

"Kinda late, huh? Where ya folks at?"

"We're not babies, stranger. We's stay up as late as—heeey, she in't got wings! Why in't she got wings?" The other children turned around to gape at Matil.

"She got 'em ate off," Dask said.

A girl's mouth dropped open. "Ate off?" she gasped.

"Ate clean off."

"Naw," the boy said.

"Truly."

The boy turned to his friends, looking impressed. "Ate off!" He crossed his arms. "By what?"

"Oh, it was a…a big badger. We saw deh badger eatin' off her wings and bam bam! A little magic scared 'im away. I wouldn' bet on anudder fight, though. Heeey, I wonder if dat *badger* is in your hole?"

After a quiet pause, a low, vicious growl came up from the hole. Most of the children screeched and hopped right away, flapping their small wings but not able to fly completely. The curly-haired boy and some of his friends seemed frightened, but they stood their ground.

"It's prob'ly a mouse," the boy said.

The growling became louder.

"I'd get clear if I was you," Dask said.

The rest of the children wasted no time in leaving.

There it was again. He lied.

They walked up to the hole. The growling continued and Dask stretched his neck, trying to see inside.

"You don't think there's actually a…" he said.

Something lunged out of the darkness. They both screamed and turned tail without looking back. Could they run fast enough? Would Matil be eaten because she couldn't fly away?

"Whoa, haha, wait up!"

They stopped themselves and looked around.

It was only Khelya, her shoulders shaking with laughter.

5

Elders and Thieves

Matil took her hands off her thumping heart. "Um, hello."

Khelya snorted mirthfully. "Sorry I scared you, but that jape was too good to pass up. Didja hear him squeal?"

"I didn't squeal," Dask said, "I was reasonably losing my nerve. It's natural when you think there's *a badger coming to eat you*."

"Still, it was pretty hilarious."

"I'm laughing over here, I really am."

They would go back and forth for half the day if Matil let them. "We won't get anywhere like this," she said, "so... Khelya, I asked Dask earlier to, uh, be agreeable toward you, and he said he'd do it if you're good to him. What do you think?"

"I s'pose it'll work better that way."

Matil beamed.

"Let's get outta here." Dask looked around. "We don't want those kids coming back."

"Hold on. Say my name right," Khelya said, eyeing Dask.

"Really? Aren't you being a little childish?"

"Maybe so, but you're not above that, now, are you?"

"What? I'm more mature than—"

"Just say my name."

Dask pressed his lips together in concentration. "Khel… Khel…Khelna. That's your name. Definitely."

"You're about as mature as Dyndal, you know that?"

He responded with a big grin.

"Never mind." Khelya tightened the knot on her headband. "So, what'd you find out?"

"We think that Matil might have something to do with the Book of Myrkhar."

"Huh? How'd you figure *that?*"

"When I heard that name," Matil said, "I remembered it. I know it from before."

Dask nodded. "Alva have been saying that the Book was stolen and now there are Sangriga at the border, trying to go across. They won't tell anyone what they want, though."

"So we're going back west?" Khelya said.

"Up to Loda's Brug."

"Aw, another Ranycht town? When will I get to do something?"

"We're not going into Loda's, we're going near it," he said curtly. "Anyway, we might need your help there. *Maybe.*"

* * *

They looked at Khelya's map and set off, mostly avoiding the trails and little Ranycht villages speckling the tree branches. Passing close under one of the villages, Matil was surprised. She didn't hear working, playing, laughing, or talking. Then she remembered what Dask had told her about Ranycht. They must be asleep. She wondered what it would be like here at night.

The heavy forest ceiling that shielded against the sun soon thinned. Light shone through the gaps and blinded Matil when she accidentally walked into a ray of sunlight. They walked a long way until the sun was high in the sky. All of them agreed that it was time to rest, and they sat down in a secluded area. Khelya brought out the food and water.

"What's an Elder?" asked Matil.

Khelya looked at her in surprise. "Oh, thiffen, you don't know. Elders are powerful alva – well, more'n alva, really – who directly serve Thosten. They—"

"Who is Thosten?"

"Don't tell me you forgot *him*."

Matil faltered, wondering what she should say instead.

"He created the world and everything in it," Khelya eventually said.

"He did?"

"Yeah. The Elders used to watch over us, but the Elders who went bad, the Saikyr, needed to be locked away. They kept coming back and the only way they would stay gone was if the good Elders, the Heilar, were also gone. Then

Calo of the Heilar put them all into the Great Hibernation and they haven't been seen since. Neither have the Saikyr, though, so their plan must've worked."

Dask laughed.

"What is it, floppy-ears?" Khelya said irritably.

"Those are just bedtales mothers tell their children to get them to behave," he said. "Don't believe it, Matil."

"Oh." Matil scratched her head.

Khelya looked between the two. "They are not!"

"How can you prove they aren't?" Dask said.

"How can you prove they are?"

"*Hm.* Even if Thosten does exist, he hasn't done me any favors."

After lunch, they continued on their way. Matil learned that Khelya had grown up on a big farm and hadn't traveled much, so all this moving around was new to her. They walked in quiet for a little longer.

Finally, Matil heard voices. She and Dask crouched lower and Khelya, looking down at them in confusion, followed suit.

"Something wrong?" she asked them.

Dask took the map from a pocket on Khelya's pack. He looked it over, then cocked his head toward the voices. "I think we're at the camp. I'll go in and see what I can get out of the guards."

"Can I come?" Matil said.

"I don't think it's safe. You don't have any wings and they'll ask questions and probably lock us up." He nodded in agreement with himself.

"I'll…stay, then. Good luck."

Dask disappeared through the underbrush. Matil heard raised voices close by, and then he slipped back to them.

"Yeah, I'm not getting in there," he said, pulling a face. "They told me to get lost. That wouldn't have discouraged me, but security's too tight to sneak in."

"Sneak in?" Matil said worriedly.

"I said I couldn't. Anyway, there's supposed to be a camp of alva waiting to get in on the other side of the border. And this one's got Sangriga and Obrigi. It should be a perfect first mission for our friend Khel."

Khelya looked at him blankly. "Huh?"

"You go. Into Obrigi camp. You get. Information. About Book of Myrkhar. Okay?"

"Hey, I'm not simple!"

"I know what you *are* and, honestly, simple's an understate—I mean, yes, you're not simple. Sorry. You can stop looking at me like that, both of you. I was just joking."

"I'll pretend I didn't hear any of that," Khelya said. "So, I go and ask the Obrigi about the Book?"

"No, they'll get suspicious and take you in for questioning if you straight up ask about the Book. The rumor about its theft hasn't gotten around yet. Ask what they're doing there and follow up with a bunch of questions. But don't sound too eager or they'll get suspicious."

"That's a little complicated."

"It'll get the job done and done well, as long as you play it right. Oh, yeah, and you can't just be yourself or they'll get—"

"Suspicious."

"Yeah," Dask said, looking pleased. "What you need to do is make up a story. Like, um, you're a farmer near the border between Obrigi and Tyrlis. Some Sangriga recruited you to send a message to the camp over here and…your message is…"

"That's dumb."

"And it's lying," Matil said.

Khelya continued, "All I'll say is, I'm a farmer from around here – that's true enough – and I'm just curious what's going on. Nothing suspicious about that."

"Listen, I have a lot of experience with the authorities. You need to have a *reason* to be there. So your message is that you need a report to bring back to Gevan City. Simple. Try to talk to somebody who looks low-ranked. They don't have as many connections and will ask the least questions."

Matil was worried. "Does she have to lie?"

"Yes, otherwise it won't work. I just explained that."

Khelya sighed. "Okay…But what if they say no? *What if they question me anyway?*"

"Use your feminine wiles," Dask said exasperatedly.

"My feminine *what?*"

"I don't know! Just go!"

Khelya bit her lip. Matil gave what she hoped was a reassuring smile. "Good luck, you'll be fine."

"Thanks." Khelya took a loud, shaky breath and proceeded to stomp away through the bushes.

Matil wound her hands together tightly and started pacing. She suddenly regretted sending Khelya into possible danger on her account.

Dask had sat down and was staring into the forest. Matil wondered what he was thinking about. He seemed nice, but there were a few things he said that weren't quite right. What was his job? Why had he given it up?

Was Khelya all right? If she had already been arrested, how would they know? If they waited for a long time, it might be too late—

Matil jumped as she heard heavy footfalls approaching.

Khelya stepped out of the bush. She looked like she was about to faint. Matil ran over to her.

"Are you okay?" Matil said. "Sit down, sit down."

The two sat down next to Dask.

"So," he said, "how'd it go?"

Khelya wiped her brow. "When I walked into the camp, I- I forgot everything you said. They already saw me, though, so I couldn't go back. One of the guards asked me what my business was. I told him I was a farmer and asked why they were there."

Dask hit his forehead with his palm. "Couldn't you have made something up?"

"That kind of thinking is *hard* for Obrigi! It's much easier, much more practical to just say what you mean."

"Ugh. Go on."

"The guard said that something had been stolen from the

Sangriga. They chased the thief all last night and saw him castin' some sort of spell in Nychtfal. Nobody's sure what the spell might've done, but they do know it was makin' wild lights and sparks. They ran the thief and his buddy off in the middle of it all and the lights exploded like crazy. The Sangriga got blasted away and were pushed out pretty quick by the Ranycht guards. They're trying to cross over again, though, 'cause they want to check out the place where the spell was cast. The Obrigi militia came just this morning to make it more official."

"Wow," Matil said. "Great job!"

Dask raised his eyebrows. "You got all *that*? How?"

"I don't think the guard was very bright."

"Well, it's too bad we don't know where the thief cast the spell or we could go investigate."

"Actually, the guard told me the place was a few greatlengths in that direction." Khelya pointed.

"Let's go, then!" Matil grinned. They had already found out so much.

"We have to sleep sometime. It's just about sunset."

Khelya was right. Matil couldn't see the sun through the thicket that surrounded them, but the light was taking on a reddish hue.

"Let's travel until it gets dark," Dask said. "Then we'll make camp."

They pushed through the thick leaves. Matil felt a spring in her step. She couldn't wait to find another clue to her past.

* * *

A short time later, Matil suggested they stop for the night. The other two emphatically agreed. She hadn't realized how tired she was until just now. The excitement of a purpose had kept her going throughout the day.

After a dinner supplemented by bits of a wild carrot that Dask had found, Khelya passed out blankets to sleep in. Dask fell asleep bundled up messily in one of the huge blankets. Matil and Khelya took the time to spread theirs out more neatly and share some companionable conversation.

Matil's whole body ached and it was a relief finally to lie down. She looked up at the small patches of stars that showed through the forest ceiling. "The night is so beautiful." A firefly flitted across her vision, leaving her blinking from the light.

Khelya turned to see the sky. "My ma used to tell me that the stars were candles floating in the sky."

"Mm," said Matil groggily, "that's a nice thought. Who lights all of them?" She closed her eyes.

Khelya yawned. "Thosten. He pulls the sun down to him, gets some fire from it, and uses the fire to light the candles one by one."

"That's so much work, though. Why does he do it?"

"He does it because he has to. If the candles aren't lit, the night'll be too dark. 'Sides, who else is gonna?"

6

Seeking the Past

Matil looked up worriedly. The sky was still dark, but she knew it had been darker a moment ago.

"We have to get home before dawn, remember?" she said.

"Oh, you act like a mother at the worst times," came a high-pitched voice. Out of a nearby bush burst a Ranycht girl with vivid blue eyes. She clutched two shiny hummingbird feathers in her arms. "Got them!"

Matil spread her wings and flew up to the girl. "Let's hurry."

"O-*kay*."

They sped through the forest, low to the ground and swerving around the vegetation.

"We'll be late," Matil said despairingly.

The girl giggled and ducked under the branch of a bush. "You're such a fussbird—" She squealed as she smacked into something big.

Matil tried to slow down, but she, too, collided with someone's wings.

"Ow!"

"Hey!"

"What's going on?"

"Fly! They caught us!"

"Wait…these are just babies."

Before them stood a group of three slightly older Ranycht boys. Matil recognized the boys, but didn't know them.

"We're not babies," the girl pouted.

"You're not?" A boy with dark eyes yanked the feathers from the girl, threw them on the ground, and stepped on them.

"Don't!" The girl began to cry.

"You cry just like a baby," the boy observed. The other boys laughed.

"Stop it!" Matil stood up and punched the dark-eyed boy. He pushed her and she sat down hard. Tears threatened to spill, but Matil didn't want to be teased. She held them in. Standing up to help the girl, Matil noticed some dungbasks, stinky wads of animal droppings, behind the boys. "Hey, you're not supposed to make those."

"So? It's just a dumb rule that nobody pays attention to."

"I'll tell."

The boys looked worried. "No you won't," the dark-eyed boy said.

"I *will*."

"No you *won't.*" The boy pushed her down again and kicked her. The other boys did the same to the girl. "We'll stop when you promise not to tell!" one of them said.

Matil and the girl cried uncontrollably as they were kicked again. They tried to promise, but they couldn't say it through their sobs.

A boy's voice commanded, "Leave them alone." Matil could hear a brief scuffle and then silence.

Wiping tears out of her eyes and looking up, she saw a boy's round, grave face. Despite his solemnity, his hand was open and his deep orange eyes were kind. "I'm Crell," he said.

* * *

Matil opened her eyes. Clear sunlight filtered through the trees, casting rays that sent a shiver through her. The rays reminded her of something. Something bad.

Khelya sat at a small fire, grabbing dewdrops from a bent-over blade of grass and scrubbing her face with them. She watched over a few slices of bread toasting on a twig. "Mornin'," she said amiably.

Dask was huddled in his wings on the branch of a bush, picking the drupelets off of a blackberry. With a smile and a nod he acknowledged Matil, then popped a small drupelet in his mouth.

Matil rubbed the sleep out of her eyes. "Good morning. I had such a strange dream."

"Dreams are normally strange," Dask said with a shrug. He stretched down and held a drupelet out to her. "Want some?"

"Yes, please." Matil took it and bit into it. The juice was refreshing and tangy. "I don't remember any dreams I had before. In this one, I had wings! Do dreams always make you feel like...like it's happened before?"

"Sometimes, I guess."

* * *

The group continued to head east, avoiding notice as much as possible. It wasn't too hard. Once again, most Ranycht were asleep. Matil liked that. When her search was over and she could settle down, she would sleep during the day and spend the night in cool darkness.

By the time Matil's stomach began to growl, she and Dask heard many voices farther ahead. They fell back and looked for another place to hide Khelya. She complained about it as they covered her in dirt and leaves between the roots of a tree.

Matil watched as Khelya bent her head forward, closed her eyes, and began muttering under her breath. "Is something wrong?" Matil said, a little worried.

"No, no. I'm just asking Thosten to protect us."

"You can do that?"

"He's always listening."

"Oh, Lord Thosten," Dask wailed. "Make me rich! Send me one thousand sgelds." He bowed his head reverently.

Khelya scrunched her nose up at him. "Aren't you hilarious?"

Matil and Dask soon left Khelya and made it to the site of the thief's spell, only to be greeted by a discouraging scene.

The spell had been cast in a small clearing, but it couldn't truthfully be called a clearing any more. In the center, Ranycht in robes and long coats swarmed what Matil could just barely recognize as some sort of symbol burned into the ground. They all concentrated very carefully on the symbol and took notes. Many guards – more disciplined by far than those in Lowen – were stationed around it and patrolling above, where they kept out the swarm of over-eager Ranycht citizens.

"This makes things more difficult," Dask muttered.

Matil sensed that she had to get to the symbol. There was something sizzling in the air. It surrounded her and pulled her toward its center. *The symbol.* "I know what to do. I need to be close to it," she said, staring into the clearing.

He pushed his mouth to one side consideringly. "This crowd could work to our advantage." He gave Matil a crafty smile. "Just wait, I'll be right back."

He left her in the shadows at the fringe of the crowd. Nobody paid attention to her, for which she was glad.

Dask returned carrying several hooded cloaks that also tied below the wings, and he handed one to Matil. "Roll some of these up on your shoulders and put one over them. It'll be hot, but it should keep alva from noticing that you don't have wings."

"Where did you get them?" Matil had seen some enterprising Ranycht hawking snacks and water, but not cloaks.

"Don't worry about it," Dask said.

Matil nodded slowly and put the first cloak on. He probably just didn't want her to know how much he had paid for them.

Dask helped her get the rest of the cloaks on until it looked like she did have wings folded up under them. He took her hand and pushed through the crowd. "Stand here," he said. "When you see a commotion, run to the center, do…whatever it is you need to, and then get out as fast as you can. I'll find you afterward. Got it?"

Matil looked past the guards, to the center of the clearing. "Got it."

"It might be hard to run in the cloaks, but don't take them off. The guards would definitely nab you then. Good luck. I'm off to work my magic." Dask disappeared into the crowd.

Matil watched the circle of guards tensely. The alva pressed around her, flew above her, kicking her head accidentally, trying to push her out of the way. Wings flapped all around and the cloaks got warmer and warmer…

She had to concentrate.

Was anything happening yet? No.

Now? No.

Now? N—*ah!* A commotion!

She could hear Dask's faint shouts over the crowd, "There's an opening over here! If we all push, the guards can't stop us!"

Alva suddenly vacated Matil's vicinity, eagerly chattering about the to-do. The guards grunted with displeasure and zipped over to the pressing throng on the opposite side of the clearing. Nobody was watching Matil. She cautiously avoided the gazes of the guards and bolted toward the strange force that called her.

A cloak slipped off her shoulders and her feet pounded the damp dirt. The alva analyzing the symbol cried out as Matil skidded to a halt, knocking over one of them.

"Sorry," she said, wincing. She tried to get to the symbol but they were blocking her path. She *needed* to touch it.

"You shouldn't be in here," someone said. "Guards!"

Matil steeled herself and pulled out her dagger. "Please! Get out of my way!"

They gasped and ran for the guards, who were occupied with the stampede of Ranycht threatening to overrun the clearing.

Matil stepped forward. As her foot landed in the smeared scorch-mark symbol, she froze. A rushing sound roared in her ears and her vision grew hazy. The symbol siphoned a crackling bolt of lightning into her which shot back out, stretching on and on through the forest. The sound died down and once more, she could see clearly.

But the path of lightning remained.

7

Dodging the Present

Matil followed the trail of magic, running with purpose past all the alva stupidly making noise about things they didn't understand. The forest swallowed her up and she ducked and dodged the rocks and plants and insects in her way. The cloaks fell off all at once.

A Ranycht flew up beside her. "Hey, slow down! You're going past Khelya!"

"We have to hurry, Crell!" Matil panted. "The Book is this way."

"Crell? Who's Crell? Wait, Matil, *stop!*" He landed in front of Matil. She pulled up short, surprised.

Matil grew irritated. She had to follow the trail. "Out of my way!" She pushed past him.

"Matil?" He sounded shocked.

That made her stop. Her head swam and her limbs grew heavy. She sat down numbly.

"Matil, what's wrong with you? You want to get Khelya, right?"

Matil blinked. Khelya?

"If you're saying we should go without Khelya, I'm all right with that."

Khelya.

"I mean, really, she's just an Obrigi. How are we supposed to stay unnoticed with a big lump like her following us, anyway?"

Khelya, Dask, Matil. "No!"

"Hm?"

"No, no, we aren't leaving Khelya behind!" Matil put her head in her hands. "What happened? It felt like I was someone else."

Dask leaned back in disbelief. "You called me Crell and said that the Book was this way. But this is the way we came, isn't it? And it's the way the thief would have come. Unless…oh, that's clever." He laughed. "The thief could have dropped the Book off somewhere in Obrigi or Tyrlis – the last place the Sangriga would look! But how did they cast the spell? You know what, I'll bet they brought the Book here and *then* flew back to Tyrlis with it."

"Crell…he was in my dream."

"Oh. That's actually a pretty good lead. Maybe you remembered Crell from your past. I know a few Crells. We could find them, see if one remembers you."

"No, when I stepped in the symbol, I knew where to go. It's still there. We have to follow it."

"Then let's do that. We can look for Crell later."

Matil looked around. The forest wasn't familiar at all. "Where are we?"

"Don't be scared. I know how to get around Nychtfal. We're not too far from the clearing right now."

"And Khelya, where's she?" Matil stood up despite her tired body. The trail of lightning was making her fidgety.

"Aw, fine. Follow me." Dask jumped into the air and flapped forward, only to stop. There were two Ranycht men in his way.

One of them wore a wide-brimmed hat and a patchy vest. "Dask," he said. "Really great to see ya here." He grinned nastily.

Dask gave the men a sheepish wave. "Hey."

The other was burly and had no shoes on. He folded his arms. "Whaddaya doing out here?" he grumbled. "I thought you was gonna be in the Brug by now."

Were these alva from Dask's job? They didn't seem very pleasant.

Dask hunched his shoulders and took on a submissive tone. "I just wanted to see what all the fuss with the Book of Myrkhar was about. I was on my way back."

"And you got the goods?"

"Yeah. I hid them around somewhere so nobody would grab 'em."

Matil didn't remember them hiding anything except Khelya.

"You *hid* them?" the shoeless alva said, bristling. "That's the stupidest thing you've ever done! Listen, *I'll* take them the rest of the way. I don't know what's up with you, but you'd better deal with it before your next job or it's back down to street duty."

"I will, I will."

"Who's that?" he said, noticing Matil. "And what's wrong with her wings? For your sake and hers, I hope you didn't tell her anything."

"Oh, no, she's from Lowen. She's Kerl's granddaughter. Wanted to see Nychtfal. Got really sick when she was a kid, wings fell off. You can be sure I haven't told her anything."

Matil shifted on her feet, her heart racing more with each lie. At least the last part was true. She lifted her eyebrows with surprise. Dask *hadn't* told her anything about this.

The shoeless alva frowned. "You keep it that way."

"So, where's the stuff?" the alva in the vest asked.

"Why doesn't he just show us?"

Matil wanted to run away. Dask must be lying about this 'stuff'. And he would get in trouble because of it. This was his problem, not hers! It was his mistake. His mistake, but he *was* helping her. Maybe she should help him.

"Uh, yeah," Dask said. "Just over here."

Where was he going? She could just bolt and hide. Those creepy alva might not care. But…would Dask care? *Would he?*

They had already begun flying ahead.

Dask stopped. "Ma—" His eyes shifted toward the men. "Marga? Are you all right?"

Matil forced herself to walk forward. "I'm fine." She would trust him for now. Even though – she hated to think of the possibility – he might not be trustworthy.

* * *

Every tree looked the same. As they walked, Matil wondered how Dask could make his way around. But he did, and they found themselves standing next to the tree under which Khelya hid. Matil could remember that much.

Why were they at Khelya's tree? Wasn't that dangerous? Dask probably knew what he was doing. Probably.

"It's right around here somewhere..." Dask said.

He had no clue what he was doing, did he? Matil tensed up and surreptitiously checked that her dagger was ready to draw. She wasn't sure what would happen when their act was exposed, but she would be as ready as possible.

The shoeless alva's face contorted monstrously. "If you lost the shipment, your wings'll be hanging up to dry."

Matil looked at the ground. She couldn't watch this.

"I didn't, I promise. I know it's around this tree. It's heavy, though. I'm going to need some *help*. From a *large someone*."

"You mocking me, kid?" he growled. "I've had enough—"
Thunk.

Matil looked up in shock to see that the alva had been knocked down by Khelya. Khelya with a big stick.

"Boss? Whoa!" The alva in the vest dodged Khelya's stick and darted up toward the treetops.

Dask muttered something and took off after him. The two disappeared into the leaves.

Khelya lowered her stick. "Thosten willing, Dask'll get him. Who were those dirtwads? Hey, you look like you're about to keel over. You okay?"

Matil nodded. But now that the scary shoeless alva was lying on the ground, unconscious, and everything had happened without her doing anything, the tension felt like leaving. Along with her breakfast.

Khelya dropped the stick and made her way over to Matil in a few short strides. She knelt and put her thick arms around Matil. Matil sniffled and laid her head against Khelya's expansive shoulder.

Presently, Khelya pulled back and regarded Matil with solemn eyes. "You looked like you needed a hug. What's wrong, anyway?" She sat down and glanced at the trees above them. "Is this all Dask's fault?" She picked up her stick again. "I can beat some sense into him, if you want. I could even beat the sense outta him if it was that bad."

"No, I—well, yes—but…" Matil launched into a quick description of everything that had happened since they left Khelya. As she finished, she said, "Lying…I think it… frightens me, and it's very hard to trust someone who does it all the time."

"You don't have to trust him. You *shouldn't* trust him. From what it sounds like, he doesn't exactly follow the rules. And I knew it, too."

"But if we're going to be traveling with him, we can't always suspect him of the worst."

"We can and we should. I don't wanna wake up one morning to find that he's gone, along with all my stuff. He would do it if he didn't want to travel with us anymore."

"He would?"

"No question. But you know what? We don't need him anymore."

"What do you mean?"

"We have a path that goes straight into Obrigi. What use is a Ranycht there? Obrigi is my territory."

"I don't know…"

Matil heard a rustle above them. To her relief, it was Dask coming through the leaves. As he flew closer, she could see that he looked glum.

"I lost him," he said when he landed.

Khelya patted Matil on the shoulder, then heaved herself up. "Think about what I said."

"Hm?" Dask looked between them. "What did I miss?"

"Stuff you needn't be concerned with."

"…Whatever. We need to get out of here before Mister Grumpy wakes up or more of my old buddies come looking for me. The other guy saw Khel. They know my name and now they know I'm traveling with an Obrigi *and* a wingless Ranycht. I couldn't be more visible." He ran a hand through his sweaty hair, causing it to stick up. "You lead the way, Matil, you know where the Book is."

Matil eyed him uncertainly. *You shouldn't trust him.* What should she do, then? Send him away? For now, it was time to be on the move again. While her body protested and begged her to sit down, the trail she felt in her mind was urging her onward. "Let's go."

As they set off, Dask said, "So, um…did you want to know what those alva were all about?" he said.

Matil looked down. "Sure." Not really.

"The one who flew away was an assistant to the big one. The big guy wasn't my boss, but we worked in the same… company, and I'd done some jobs for him in the past. Now, we had a shipment we were expecting. That's what I was supposed to get. But then I quit. I didn't want to tell *that* guy I quit because he's pretty mean. Nobody likes him. I just wanted a clean break."

"You brought him to Khelya so she could knock him out because you didn't want to tell him you quit?" Matil said.

"I…yeah. It sounds bad, but the company was really expecting that shipment and I would have been in a lot of trouble. You heard that guy threatening me. Just don't worry, Matil."

Her stomach twisted as she realized that she couldn't help worrying.

So that was what it felt like to distrust a friend.

8

Large Country

The day ended in Obrigi, not long after they slipped past Ranycht and Obrigi border patrollers busy trading jeers and mockery from their respective posts. Matil had begun this leg of the journey with an urgent feeling, but she relaxed as they followed the trail. When they found a safe place and decided to bed down for the night, it was early. Everyone was exhausted and sleep came easily. Matil awoke in the morning with the faintest wisp of a dream that soon faded away completely. She had slept too deeply to remember.

As they went on, Matil found things sliding into monotony a few times, but the presence of her new friends and their abundant conversation warded off boredom. Dask kept making subtle jabs at Khelya, while the Obrigi occasionally used not-so-subtle wording. They didn't get angry, however, so Matil eventually gave up telling them off every time Khelya called Dask 'birdface' or Dask flew up and stepped on Khelya's head, wings flapping merrily.

The forest continued in the formula she was now used to. In Nychtfal, the woods were thicker and darker. The trees in Obrigi were farther apart and the sun dappled the wide meadows cheerily. Matil could have done without the dappling. Dask's squinting and scowling suggested that he felt the same way.

Each of them tried their hand at hunting for food. Dask was the expert because he had often traveled through the wilderness. Khelya didn't have as much experience with that, but with the help of Matil's knife attached to the end of a long stick, she did take down a small squirrel. The fight left her with a few scratches, which worried her, though Dask didn't think the squirrel was diseased.

Matil tried skinning and discovered that she couldn't do it without feeling queasy. Cooking the meat, once Dask taught her the basics, wasn't as difficult to her. She enjoyed it, too, making sure the meat was roasted just right all over – but her first attempts were very charred. They had plenty left after lunch and even some after dinner. Dask mentioned the possibility of selling the skin, but it was too big to carry with them.

When they had a free moment, in the mornings, evenings, or during breaks, Matil and Dask took up sparring with twigs in place of their daggers. It further unearthed Matil's knife-fighting instincts and skill, and gave her practice dealing with a flying opponent.

With Khelya and her map guiding them, they managed to stay away from the more settled areas. There were still enough Obrigi around, though, that Matil and Dask occasionally needed to go unseen. Khelya bought a rickety handcart in which she could hide them under the blankets. The Obrigi, from what Matil could hear of their ready greetings and boisterous voices, were quite friendly. When she caught glimpses of them, she was surprised. Khelya was short for an Obrigi. The others tended to be at least a head taller.

Another thing that struck Matil was how similar each Obrigi's clothes looked. The colors didn't go beyond various drab shades of red, brown, white, and green. Shirts for man, woman, and child alike were all in the same two or three styles. The outfit Khelya wore was only slightly different from those of the other Obrigi.

Khelya seemed to continue longer between rests when pushing them in the cart than when they traveled by her side. Dask explained that Obrigi could keep going for a long time without wearing down much, provided they didn't stop. When they finally did, the exertion crashed down on them. Matil believed him; on their lunch breaks, Khelya fell asleep.

A few times, they crossed bridges over streams. Matil had peeked out of the cart the first time so that she could see, but the water, reflecting shattered bits of sunlight, quickly drove her back under the blanket.

The trail turned north a short way into Obrigi. Dask wondered why the trail didn't just lead straight to the

Book, but Matil guessed that it was following the way the thief had gone. As they went past farms, she enjoyed looking out of the cart at the huge houses. Most of them were in the style of Khelya's ruined house; stout and sturdy, with slanting walls and thatched roofs. Children as tall as Matil played on the fortress-like 'low' stone walls, and plump, brown-and-white quails shuffled around in large pens.

At the end of the second day in Obrigi, they found another safe place to rest. It was a cozy area in the middle of a ring of five thin trees whose branches had grown twisted together. Bushes encircled it, providing plenty of cover. They didn't build a fire, but made do with cold leftover meat and berries.

"It doesn't feel safe, sleeping on the ground," Dask said.

Khelya spread out her blankets. "If we had more knives, I might be able to get up one of them trees. But we don't, so I won't."

"What? Knives?"

She ignored him.

"You're weird, you know that?"

Matil couldn't sleep with the trail burning in her mind. They were getting close. She wanted to tell them all to get up and march. But it was only one night. She yawned. Maybe she should pull another blanket over herself. She'd be warm and toasty then…

* * *

"How do you do, Magistrate Crell? It's been a long time."
Matil curtseyed. "This is my important guest, Princess Arla.
She's from Vangara." Her vision came into focus and she saw
the boy named Crell and the blue-eyed girl, Arla. They stood
in a small yard of sparse, dark grass raggedly cut down to the
height of their waists. Father's herb garden nearby filled the
air with crisp scents. At Arla's feet was a walnut-shell filled
with water. A house made of woven plant fibers sat nestled
between two young trees a few lengths away.

Crell bowed awkwardly to Arla.

Matil leaned over. "Say, 'You're a Nervoda?'"

"You're a Nervoda," Crell recited blandly.

Arla nodded. "Yup. I'm a *princess* Nervoda." She cupped
some water in her palm and threw it at Crell. She giggled
as it splashed his face.

He wiped it away sullenly. "Can we play bandits now?"

"Shhh!" Matil said. She cleared her throat. "Dear
Magistrate, why don't you tell the princess all about the
old days when you fought robbers in the woods? Oh no!
Look, there are some bandits now! Please teach us how to
fight them!"

Crell gave her a gap-toothed smile.

His punching lesson was coming along well when a man's
voice interrupted.

"Where did those flightlings go?"

"We're out here, Father!" Matil shouted cheerfully.

A bearded man with purple eyes flew over the house
and landed next to them. "I think it's about time you came

around back to see the surprise I've got."

They all followed him eagerly around the house. Matil searched the empty little yard, confused; nothing was out of place. But the rose bush…

There was a hole in the rose bush!

Matil, Crell, and Arla ran over to the hole and peeked in. It was a tunnel made of sheets of bark and was almost as tall as Father.

"Be careful you don't hurt yourselves on the thorns," Father warned.

"What is it?"

"Go in and find out."

Matil walked through the tunnel, the sweet smell of roses floating all around her. The tunnel ended in a small room with a table, chairs, and her favorite toys. She squealed in amazement. It was her very own little house.

"Thank you Father! *Thank you thank you thank you!*"

She heard his golden laughter as he walked in behind them and put his arm around her.

* * *

Matil woke up with tears in her eyes. She sat up, bewildered, and wiped them away with the blanket. Neither Dask nor Khelya were awake yet. She gazed blearily around the little stand of trees. Morning light filtered in through the leaves. Birds sang loudly. Fat drops of dew speckled everything.

And someone else was there with them.

Matil met the gaze of what looked like an alva.

He wore a tattered shirt and pants, and his brown hair was so shaggy that it nearly covered his dark eyes. He was smaller than Matil, but also had no wings. His ears were large and rounded and positioned higher on his head than normal. With his back hunched and his face twitching with nervous energy, he almost looked like an animal. Matil stared for too long before she noticed that he was holding Khelya's bag.

What should she do? She began to stand up slowly.

In the blink of an eye, the alva grew fur all over, his face lengthened out, and his hands and feet became pink paws. As Matil gaped in shock, he bolted.

"H-*hey!* That's ours!" she yelled.

Dask launched himself out of his blanket. "Whas goh non?" he said with a dazed look.

Matil ran to the edge of the trees and peered through the bushes. The alva was gone. She turned frantically to Dask. "There was an alva who turned into a mouse and left with Khelya's bag!"

Dask settled back down glumly and folded up his wings. "We're not going to catch it. Those things won't be found if they don't want to be found, and I'm not a great tracker."

"What was he?"

"I think we talked about them before. They're called Kyndelin. They can turn into an animal."

"Any animal?"

"No, only one. It's inherited or something. They're kinda like the Skorgon except, you know, not bugs. Anyway, they're not seen very often. Better at blending into the forest than most Ranycht." He looked at the spot where the bag had lain until recently and asked dispiritedly, "What did we lose?"

"The map, definitely. The rest of the food, too."

"Talrach," he muttered. He shook Khelya's shoulder. "Hey," he said grumpily, "are you a log or an Obrigi? Oh, wait, that was redundant, wasn't it?" He snickered.

Matil lightly swatted him.

Khelya mumbled unintelligibly and turned over. She opened her eyes and looked up at them without saying anything.

"Your bag was stolen by a Kyndelin," Dask said.

Khelya sat up quickly. "*What?*"

"In your mind, repeat what I just said. Then you'll have the gist of it."

Her shoulders slumped. "At least we still have the cart and the blankets. And it's the season of Briden, so food shouldn't be hard to find. You know what? Things aren't so bad."

"Still," Dask said, "I should've set up a watch. We were all so tired and I thought we were hidden well enough. It was only a Kyndelin, though, could be worse."

Matil smiled. They began their morning with a minor disaster; they ended it with optimism. That was how real teams worked together.

Khelya leaned back against a tree. "Now go fetch us some breakfast, Dask."

"Hey, I foraged the last two times. I'd say it's about time you get us another squirrel."

"My scratches haven't healed all the way yet, not to mention that was a lucky find!"

"Sure, but you can go find berries just as well as I can. So…shoo." He waved his hand dismissively.

"Stupid, dumb, idiotic…Matil, come with me, we're gonna get breakfast."

9

Caught in a Downpour

After a scant breakfast of berries and a cricket, they left the ring of trees with haste. Matil had shared her feeling that they were nearly at the Book, and that was good news to all of them.

Khelya looked up at the sky and heaved a sigh.

"Clouds're coming in," she said.

Unsurprisingly, she was right. The light was dimmer and the clouds gave everything a sharp, cold cast to match the dropping temperature. For some time the wind had been picking up and now it pressed powerfully against the group as if urging them backward.

"Rain?" Dask said.

"Rain." Khelya watched her feet. "I would be inside today, warming my hands by the stove. The rain would start to fall outside and I'd be so excited 'cause just a couple days earlier, I'd have sown the last of my seeds."

Matil bit her lip. "I'm really sorry."

"Not your fault. I'm just going to have to get through it. Might've happened to me sometime later anyway. Farmers have to deal with stuff like this." She set her jaw and nodded firmly.

The Book's trail led past a relatively small village – where Matil and Dask hid in the cart – and wound through a blackberry thicket, which they walked around to avoid the thorns. Since they had lost the map, Khelya didn't have any clue where they were. However, Matil was confident that what was at the end of the trail would solve their problems.

That feeling grew stronger as they walked until…until it was just a few lengths in front of them.

Matil could think of nothing else. It was so important. She had better run for it.

"Hey!"

"Matil!"

The Book was close. Matil sprinted as fast as she could, sliding under a root and pushing past leaves. *Almost there.*

She skidded to a stop in a tiny meadow. The trail was gone. An overwhelming feeling of loss filled her. She looked around, but couldn't see where the Book might be.

Khelya pounded into the meadow, pushing the cart. "What's wrong? You look terrible." Dask flew in behind her.

Matil stared blankly. "There's no…" She walked back a few paces and was immediately gripped with a sense of purpose. She *had* to find the Book. It was right in front of her. If she just walked over—

The trail was gone again.

She tried one, two, three more times as Khelya and Dask looked on in confusion and asked her what was wrong.

"The trail ends here," she finally said.

Dask grinned. "So the Book is around here somewhere?"

"Maybe?"

"What do you mean, 'maybe'?"

"The trail just stops. There's nothing left. If the Book were really here, wouldn't the trail lead right up to it?"

He looked thoughtful. "I don't know much about magic, but you might be right. In that case, we just wasted half a week. A whole week, including the return trip to Nychtfal."

"But if the Book isn't here," Khelya said, "what's the trail for?"

"It *was* a trail to the Book. I could feel it." Matil sat down wearily in the dirt.

Dask crossed his arms, opened his mouth, and paused. "I'll bet it was a trick."

"Why would it be a trick?"

"The thief made the trail to mislead anyone who magically examined it. At least, that's how I see it."

With an irritated look, Khelya pushed up her cloth headband. "What do we do now, then?"

"When Matil first got the trail, she called me Crell."

"Oh, right. When she went crazy?"

"I didn't go crazy! I just…wasn't myself."

"All right, when she 'wasn't herself'?"

"Yeah. Anyway," Dask said, "I know a lot of alva and some of them go by the name Crell. I thought I'd see if Matil recognizes any of them."

"Fair enough."

"We're going to have to leave Khelya in Obrigi, though."

Matil's mouth dropped open. "But—"

"It's more trouble than it's worth to hide her all the time. And now that she's been noticed in Nychtfal, it'll be even more dangerous."

Khelya sighed. "He's right. We can work something out so you can get in touch with me when you're done in Nychtfal."

"Well…all right." Something ice-cold hit Matil's head, dazing her. After a moment, she realized that her entire upper half was dripping wet. "What…?"

"Oh, no," Khelya said.

Dask pulled Matil to her feet. "Let's get cover."

"Agreed."

"That's rain," Matil said, awestruck. She shivered. Drops began to gently thud around them. Khelya recoiled from one hitting her hand.

"Yes, it is." She shook her arm. "And it looks like you got the worst of it. Grab one of these blankets and dry yourself off as we run. The rain hasn't really got going yet." She tossed a blanket down to Matil.

Matil caught it and wrapped it around herself, rubbing her ears dry.

Dask pointed. "I think I see a cave under that tree. Should be a good place to wait out the storm."

They all dashed across the meadow until they reached a cave tucked under the roots of the tree. Khelya was still pushing the cart, but Dask convinced her to leave it outside. The opening was just big enough for Khelya to fit through.

Inside, it was dry and much bigger than the entrance. A few tunnels branched off, but the trio decided to stay in the main cavern because Dask and Matil could hear breathing coming from the tunnels. They didn't want to intrude on ill-tempered animals.

Matil found a small alcove and sat in it while she squeezed the water from her tunic. She was glad for the cave, but couldn't shake the depression of leaving the trail. Khelya and Dask sat down on each side of her. They all listened to the rain pouring outside and the wind picking up. Matil's ears twitched and dread made the back of her neck prickle. Soft, crunching footsteps bespoke another presence just as four Obrigi men came into view, almost walking past the alcove.

"Weapons ready!" one of them said suddenly.

Matil filled her mind with thoughts of shadow in an attempt to fade, but jumped back when the giants lowered large spears. They advanced swiftly and cornered the group in the alcove. Dask edged away slightly and had to dodge a spear jab.

"*Watch* it!" he said.

The Obrigi who had shouted the order now watched them in bewilderment. "Well, Olen blind me. What're Ranycht doing in Obrigi?"

Khelya's mouth hung open. "Uh…I caught these two sn-snoopin' around on my farm. I was gonna- gonna bring 'em to the authorities, but it started raining, as- as you can see."

"Staying by your side pretty as you please? They're sure tame for Ranycht. I don't see any leashes on 'em, and if what you say is true, they'd be gone by now." He was an older alva with a strong jaw and large, drooping nose.

The four Obrigi wore leather armor and light-colored sashes with a strange emblem on them. The emblem resembled a sun, with a small letter in the center. Hanging from their belts were ropes tied to three round weights. The soldiers' hair was close-cropped and their eye colors were all strangely dull or dark like Khelya's. Their eye coloring and lighter skin appeared to be common among Obrigi.

One of the Obrigi smirked. "What are we gonna do with them, Dron?"

"We'll bring them all to the camp when this rain lets up."

"Can we knock the Ranycht around some?" another one said.

Matil shrank back, eyeing their big fists and feet with panic.

"Not until the captain's given orders about them."

"Not even a little?"

"No," Dron said, steel in his gaze. "Do any of you have respect for your superiors? We'll be back at camp by tomorrow and then the captain will decide what's to be done. You can wait."

The four Obrigi stationed themselves at the tunnels and the entrance to keep their prisoners from escaping. They taunted Matil and Dask for a little while and made disparaging remarks about Khelya. Dron didn't join in, but he smiled indulgently and shot disapproving looks at Khelya. Poor Khelya kept her eyes on the floor the entire time. Matil and Dask sat across from her and didn't speak very much.

Here they were, captured with nothing to show for it. That someone had left a false trail…it turned Matil's stomach with bitterness.

The traveling of the past few days caught up to her and weighed down her eyelids. She folded her blanket, set it on the cave's hard floor, and used it as a pillow. As she fell into the mist between wakefulness and dreaming, she heard the smallest of whispers from Dask to Khelya.

"…*a tap on the arm…you pick her up…*"

Soon, the splashing of the rain outside coaxed Matil to sleep.

-

Blistering heat, glaring light. Matil's throat, so dry and scratchy that swallowing was painful. The only thing she could see was Arla. It was too bright to look anywhere else. The Ranycht girl sang sweetly, something about 'green' and 'sparrows'. Her voice faded slowly into a ceaseless background noise that Matil couldn't place.

Now she heard Crell's voice echoing around her, but couldn't see him. The words were choppy and mixed together, almost overpowered by the crackling and whooshing.

"*You made it! ...gone...get out? ...Thosten now...Can't stay...Before the fire catches...*"

The fire.

Now she could see it. The blaze was all around, the light as though the sun had descended to burn out her eyes. Heat and smoke pressed down upon her.

She tried to shout for help, but couldn't.

"Shut her up."

A gentle hand on her arm, cool and reassuring.

"Hjarth, mu olrin." That soft voice. So familiar. "Hjarth...hjarth."

Who was that?

Dask...?

* * *

"It's stopped raining for now."

"Good. Get up, you three, we're leaving."

Matil forced her eyes open and looked out the cave entrance. It was still gray and dark, but only the occasional drip indicated rain. She sat up. Dask was idly poking himself in the forehead with a feather that had fallen from his wing and Khelya slumped to the side on a blanket of her own, snoring loudly. Matil lightly shook Khelya's shoulder. She turned over and mumbled something. Dask jabbed her in the ribs with his foot.

"*Hey!*" She shot up and scowled at him, rubbing her side.

He held his hands up innocently. "Time to go."

They exited the cave and began marching through the damp grass, trying to stay underneath trees and bushes as much as possible in case it began raining again. The four Obrigi flanked Matil, Khelya, and Dask, watching them carefully.

Dask's eyes flicked around at their guards. He leaned ever so slightly toward Matil's ear. In an almost imperceptible whisper, he said, "Listen, we…" He paused. "Never mind."

"What?" Matil whispered back.

"There's an opening, but Khelya couldn't…it's nothing. I know what you'd say."

"I don't understand."

"Don't worry. We have a plan." He looked ahead.

Matil suddenly remembered something that faintly drifted in the back of her mind. "You said something when I was sleeping, didn't you?" she said out loud. "What was it?"

"Huh?"

"When I was…" Fear flitted around the edges of her mind. "When I had my nightmare."

Was Dask blushing? "Oh, yeah, that. Hyarth moo ohl-rin," he pronounced slowly. "It's something my mother used to say to me when I was scared or had nightmares."

"You have a mother?" Khelya put a hand over her open mouth mockingly.

"*Had*," Dask snapped.

She paled and glanced away.

"What does it mean?" Matil said softly.

Dask's angry look melted. "I'm not exactly sure. But I think it- it means something like…'Be calm, my child.'" He shifted his wings so that his face was hidden.

10

This Is the Army

Khelya stared as they ascended the rocky dirt rise of the Obrigi camp.

"I didn't realize we were this far along," she said in a low voice.

Dask cast a look of disgust around the encampment. "What do you expect the Obrigi to do when they're on the verge of war? Spend their days petting caterpillars?"

There were identical canvas tents set up in neat rows under the gray sky and arching branches. The camp was dotted with small fields full of straw dummies of many sizes. Every Obrigi wore the same leather gear as the prisoners' escorts. Many of them wielded huge spears with long blades and were engaged in the activity of stabbing the dummies. Crates and barrels were stacked all over the place and Matil noticed an Obrigi pulling a bundle of arrows out of one. He brought them to a field where others used bows nearly as tall as themselves to fire at targets on the other side.

Some of the soldiers jeered as Dron led the group into the camp. They held their hands up to their heads in mockery of Matil's and Dask's large ears. A line of soldiers marched past in perfect time, chanting something monotonously. Matil listened to the words – they were shouting about an Obrigi saying colthal to his family for the last time – and realized that it was a song.

"I don't know," Khelya said, bringing Matil's mind back to her companions. "I just didn't think it was so close. Oh, thiffen, I'm gonna have to move, ain't I? I'm too close to the border."

Dask raised his eyebrows. "Let me say that if we weren't in the dastardly clutches of the Obrigi Army, you'd actually be set if you wanted to move. You have nothing *to* move. Remember that little fire?"

Matil shuddered at his mention of fire. She wished she could forget that dream. "Dask," she said apprehensively.

"It's true."

"It's rude," Khelya huffed.

"Stop chattering back there," Dron said. He turned to his men. "Report to mess tent immediately." They made relieved noises. "I'll tell the captain what our patrol rustled up, and you fellas will be the first to know if the Ranycht can play."

"Yes, sir," the soldiers said enthusiastically. They plodded in the direction of one of the largest tents.

Dron looked back at Matil, Khelya, and Dask. "Let's move." He turned and walked forward.

"Okay," Dask said.

The next thing Matil knew, she had been yanked into the air and thrown over Khelya's shoulder. She let out an involuntary squeal as Khelya began running. Dask flew overhead.

Matil looked up to see Dron spinning his weighted ropes above his head. "What's going on?"

"We're running!" Khelya wailed back. "I'm gonna die!"

Dask flew erratically, dodging the weights and a couple of arrows longer than Matil's arm. He would make it, he would make it…

Khelya skidded to a stop as Dask landed in front of them in a crumpled heap, the ropes tangled in his wings.

* * *

"These are the troublesome alva? Now that's strange," Captain Barden said slowly. "No wings. And one of our own helping the birdfaces out."

"That's right, sir."

From what Matil had seen when Barden entered the infirmary tent, he had on a chain mail shirt and wore impeccably-kept side whiskers. It was hard to tell if he'd be merciful or…not.

She ignored Barden and Dron now as she watched an Obrigi man bandage the top of Dask's right wing. Dask had been brought down by the weights, but an arrow grazed him and the resulting cut bled heavily. The Obrigi's large fingers kept stumbling and poking – accidentally, she hoped – Dask's wounds. Every time that happened, Dask shifted and made indistinct noises in his unconscious stupor. He had passed out upon landing.

They had taken Dask's and Matil's weapons. It was the first time she'd gone without her dagger. She felt vulnerable.

"…will be executed, the Obrigi will be tried for treason, and the wingless one…We'll take her up to the Council, see what they wanna do with her. How's that sound?"

Matil looked up, worried.

"Fine, sir."

"Treason?" Khelya whimpered.

Captain Barden nodded. "I mean, you going around with Ranycht is pretty treasonous by itself. But near one of our training camps *in* Obrigi? I'm wondering what your plan was."

"No plan, sir," she said earnestly. "I was just doing my friend a favor." She put a hand on Matil's shoulder.

Barden's eyebrows drew together and Dron glowered at Khelya. She quickly pulled her hand away. Matil watched disbelievingly.

"What favor was that?" Barden drawled.

"My…my friend, she…" Khelya hesitated.

Matil wondered whether they should tell the Obrigi everything they knew. Dask might not like it. Maybe she could try to explain some things without saying all of it. "I don't know who I am," she said.

Barden and Dron looked at her in confusion.

"I woke up near Khelya's farm a few days ago. We were attacked by Skorgon, Khelya's farm burned down, and she decided to help me find out who I was."

The tent was quiet for a few moments and Matil realized that the Obrigi doctor had moved to the other side of the tent to work on someone else.

"What about this idiot?" Barden said, gesturing at Dask.

"He was there, too."

"In Obrigi? He illegally crossed the border?"

"It's not very hard to cross—"

"*She means*," Khelya said, "that, uh, he was chased across by some of his own at around the same time I f-found her."

"Mmm…hi," Dask mumbled.

Barden folded his arms. "And I assume you don't know where your wings went?"

"I don't, I'm sorry."

"Or why there were Skorgon in Obrigi?"

"No."

He turned to Khelya. "Listen, you show us on a map where your farm is and I'll send someone down to look for clues. Skorgon could be a real threat. Not to mention Ranycht crossing whenever they well please. All the more reason to tighten up our borders," he added under his breath.

"What- what are you gonna do with me?" Khelya said quietly.

"You'll be investigated. If no evidence is found that points to treason, you can go free."

Matil gave him a pleading look. "And Dask?"

"This guy'll be questioned, but if he doesn't seem like a spy, he'll likely be sent to the Council along with you. I don't like executing those who seem innocent. Council does it a lot better."

"*Executing?*"

"That's what I said."

"Can't you let him go if he's not a spy?"

"He might not be a spy now, but when he got home he'd tell everyone what he saw."

"But—"

"We're in dangerous times. I won't take foolish risks just 'cause you're making your eyes big. Besides, you and your friend, if he's not a spy, won't be my problem anymore. If you really want to save him, you'll have to convince the Council. Dron?"

"Yes, sir?"

"Get these two under guard. Questioning for this one begins immediately." He grabbed the front of Dask's vest and heaved him up off the ground.

Dask twitched and began struggling and flapping his wings. "Wha—hey—ow! Where—*ow!*"

Barden strode out of the tent, holding Dask.

11

Loose Lips

Dron grabbed Matil and Khelya by their arms and marched them out to a thick branch driven into the ground behind some tents. He ordered them to sit, then tied their hands and secured them to the branch, at a height above Matil's head.

"You," Dron barked.

A young Obrigi man nearby turned around in surprise.

"Get over here."

"But, sir—"

"Watch these two. Like an owl."

"Uh, sir, how long should I watch them? I need to get these—"

"Indefinitely."

"O-of course, okay, yessir."

Dron walked off, muttering, "Insubordinate…"

The Obrigi gloomily assumed his post next to the branch.

"'Scuse me," Khelya said timidly. "You have to believe that we're innocent."

"Doesn't matter if I do or don't."

"But I mean…you could…let us go."

He laughed. "Thanks for that, you really lifted up a bad day."

"I'm serious."

"Too bad, then. No chance you're getting free on my watch."

They settled into silence occasionally broken by quiet chatting between Matil and Khelya. Time went on and the gray clouds floated overhead. Matil's arms were getting tired of hanging from the branch; Dron had tied them too high.

"Whoa, hey, the wing still hurts!"

She looked up to see a sour-faced Obrigi with a messy beard unceremoniously pushing Dask forward.

The Obrigi guarding them looked up hopefully. "Sir—"

Dask's escort went past dismissively and bent down to tie Dask to the branch. "When I get back, yer next, *traitor*," he sneered at Khelya. "Don't get comfter-bul." He ignored the guard's mild inquiries and stalked away.

Matil smiled. "How did it go?"

"Wish I knew." Dask rolled his shoulders awkwardly. "I think I did a good job."

"What do you mean?" Khelya said. "All you had to do was tell the truth, right? You're no spy. *Or are you?*"

"No, I'm—"

"*That's* why you were in Obrigi in the first place, wasn't it? I can't believe you fooled us." Khelya shuffled away from him and spat on the ground. "I knew it, though, didn't I? All along, I knew you were a slick, lyin' Ranycht."

"I was in Obrigi to pick up that thing, remember? I know I haven't been...you know..." Dask hesitated. "I'm *not* a spy! I work..." He shook his head. "I don't spy."

Matil looked down in disappointment. He couldn't even say what he did.

She wished she could wipe Khelya's spit spray off of her boots, but her hands were tied. The boots were very dirty anyway. They had come a long way in such a short time.

"So..." Dask said to Khelya. He lowered his voice to a whisper. "Keep quiet about the *you-know-what.*"

"Huh?"

"The thingy."

"What?"

"The...you know, the...*Matil's book.*" Dask's eyes darted around covertly.

"Oh."

"Anyone links it to us and we'll be carted off. That means no more farm for you."

Khelya whimpered.

"They'd lock us up and force us to do their will. So don't say anything about it."

She swallowed. "I won't."

* * *

As Khelya was tied back up, she avoided looking at Dask.

"I don't know what you three have gotten yourselves into and I don't want to know," Barden said. He had brought her back after the interrogation. "Miss Khelya's going with you to the Council."

"What? But Khelya was going to go free," Matil said.

"Not anymore. Listen, with the exception of the winged mudskin over there—"

"You have a nice complexion, too," Dask muttered.

"—*you seem genuine*." Barden gave him a withering look, then turned to Matil and Khelya. "As in, I don't think you signed up for this…stuff. Whatever it is, you're stuck in it, and that means you both go to the Council. But I wouldn't say you were spies or even meant any harm. I could be wrong. But that doesn't happen a whole lot." He turned to go.

"What happens to me?" Dask cringed apprehensively.

"You're a shifty fella, but I can't pin anything on you and I'm not one to mess with the evidence. You're safe until the Council can have a good look at you." He nodded and left them.

"You told them," Dask said violently under his breath.

Khelya shook her head quickly. "No, I promise, I didn't! I just…got a little jittery. The alva questioning me – oh, he was snaky – he had it out for me. And he got all upset when I said some things that were a little tiny bit…weird. Told the Captain to execute me along with Dask."

"No! They wouldn't do that, would they? What were the weird things you said?" Matil said.

"I mentioned your magic trail and talked about going into Nychtfal. I, uh, also confessed to hiding you two while in Obrigi." She cleared her throat. "That can't have—"

Dask groaned.

"—helped."

"Is it very bad?" Matil said.

Dask looked at her incredulously. "No, no, the Obrigi and the Ranycht are only this close," he held up his forefinger and thumb and touched them together, "to killing each other's heads off. Why would a little thing like smuggling Ranycht into Obrigi be bad? *'Is it very bad'…*"

"Then why'd you agree to it in the first place?" Khelya said in a frustrated voice.

"Because," he whispered vehemently, "I didn't think we were going to get caught. In fact, I was starting to think maybe you were trustworthy. That maybe you could actually handle life outside your little farm. I was wrong, apparently."

"Dask," Matil pleaded.

Even sitting, Khelya suddenly seemed as tall as a tree. "*Trustworthy? ME?!* Look at *you*, lyin' down to your *boots!* Just ask Matil how *trustworthy* she thinks you are!"

"What?" Dask turned to her. "Matil, do you think I'm…?"

Matil looked down and her face grew very hot.

"Matil, what do you think of me?" He sounded hurt.

Something sharp but foggy swept through her violently and, to her surprise, she was saying exactly what she thought.

"I did trust you, I did," she said in a low voice, "but you keep answering my questions only halfway. I don't know why you sound all sad when you *have* been lying! You lie to everyone and you tell us to lie, too."

Dask sat back in shock. "I—well, I...Those lies were all necessary! To keep us out of trouble! And I knew you would act like this, so, yeah, I didn't say everything about myself! Is any of that so wrong?"

"Accordin' to the Chivishi wol Thosten, it is!" Khelya looked with respect at Matil.

Matil looked back in confusion. "What's the hee-vee-shee?" That word was something else she had heard before. Something that filled her with a strange melancholy.

"Thosten's directions to us and the Elders."

"They're the rules, hung up in alva's houses as if they actually follow them." Dask let out a loud breath. "Listen, I'm not part of that. Lying is what I do for a living. What I did."

"What *did* you do?" Khelya demanded.

"I ran errands for my gang. Guard duty, smuggling, stealing, stuff."

Each word hurt Matil's heart. He wasn't just a liar. He was a thief.

Khelya gave him a sidelong glance. "Have you... murdered anyone?"

"Never. Sometimes I had to hurt alva, though. Just until they got the message."

And he was a thug.

He had been so nice to her, though. Matil remembered the things he said when they were first planning in Khelya's house. Dask had talked about his job. "You said that you wanted to leave, right?" she said.

He eyed her inhospitably. "It didn't end up being a great idea, did it? I've had to spend the last week with an Obrigi, *on the run*. And here I am now. Tied up and headed for Corwyna. The City of Light. More like the city of 'hello, I'm a Ranycht, oh, wait, where'd my head go?'" He scooted as far as he could away and huddled up, surrounding himself with his wings.

Matil caught one last mutter from him.

"All because of you."

12

The Ritual

Matil spent a long time staring into space hopelessly. Khelya had taken to drawing the blueprints of her house in the dirt and Dask was still covered in his wings.

Dask was upset and it *wasn't* Matil's fault. He decided to come along and she was grateful for it, even now that she knew what he'd been hiding. So when had their search gone wrong? It was that stupid, fake magic trail. She wished she could find the alva who stole the Book and…and…punch them or something.

At some point, it started pouring rain again. They were moved into a tent guarded by two soldiers who flicked wet soil at them as part of a game. The first guard had finally been allowed to leave. Lunch had not been a priority, so it was a while later when another soldier brought dinner for everyone in the tent.

Matil marveled at it. Huge bowls of a warm golden liquid that she was wary of until Khelya told her it was called quail broth. It was a small serving to Khelya, which she complained about heartily, but plenty for Matil and Dask. The broth was delicious and drove back the chill of the evening rain. Though it wasn't very filling, Matil shared some of hers with Khelya.

Dask was silent throughout the meal. He ended up with a puddle of broth in the bottom of the bowl, into which he lowered his spoon, brought it up, and lowered it again without taking a sip. He frowned and shoved the bowl at Khelya.

"Uh…" she said, but Dask was already huddling back up.

The soldiers chose that moment to resume the game and their latest projectile fell into the bowl to a round of sniggers.

* * *

Footsteps and the laborious breathing of their guide was all that Matil could hear. A scratchy blindfold covered her eyes and it made her heart pound rapidly. She couldn't see. Couldn't see anything. She wiped her hands on the skirt of her tunic. Not long after, sweat slicked her palms again. "C-Crell?"

"*Hush!*" said the guide in his harsh voice. "Outsiders do not speak!"

A comforting hand closed around Matil's shoulder. He was there. Good.

Matil loved the dark, but being blind left her vulnerable and helpless. What if somebody crept up and decided to kill her right then and there? She had made a few enemies in the past years. What if their guide was leading them to a room full of conspirators plotting revenge?

A splash echoed in the space and she whipped her head around. She swallowed and strained her ears. It had been a mistake to trust these death-worshipers.

She jumped as their guide rasped, "We enter the inner sanctum. One word spoken inside may kill you! We are channeling powerful forces."

A door creaked open and they walked in. Matil's ears filled with the subdued sounds of many voices chanting quietly. Her skin tingled. The guide ripped off her blindfold and, with great relief, she took in everything. She and Crell were in a low-ceilinged but large room filled with Ranycht. They all wore plain brown robes lined with red, and hoods that fell low over their faces. Their wings were shrouded in cloth. Another measure to conceal their identities.

In the middle of the chamber loomed a round stone platform. Carved into it was a familiar symbol: a circle in the center of a larger broken ring, open at the bottom, and the two attached at the top by a line. Standing in the symbol was a tall, robed alva wearing a burnt-orange mantle. That must be the 'high priest' Matil heard so many rumors about.

"Will the petitioner stand in the Heart?" the high priest said in a strangely delicate voice.

Matil knew that the symbol was the Heart. She stepped forward uneasily. She didn't like being surrounded. A flutter of her wings and she stood next to the high priest on the dais. The tingling grew into an uncomfortable prickling.

"The Gatekeeper likely stressed the importance of silence in this chamber." The high priest's voice was soft, but it carried. "However, his warning is occasionally unheeded. Alva do not believe that we possess real power. Now, some startling things may occur. Many petitioners and uninitiated have succumbed to the temptation to cry out. They were savaged by the spirits we called forth and no remains were left behind." In the shadow of his hood, the high priest smiled. "Remember, not a word. Not even a syllable."

Matil nodded, attempting to look less troubled than she was.

"Your arm."

She lifted her arm and he took hold of it, pulling it out over the Heart. From his robe he produced a simple knife. Matil stiffened. In response, his grip tightened and he raised the knife. "*Sholsi, thokir, en drihol wol dek alva*," he said with a quick downward slash. Blood dripped onto the Heart from Matil's arm, and smoke rose up with a sizzle.

It violated her every instinct to stand still, but she braced herself. *For family.*

The high priest clamped his hand down hard over her wound, hurting far more than the swift knife had. One of the cultists handed him a strip of cloth with which he promptly bound her arm. He then knelt down and wiped his bloody hand in a small circle in the middle of the Heart.

Standing up, he raised his arms and said in a resounding voice, "Lord Myrkhar, please deign to send a servant to speak with us!"

From the smoke that still floated up, an animal's head formed. Antlers spread out above its large ears and long snout. A stag. It regarded Matil with white, fog-like eyes.

The high priest gasped. "My lord!" He grabbed Matil's arm again and pulled her into a bow alongside him.

"Yes," the stag said lazily. "I am." Was this Myrkhar? His voice was almost *too* deep, and for some reason it reminded her of the nightmares she'd had since…

"Uh, my lord, it is an honor and a surprise to meet you at last! If I may ask, are we serving you well?"

"You may not ask." Myrkhar glared coldly at the high priest. "But if you must know, I like my sacrifices with a bit more *spice*. Perhaps you need some juniper berries?"

"Ah…y-yes, my lord?"

Matil felt chills run down her arms as Myrkhar's spectral gaze flashed over to meet hers. She looked down.

"My dear child," he said. "I sense your need."

He sounded genuinely concerned. Matil looked back up in surprise.

"Go on. What troubles you?"

Matil opened her mouth, and then turned to the high priest. If she could have seen his eyes, she was certain they'd have been blank and bewildered. He stayed silent.

Could it be a trap? Was Myrkhar trying to trick her into saying something so that he could devour her?

He watched her closely. "You have nothing to fear from me."

Matil was speaking with the villain of all her childhood stories. Only he had the power to help her. That was why she had come in the first place.

Still bowing, Matil said in a small voice, "Thank you." The high priest tugged on her arm. "Lord Myrkhar."

"Think nothing of it. You intrigue me, child."

"I…" She took a deep breath. "I need to destroy them. All of them."

"Hmm." The sides of Myrkhar's mouth lifted in a foreboding smile. "Perhaps that can be arranged."

* * *

Matil's eyes flew open. She sat up and pulled the scratchy blanket around herself with shaking hands. Khelya and Dask were still sleeping. Two new guards sat in the tent, looking bored. They ignored Matil.

She lay back down.

The symbol in the dream – the Heart – she had seen it before. It was the symbol in the spell clearing that had given her the magic trail! Were these dreams her past? Her memories? They *couldn't* be, she would never…

Myrkhar.

She pressed her eyes closed and an image appeared in the blackness. A stag's head made of smoke.

* * *

Later that day, they were loaded into a large covered wagon pulled by a snuffling mole. In the wagon bed, benches ran along the sides. Dask and Khelya sat on either side of Matil, and a few soldiers sat across from them, leaning back against the sideboard. Matil's and Dask's feet dangled above the floor. Dron was in the wagon, too; he was in charge of the group going to Corwyna.

Dask still wouldn't meet Matil's eyes. She had almost said something a few times. "Good morning," or "Did you sleep well?" But she stopped herself because she was a little afraid of initiating conversation with him and his sulking annoyed her.

So she continued to ignore him. Even though he was sitting right next to her.

"The only games we Obrigi have to ourselves," Khelya was saying, "are the kind where kids pretend to do jobs that adults do. Playing house an' stuff. Everything else comes from the other alva. Catch the Crickets is a fun one. Really simple. You pick who the catcher is and he runs around trying to get the other kids – the crickets."

Matil forced a smile, trying to take her mind off Dask. "That sounds fun."

"We could try it sometime. If we all live long enough. And we'd need more players than just you, me, and Lord Magistrate Fluffywings."

The soldiers had been glaring pointedly at the prisoners or joking among themselves, but now they all chuckled.

Khelya blushed and, out of the corner of her eye, Matil could see Dask scowling. She looked away dismissively, but then remembered last night when Dask gave up the rest of his broth. For Khelya, of all alva.

Maybe he didn't know how to say it.

Matil bit her lip, held her hand out palm-up, and looked at Dask. He glanced at the hand and then looked at her, puzzled. His eyes widened slightly. Reluctantly, slowly, he lifted his hand and put it on hers.

"…I don't regret it," he whispered. "I'll try finding us a way out."

After that, Dask grew more and more sociable. It was good to see him smile again and, though unsettling, just as good to see his eyes scanning the wagon, taking in everything he could. They needed to escape. She put her brain to work, puzzling out different ways they could leave the company of the Obrigi without being recaptured. A distraction, maybe? Matil and Dask fading? Nothing seemed practical.

Outside of the wagon, viewed through a gap between the tarpaulin and the sideboard behind her, rays of sunlight were poking through the clouds. Greatlengths of damp meadow and farmland rolled by; squirrels, mice, rabbits, and other large creatures gallivanted on and around the sparse trees and bushes; and Matil swore she spotted an alva that turned into an owl. If only she could do the same.

Everything was tinted with a brilliant orange as the sun set. The wagon began to pass smaller, more delicate houses than the ones where the Obrigi lived. Pale alva floated around on strange wings that looked like shafts of light shining from their backs. They were a lot smaller than the Obrigi, but most of them seemed to be taller than the Ranycht. Their ears were thin, rigid, and long enough to stick out behind their heads.

Matil watched them warily. At the sight of their wings, an unnerving feeling resonated deep within her that she couldn't recognize at first. She wanted to go back, as far as possible from these creatures. The feeling made her think of Myrkhar's hazy visage, and she realized what it was that struck her bones with such ice.

Fear. Heart-thudding, soul-wrenching fear.

She tore her gaze from the glow-winged alva and took a breath, trembling.

"You all right?" Dask said.

Matil didn't look up. "I'm fine."

"Really?"

"*Yes.*"

"…Okay. If you say so."

She had probably sounded kind of rude, hadn't she? She looked up with a smile that she hoped would hold. "So, are we in Teer…um, Teer…"

"Yep. Tyrlis," Dask said. "Home of the ultimate snoots."

"You have no right to call them that," Khelya said angrily.

"Why do you protect them? On top of thinking they're better than every alva in Eventyr, they're murderers!"

"Shut your mouth," one of the soldiers said, swiping Dask in the head with the handle of his knife.

Dask winced.

"Only that rogue group!" Khelya said. "Besides, what about you? You're all kinds of criminal!"

"'Only that rogue group.' Then why are some of them still walking free?"

"It was found that they weren't involved."

"Ha," Dask said, so quietly that Matil was the only one to hear him. "I wonder if money changed hands…" Out loud, he said, "And I'm…a criminal, yeah, but at least I've never—" He stopped with a bleak look in his eyes. "At least I haven't done what they did."

"Good for you. Wanna know the reason the Sangriga are some of the best alva in the forest?" Khelya drew herself up. "They keep us from becoming *intellectually stagnant*." She pronounced the last words carefully.

"Recited like a good little Obrigi schoolgirl."

"There's a reason for it! Without the Sangriga we'd be ten steps behind the rest of Eventyr in technology and culture!"

"Okay, okay," said Dask. "But that doesn't mean you have to worship them blindly."

"I don't know what you're talking about!"

"You do. You just don't want to admit it!"

"That's enough, you idiots," Dron said, scowling.

Matil eased her hands off of her ears where she had shoved them to block out the noise.

13

The Secondhand City

Houses and farms were closer and closer together as they made their way down the road. Carts and carriages pulled by voles or glossy beetles passed them more often. Matil's apprehension about the Sangriga settled into the background of her thoughts. The night came, and with it, peace.

Eventually Matil looked out of the wagon and tried to comprehend what she saw.

A long expanse of featureless white stuff seemed to be taking over the horizon. She pressed her face up against the gap so that she could see better. The white stuff was a tremendous wall. At the top, lights of various colors shone through the night, giving the wall a festive appearance.

They stopped at the city's giant gate where well-dressed Sangriga guards took a look inside the wagon and Dron relayed his orders. The gate was opened with loud creaks and squeaks, and Khelya began to mutter.

"I'll bet the gate didn't sound like that in ancient times," she said to Matil. "As good as they are, Sangriga don't know how to care for Obrigi stuff. They won't let any of us near the ancients' work, though."

A rumble of agreement came from the soldiers who had heard her quiet voice.

Matil peered out of the wagon with awe as they entered Corwyna. The wall was massively thick, and after they passed through it, she could see that the buildings – also very large – were made of the same white stone. Everything was carved and decorated beautifully, with many domes and a blockiness to the architecture that she hadn't seen in the Sangriga towns they had passed. All the windows were dark.

"The Obrigi built this city?" she said.

Khelya nodded with a yearning expression. "A long time ago, when we could make amazing things that looked nice. We had the blessing of Falgar. He's an Elder, the greatest warrior and artist in Eventyr. I studied the ancient Obrigi a lot when I was in school. Tried copying their designs a few times, but it just didn't look the same to me. Maybe I was bein' picky." She yawned. "It's good to be in Corwyna, despite the circumstances. Always meant to come back here."

Matil looked at the city again. They went past a tree root and she leaned to see farther. The tree was wide and tall, rising high above the tallest buildings. Windows and doors had been carved into the trunk, and balconies had been added in many places. Wide ramps connected several of the balconies. Matil wondered what it was like on the inside.

She was used to Obrigi-sized everything, but Corwyna was even more impressive than what she had seen so far. This was a city built by giants, but it looked like it had been made for creatures much larger. The occasional Sangriga guards patrolling the dark streets were ridiculously tiny in comparison.

Matil saw more tree-buildings like the first one. Some trees were linked by long bridges adorned with elaborate scrollwork. The buildings became smaller and smaller as they clattered down the cobbled roads until eventually they turned and entered a subdued walled compound.

The wagon stopped and they were led out. Matil's knees felt weak, but she stretched them while she walked. Suddenly worried, she turned to Dask. She had been so intent on seeing Corwyna that she only just realized he had been quiet the entire time.

Dask's ears were drooping, his shoulders were slumped, his feet dragged, and his face was full of despair.

Matil guessed that he, like her, hadn't had any luck finding a way to escape.

Khelya didn't look like she was about to die, but her cheeks blazed red and she bent her head as they went into a building marked with a sign that said, '*Holding Cells*'.

"I hope my parents don't find out about this," she said woefully.

The inside was brightly lit, both by glowing balls of light in shallow alcoves in the walls and by the wings of the four guards sitting around. There were only a few items of furniture in the front room – a table, chairs, and a large chest. Dron spoke to one of the guards and then left with his men. Matil, Khelya, and Dask were each taken by a guard and pushed through the door in the back wall.

The next thing Matil knew, she was led to the left, and Khelya, Dask, and their guards were going down separate hallways. She had a brief moment of panic. Why were they being separated?

"Don't worry, Matil," came Dask's voice. "Good night!"

"'Night!" said Khelya.

Matil relaxed slightly. "Good night!" she called behind her. The guard shook her.

"Quiet down," he grumbled.

* * *

Matil rolled over in her scratchy blankets and pulled them up to her chin. Faint sunlight came in through her small, barred window, and chittering birds and the commotion of a city could be heard outside. She sighed despondently.

Last night, she made her way to the cell's bed to sit and sulk, but almost immediately fell asleep. She couldn't really remember last night's dreams. The only thing that came to mind was her, sitting on a branch, with the most desolate feeling she'd ever had filling her mind. She had looked down at the forest floor and wondered…wondered if she should tie her wings shut and then jump. The thought was interrupted by Crell flying to her side with breakfast.

Tears welled up in Matil's eyes. Why would she consider doing something so terrible?

She was startled by a clatter and she turned to see that some real breakfast had been slid through the door on a tray. Her stomach growled and, though she wanted to stay in bed longer, she got up and took the tray.

The food was likely meant to be dull prison fare, but Matil was excited. It was different from what she had been eating all this time. She regretted the silence, though. It would be nice to share this meal with her friends.

A small bowl of some kind of spicy cabbage soup, a stale but sweet bread roll, a cup of water, and a dingy metal spoon had been provided. Matil ate the dripping cabbage first and used the bread to sop up the rest of the soup. The spice lingered in her mouth and she savored the tingling sensation with delight.

When she was done, she took a good look around. The cell was very small, with the entire length of the back wall filled by a low, built-in stone bed just large enough for an Obrigi to sleep on. Set into the front wall was a wooden door with a viewing slot. A metal bucket with a wide rim sat in a corner opposite the bed. Matil knew what the bucket was for, and made a mental note to clean it off before using it.

Attached somehow to the ceiling like an aphid was another ball of light. This one was outshone by the sunlight coming through the small window above the bed. Matil moved the thin mattress to the side and climbed onto the bed to look through the window. There wasn't much to see but the courtyard of the prison compound and Sangriga floating from place to place.

She hoped that something would happen soon or this would be a long day.

14

The Council Convenes

Matil spent a while sitting on the bed and contemplating the near future. Would they lock up Khelya and her and execute Dask? Oh, she desperately hoped not. Would they just lock up all of them? Execute them? *Would she ever see Khelya and Dask again?* What if they had already been dealt with?

She slid down onto the lumpy pillow and clenched the blanket in her hands. That would mean that the last conversation they had was an exchange of good nights. Not such a bad thing to end with, but she didn't want it to be the end.

What could she do? Nothing.

She suddenly remembered when Khelya was asking Thosten to help them. Would that work? Well, if he was listening…

"Please let me see my friends again," she whispered, "and please don't let any of us be executed."

She fell asleep afterward and had a chilling dream. In it, she heard voices speaking but couldn't understand them, and that symbol, the Heart of Myrkhar, became white-hot and branded her arm.

The sound of the door scraping open jerked her to consciousness. One of the guards walked in and ordered her to stand. He bound her hands in front of her with cloth and rope and led her back through the prison.

Outside, Matil was immensely relieved to see her friends waiting.

"Matil!" Khelya said with a huge grin on her face.

Dask was even grimmer today, and the darkening stubble covering his jaw gave him an older look. He managed a weak smile. "Hey."

"I'm so glad…" Matil said. "I wasn't sure if…Why did they separate us?"

Two guards shoved the group forward and they all started walking.

"It's so that we're not 'getting our stories straight' together," Dask said.

"Do you think we're actually going inside the Ambermeet?" Khelya asked.

"You sound excited."

"Last time I was here, I only got to see it from the ground, 'cause they don't just let normal alva in. You gotta be important."

"And we're real important, aren't we?" Dask said sarcastically.

"Oh…" Khelya's face fell. "Um, you know, I don't think you're great or anything, but I'm really, truly sorry."

Dask only grunted.

Matil heard and turned to them indignantly. "He's not getting executed. He's *not*."

"It's sweet of you to be so optimistic, but how exactly am I going to avoid that?"

Her face fell. "I don't know."

* * *

It was late afternoon as they walked through Corwyna. There were more Sangriga flying and, at times, walking than Matil had seen of the Ranycht in Lowen. The noise was confusing and too loud for her, but Dask didn't seem bothered. Little, pink-faced children followed them at a safe distance, prattling to each other. All of the Sangriga that went past wore incredibly fancy garb dripping with cloth and opulent trim. They didn't even bother looking at the prisoners.

The city seemed bigger today than it had last night. The streets appeared as wide as they were long, though Matil knew that wasn't the case. Looking up at the soaring buildings made her dizzy and, high above them, she could see a shiny dragonfly perched on a dome.

She was so busy watching its glassy wings tremble in the breeze that she bumped into Dask's back as they all came to a stop. The group had arrived at a large guarded door in one of the tree-buildings. The guards spoke with the prisoners' escorts and let them through.

The room beyond the door spanned the entire base of the tree. Harried-looking Sangriga zoomed to and fro across the intricate sun mural in the floor, making streaks of light in Matil's vision. The room's ceiling was very high up, and a large hole in the center continued past other floors as far as she could see. Sangriga swarmed up and down the well.

The prisoners were led to the wall, where a steep ramp gave access to the above floors for those who couldn't fly. The ramp corkscrewed up along one part of the wall and they marched on it for a long time. It went through the ceiling and then every two revolutions the group would pass by a doorway marked with a number, starting with one.

When they reached five, the prisoners were pushed through into a long, tall hallway dotted with intermittent doors. Some were even halfway up the wall, with no way to get in unless one could fly. Ahead of the group, the hallway opened into a circular balcony surrounding the well that Matil had seen earlier. Glowing forms shot past, and some of the Sangriga slowed in order to float onto this floor. The ones entering the prisoners' hall stopped completely to goggle at them.

Matil squinted down at the wooden floor. Were they only astonished because no wings sprouted from the hole in her tunic?

The group crossed the tree's diameter, ignoring the doors to the sides. At the end of the hall, they came to a door that let them out on a precarious walkway spanning the distance between their tree and another a couple of greatlengths away.

The walkway went straight through what appeared to be a giant teardrop made of amber. The Ambermeet, Matil supposed. It was suspended from a tree branch far overhead, and it shone with inner light. The walls were deep orange, murky, and filled with bits of leaves and insects. Matil stared at it in fascination as they approached. An encased mosquito stared back at her.

They entered through an ornately gilded archway. The guards standing by eyed them without expression.

As they came out of another archway and into the main room, Matil looked around in wonder at the inside of the Ambermeet. A row of seats ran along the circular wall with another row in front. The rows were crowded with haughty-looking Sangriga wearing purple robes. Their shining wings lit up everything, and Matil winced as her eyes adjusted to the glare. Gentle chatter echoed through the hall. The walls arced gracefully, connecting at the highest point of the ceiling. Upon a raised platform, flanked by preserved butterfly wings, stood a beautiful throne made of lustrous stone. It was empty.

Matil, Khelya, and Dask followed the guards out into the middle of the room where a huge mosaic – also depicting the sun – decorated the floor. A pudgy Sangriga man floated out to them as the talking slowly stopped. He whispered to one of the guards for a moment.

The man drew himself up and cleared his throat. "The Council presents three prisoners," he said in a loud voice, lightly trilling his R's. "A Ranycht and a *wingless* Ranycht," the Council began muttering at that, "accompanied by an Obrigi."

A Sangriga rose to his feet, hunched and wearing robes cloaked with gold cloth. His face was draped in an equally gold beard and he held a delicate, honey-colored staff with many small branches.

"Introduce yourselves," he said amiably.

Matil, Khelya, and Dask looked at each other.

"I'm Dask." His voice carried easily in the resonant chamber.

Khelya bowed at the waist and awkwardly tugged on her headband. "Name's Khelya."

"My…my name is Matil." Matil's gaze flickered around at the staring Sangriga audience.

"A Ranycht with an Obrigi name and no wings?" the bearded Sangriga said. "How fascinating!"

"I named her, sir Councilman, sir." Khelya's head was still bowed.

"You named her?"

"She doesn't remember who she was," Dask said quickly.

"Why ever not? Ah, let's not bounce around. Tell us your story from the beginning."

The three took turns giving the Council a general description of what had happened regarding Matil. Dask even remembered the date that they had first found her, though he'd lost track of the time since then. They left out several things, mainly at Dask's hinting, like what happened in Lowen and every mention of the Book. It made it difficult to connect certain events to each other, but Matil hoped that the Council wouldn't notice.

When they were done, the bearded Sangriga nodded. "I think the Council will agree that what you have told us is not satisfactory. You haven't anything else to say?"

Matil and Khelya hesitated.

"No," Dask said.

"Very well. Now, then, Council, what are we to do with them?"

A wide-mouthed Sangriga woman with elaborately styled hair stood. She left her staff leaning on her table. "I say we send the Ranycht jeppies off to the chopping block, and the Obrigi to the quarries."

"That is…quite simplistic, Gwened."

"Thank you," she said. She sat down with a smug smile.

Another man stood up. He had long, reddish-blond hair and piercing yellow eyes. His staff curled at the end and was studded with the occasional emerald shard. He stared at Matil, disgust plain on his face, then smoothed his expression and turned to the gold-bearded Sangriga. "Simple it may be, but simplicity is often a virtue. Is that not right, Lord Owynth?"

"It certainly can be…"

"Of course. I second Councilwoman Gwened's reasonable motion." He sat.

"I propose a change," said a woman, standing. She gripped a staff crowned with a thick metal triangle. Her hair was pulled up in a simple bun and her sea-green eyes blazed out at Matil with intense curiosity. The scowl she wore seemingly tried to hide her curiosity by silently threatening everyone in the room with a staff-thrashing.

"Please state your change, Lyria."

"This Ranycht appeared the day after the artifact was stolen. Would it not be worth our while to have our magicians examine her mind? To see if we can uncover some of her memories? Perhaps they contain a clue."

The yellow-eyed Sangriga rose again. "Is there any proof that the birdwing is connected to the artifact? No. Our magicians currently have far more worthy projects."

"My dear Nider, I do believe that this strange group has more to tell us. Haven't you?" Lyria gave Matil a meaningful look.

Matil looked frantically at Dask, trying to ask him questions without saying anything. He mouthed the word *'Book'*.

"I could sense the magic at the site of the spell in Nychtfal," she said. "And the only thing I really remember is the name 'Myrkhar'."

"Perhaps not irrefutable proof," Lyria conceded, "but certainly of interest."

"It is, it is," the bearded Sangriga, Owynth, said.

Nider shook his head slowly. "Allow me to understand this, Lyria. You wish to waste valuable time and effort on a mere Ranycht?"

The Council murmured.

"She is no *mere Ranycht*, as you can quite plainly see."

"But perhaps her wings were torn off?"

"I don't have any scars there," Matil said just loudly enough for the others to hear.

"Then she could have been born with a defect."

"I've never seen a Ranycht without wings unless they've been, you know, removed," Dask said, grimacing. "Matil's definitely got something wrong with her, but I don't think it's that. Oh, and I don't mean that in a bad way, just that she's different and…yeah." He looked apologetically at Matil.

Owynth tapped his staff on the floor and everyone looked toward him. "Lyria's point is valid, and I must admit to wondering about the origins of this Ranycht. I also see possible knowledge to hold over Nychtfal, if not a clue as to the night of the theft. Thus, I revise the motion. Work duty for the Obrigi, execution cell for the male Ranycht—"

Matil shook her head fervently. "But, sir, Dask—"

Owynth ignored her. "—and a waiting cell for the female Ranycht. All in favor?"

Well over half of the Council floated into standing positions.

"Very good. All opposed?"

Nider, Gwened, and a few other Sangriga stood. The decision was clear.

Owynth brought down his staff again, louder this time, and said, "Motion passed."

15

Enemies or Allies?

Once they returned to the prison compound, Matil sat on the waiting cell's bed and stared at the dim shadows in the corners. She would survive – at least while they studied her – and she might learn her past. But Dask's life was too heavy a price to pay.

Those last moments as they had been marched out of the Ambermeet repeated in Matil's head. Dask wouldn't say anything except for a quiet, "Colthal, Matil," as they were separated. Khelya alternated between subdued and immensely relieved that she had gotten off with work duty. She tried to make things cheerful by saying she'd try to visit, but it didn't stop Matil from crying.

Matil had noticed, though, that Khelya locked eyes with Dask and gave him a respectful nod. It was an improvement, even if it wouldn't be a very long-lasting one.

That thought brought on a fresh wave of tears.

A muffled, but familiar voice made her look up at the door.

"I would like to speak with the prisoner," came the condescending tones of Councilman Nider.

"Yes, sir."

Matil wiped her eyes and stood as the door slid open. Nider strode in. He was wearing flowing green and gold robes now instead of purple, and his wings lit up the room far more than did the little orb of light on the ceiling. He carefully slid the door closed again and turned around to glare at her with those unnerving yellow eyes. Stepping forward, he seemed to fill the room.

"What are you doing here?" he spat. "Do you think to have us both killed?"

Matil flinched away from him. "I—what—"

"You got what you wanted, so why did you come back? You are a fool!"

"I've never been here before!"

"*Now you're lying?* What purpose will that serve?"

"I swear, I don't know who you are and I've never been here before! I'm not lying!"

"You—" Nider stepped backward. He narrowed his eyes. "You're telling the truth."

Matil nodded desperately.

"Then…I mistook you for someone else. I hope that you will accept my humblest apologies."

She looked at him in apprehension. "Really?" she said.

"Of course. I was rash and I should have asked who you were before simply assuming. Could I possibly stoop any lower?"

"I-it's all right."

"Yes, yes. I shall leave you be. Once again, my apologies." He inclined his head.

Matil smiled uncertainly as Nider left the cell. The guard shut the door.

"The Council has no more need of this Ranycht," Matil heard Nider say. "I will send someone to dispose of her shortly. Let him in, will you? Take this for your trouble." There was the sound of clinking metal.

"What?" Matil cried.

No answer. She slid down the wall and put her face in her hands. Why did the Councilman want to kill her? Why had the Skorgon tried to capture her? Did she have some kind of criminal past? She was horrible for bringing Dask and Khelya into whatever this mess was. Khelya lost her farm and would be sent to work for the Sangriga. Dask would die. Now Matil would die, too, and it would all be for nothing.

She looked up. There had to be some way she could escape and find Dask and Khelya. They were all in the prison compound once again, so it wasn't impossible. Ranycht were supposed to be naturals at sneaking around, too.

Matil looked around the cell carefully. Surely there was some kind of weakness that she could exploit.

The bedding was too flimsy to do anything. The bed was built-in and all stone like the one in her last cell, so no help there. The washbasin on its stone pedestal was likewise fused to the floor. A dripping pipe came out of the ceiling above the basin, but Matil didn't know how to get it out of the moldy stone. Nothing could be done with the ceiling light. The toilet bucket was the only thing that could be picked up and used as a weapon.

What to do, then? She could hide next to the door and fade. Then, when the assassin came in, she could throw the toilet at him, dart out, dodge the guard, and leave the small building she was in. From there, she would sneak into the building with the execution cells and get Dask. Then they could escape Corwyna somehow. Matil looked at the door dubiously. It was very unlikely to succeed. But she had to do *something*. She would die if she didn't.

Matil went to the bed and then shoved the pillow underneath the blanket. She fluffed up the blanket so that it looked like someone could be underneath. Tilting her head, she heard a conversation begin outside the door.

"'Ello," said a rough voice.

"Are you Nider's man?"

"Council secrecy, mate. Don't go tossing round names, eh?" He and the guard chuckled.

Matil quietly went and crouched next to the door, all her muscles tensed. She willed herself to blend in with the dark. Trying to contain her excitement, she watched as her arm melted away, leaving only a faint silhouette.

The door slid open and a figure disguised in a hooded cloak leaned in.

"Hey," he said. "*Hey*. Wake up. Huh. This one sleeps like a rock." He walked over to the bed.

Matil threw the toilet wildly and launched herself out the door. With chagrin, she heard it clang against the wall as she ran toward the stairs that led out. A new guard was just coming down the stairs. Seeing her, he drew his sword.

She skidded to a stop, leaned from foot to foot, then turned and ran deeper into the building. Something hit the back of her head, jarring her brain painfully. She fell forward dizzily. A dull thump accompanied her connection with the floor. She could see spots buzzing around the room and everything was…gray. Had the room been gray before?

Matil realized that she was going under and felt peaceful. She wouldn't be waking up.

* * *

Matil woke up.

She opened her eyes and stared at the ceiling, wondering why she had been put back in the cell. She was supposed to have been disposed of by now.

Matil shifted onto her side. She winced at the throbbing in her head and her eyes focused blurrily on the wall. She frowned. Since when had the cell wall been blue and upholstered? She sat up suddenly, then held her head and groaned.

Leaning back a little, she surveyed the room she was in. The bed she lay on was an ornate couch. Similarly fine furniture dotted the room. The wood floor was strewn with large carpets and the walls curved gently to join the ceiling. Along one wall were several windows with curtains drawn, and a huge bookshelf dominated the opposite wall. A few small lamps lit the space.

"Ah," came a woman's taut voice. "I was just about to wake you. No need, I see."

Matil turned her head, startled, and immediately regretted it. Her head felt like a waterskin filled to bursting. To her surprise, she recognized the alva standing in the tall archway.

"Council—" Matil groaned. "Councilwoman…Lyric?"

"Lyria. You remember me. Good." She was carrying a tray of something as she strode into the room and sat down in a chair that faced Matil's couch. "I was told you tried to escape." She placed the tray on a nearby table. "Here. Some refreshments if you feel up to eating."

Matil scowled. Almost without realizing it, she pressed herself to the back of the couch to get away from the Sangriga. "I wish I hadn't missed with the bucket."

"It's for the best. You might have hurt my agent."

"*Your* agent? He wasn't working for Nider?"

"No. Now, in addition to other things, you might be wondering why you aren't dead. This is the reason. Nider acted quite suspicious at the meeting, so I had my man follow him. My agent overheard his discussion with you,

134

headed off and delayed Nider's agent, and brought you to my home." Lyria gestured at the room.

Matil gazed blankly at her. "Why?"

"I don't trust Nider. From what my agent heard, it seems very possible that he knew you."

"Even if he knew me, I don't remember him! I think he believed me when I told him that. Why would he still want me dead?"

"You were to be examined by capable Sangriga magicians. If anyone can illuminate forgotten memories, it is they. I suspect that Nider was afraid of what would be unearthed. The question is, why is he afraid?"

"All right, that's easy. Let's get the magicians to take a look at me."

"Nider will kill you if you stay past tonight. I can't even have you watched and guarantee your safety because the guards take bribes."

"Why don't you tell the Council and have him locked up?"

Lyria laughed bitterly. "If only Council politics were that simple. No, the solution is for you and your friends to leave right away. You—"

A door shut loudly in the other room and a familiar voice reached Matil's ears.

"Can I talk *now*?" Khelya said. "Where are we? What's going on?" The Obrigi stopped in the archway, squinting into the room. A smile appeared on her face. "Matil? That you?"

"Khelya!" Matil said. She clutched her head, cringing.

The archway was big enough for Khelya to walk through without a problem, but she had to wend carefully between the furniture. She sat down on one of the carpets next to the couch. "How'd you get here? Are you okay?"

"I got hit in the head, but, um, I'm okay. I think."

"*Hit* in the *head*?"

"Yeah…" Matil noticed the cloaked Sangriga man talking quietly to Lyria. He must have been the agent who came to the prison. Did he even have wings? He did, but they were curiously dim.

"You are to recover the other Ranycht," Lyria said to him. "Black hair, black wings, green eyes, on the young side. His name is Dask Rasker."

Matil's heart grew light. Dask was getting rescued!

"Right, then. Is that the last of 'em?"

"Yes, although I wish you to stay afterward. I may have further work to do."

"Of course."

"Good luck."

The man bowed his head and left the room. Lyria turned to Matil. "Would you like to relate your night to Miss Khelya? Concisely, please."

Matil nodded and told a round-eyed Khelya everything, from Nider's visit to Lyria's idea that they would leave the city.

"You shall be leaving the country, too, as soon as you can," Lyria said. "I'll provide you with transport."

Khelya grinned. "We sure appreciate this, Ma'am."

"You may not be so grateful once you've heard my plan. This is a trade. Once you have gone, I understand there is no way to enforce it…" she looked at them through untrusting, half-lidded eyes, "but in this case I must rely on faith."

Matil's brows creased with worry. "What's your plan?"

"I believe that you are the key to finding the Book so that we can return it to the Vault."

"Why would I be a key? The only thing I have is the magic trail, and that doesn't go anywhere." She sighed.

"Listen closely. The Book of Myrkhar has been kept in the Vault, here in Corwyna, since I was young. I remember well the atrocities committed in its name. As a matter of fact, there was a Myrkhar cult in my town of birth. This cult once obtained the Book, and that day, Skorgon descended on us. The Sangriga were prepared, however, and it was also the day that the Book was put away for good." Lyria became even gloomier than before, if that was possible. "That's what we thought." She noticed the untouched food tray. "Go on. Eat."

Right away, Khelya scooped up several tiny cookies and began munching.

Matil, deep in thought, slowly took a slice of cold meat. "Skorgon?"

"Indeed. Their presence at your, ah, awakening takes my theory – which you'll understand in a moment – a step further. You see, a few days after the Book was stolen, I received word that an alva leading a small Skorgon army had entered a Ranycht town and captured it. Since then, it has been reported that the Skorgon numbers are growing and this alva, known as Nychta Olsta, is in the process of securing eastern Nychtfal. She holds two towns under her sway so far."

"Why is she doing that?" Matil bit into another slice of meat, impressed. She had never tasted such delicious food.

"No one is certain yet. She uses anti-Sangriga rhetoric to agitate the Ranycht and hasn't required much violence. The Ranycht are still understandably…*upset* about the West Nychtfal Massacres and Olsta is likely playing off of their festering unrest. It's possible that she genuinely wants to garner enough support to conquer or destroy Tyrlis – a single-minded goal. It would be more probable that she's looking for power to use for some other purpose."

Lyria shook her head wearily. "Forgive my wandering. The chief concern for now is the alarming quantity of Skorgon that have been reported. They usually keep to themselves in Deep Valdingfal and rarely tend toward Nychtfal alone, much less enter it as an aggressive group. This reminds me far too much of my early experience with the Skorgon. And of what the histories say about the Book: Nearly every time an alva takes possession of it, they summon Skorgon to their side. It certainly makes the Book-readers more difficult to subdue."

Matil looked down, then at Khelya. Khelya didn't seem to be paying attention. She was still shoveling cookies into her mouth and had closed her eyes in rapture.

"So…you think that Nychta Olsta has the Book?" Matil said.

"Yes. *That* is my theory. My plan is for you, Miss Khelya, and Mr. Rasker to travel to Nychtfal, near Olsta's activity, and investigate. Track down the Book if you can, but avoid capture."

"How're we gonna find dis lady?" Khelya said, mouth full.

There was a creak as the front door opened. Everyone looked toward the archway.

Lyria smiled slightly. "The last member of your party has arrived. As to how you will find Olsta, my sources in Nychtfal can guide you. My agent will give you instructions as you leave."

"'As you leave'?" came Dask's voice. He walked around the corner with his arms behind his back, the cloaked agent behind him. "You can take your ashy hands off me. I won't fight anymore." The agent didn't move. "Matil?" Dask looked at her anxiously. "What's going on? What does she mean, 'as you leave'? Did you agree to something? If you haven't yet, *don't*. These are Sangriga. They don't look it, but they're sneakier than Ranycht."

Matil turned to Lyria suspiciously.

"You're going to trust Dask over the Councilwoman?" Khelya said. "After what we found out about him?"

"The difference between me and her is that you can trust me most of the time, but you can never trust a Sangriga!"

The agent pushed Dask. "Be quiet. There's alva we don't want to be 'eard by."

"Explain to Mr. Rasker what my proposition is, Miss Matil, and then make your choice," Lyria said. She looked sternly at Dask.

Uncertainly, Matil gave Dask a quick summing up of what had happened since they were separated. When she was done, she looked at Lyria. "What…what would happen if I said no?"

The Councilwoman closed her eyes and sat still, aside from the wrinkling of her brow and one finger tapping her palm. She seemed younger in that posture. When those bright eyes had searched the room like the moon searched the earth, Matil felt like a child caught doing something wrong. With them hidden, all that could be seen was a concerned woman.

"You would go free," Lyria said, opening her eyes.

"And we'd be recaptured as soon as we set foot outside the door," Dask said.

"No, you'd be arrested elsewhere so that it wouldn't lead back to me." She paused. "A jest. You'll be sent the way I originally planned, with supplies that ought to last until you enter Nychtfal. You wouldn't have any obligation to follow the Book."

That was generous. Matil began to understand why. Lyria knew that if Matil had come this far after the Book, she would keep going.

"I'll take your offer." She looked around at her friends. "On behalf of myself. I don't know what they'll choose and…it's all right if you don't want to come with me, Dask, Khelya."

It wasn't all right. Matil couldn't go on without them. But if they refused, what choice did she have?

Khelya folded her arms. "'Course I'm coming with you. I've seen more of the forest in the past week than I have in my whole life. You've grown on me and the traveling… it's not fun, but if that's what it takes to help you out, I'll do it."

Warmth filled Matil. "Thank you." At least she would have Khelya with her. What would Dask choose?

He looked askance at Lyria. "You're risking a lot to get us outta here, aren't you?"

"Maybe. I can manage the risk."

"Why don't you send your 'sources' to do this?"

"Miss Matil was able to pick up a magic trail immediately that the Ranycht magicians presumably couldn't. If this gives her the ability to find the Book from a distance, she has an incredible advantage over any of my agents. They won't risk their lives to sneak into Olsta's Skorgon-ridden encampments, not even for coin. It is a dangerous business, but I'm certain that being freed tonight is well worth it."

"Oh, yes, Ma'am," Khelya said. "Thank you, we'll never forget this!"

"Yeah, we got captured because we weren't careful enough, and now we're slaves. You know what they say, 'lucky are the idiots'. Come *on*, let me go." Dask jostled the agent.

Lyria waved her hand and the agent released Dask's arms. "What do you decide?"

"I'll do it." He made his way to the food tray, stuffed as much as he could in his mouth, and grabbed a plate piled high with bits of nuts, cheese, and meat slices.

"Do refrain from taking the plate, Mr. Rasker."

Dask shot her a glare and set down the plate, only to make an attempt at picking up the food pile with his hands.

Matil raised an eyebrow, and then smiled at him. "Thanks for coming with me."

"No problem," he said. Something fell out of his mouth as he spoke and he crouched down to pick it up.

"Councilwoman?" Khelya said. "Don't alva like you get butlers and maids and all sorts of servants? I always wondered what it was like, but I don't see none around here."

"Ah. Those. I dismissed them ages ago. They were a hindrance, rather than a help." After a thoughtful silence, she stood up. "It is time for you to leave."

16

Cover Up

The smile-like moon hung above, shining faintly. Matil, Khelya, and Dask were in a covered wagon, curled up under a canvas with crates stacked around them. The agent had gotten them out of the sleeping city with little incident. Now, the only things Matil could hear were the creaking and moaning of the wagon as it drove over bumps and the *tromp-tromp-tromp* of the huge beetles pulling it along.

The group was to be dropped off near the border of Eventyr, to the southeast. As they had packed themselves into the wagon, Lyria's agent spoke to them. Matil was too tired to remember what he said. Something about 'supplies', 'code words' and 'Nervoda'.

She wondered if they'd ever catch up to the Book. As she thought of Myrkhar she felt a pang, like a drop of water disturbing the surface of a still pond. Why? How could she be connected to a legendary and evil creature? She would never associate with evil. It repelled her, just the idea of it. It called up frightening images: fire, searing light, and pale faces with dark scowls.

Then why had she been to that place in her dream and talked directly with Myrkhar?

An alva shouted, jerking Matil out of her thoughts. She listened closely.

"Halt! Halt, I say!"

The wagon stopped.

"Now, what's goin' on here?" the agent said loudly.

"The alarm was raised in Corwyna. Seems some prisoners escaped. Orders are to search every wagon and buggy what's left the city recently. You were one of very few, as you can imagine."

Panic gripped Matil. They were going to get caught *they were going to get caught.*

Khelya seemed to be thinking the same thing; she was shaking.

"Hey," Dask said, so quietly that Khelya didn't even seem to hear.

Matil looked at him. What could he possibly want now? They were going to be caught and he was going to die.

"Cover Khelya," he whispered. "Fade." He moved, ever so slightly, and the shadows seemed to rearrange in order to cover him. He stretched his arms over Khelya's tightly-curled body, twisted his face in concentration, and her hair and skin faded.

Matil could do that. She could. Could she? What if she

was too nervous? She frantically forced those thoughts out of her head and focused on the darkness. It was her hiding place. A brief bitter thought crossed her mind about Dask taking charge. He knew all about smuggling. She smothered the thought. Now wasn't the time.

"…but why would the filthy birdgirl escape?" The agent was stalling.

"I don't know," the guard said impatiently.

"I think it was all pretty fair on her, considering. Oi, you look hungry. I was just about to skitch on some dumplings, myself. Care to have one or two?"

"Well…"

"Stop that," Dask whispered at Khelya. "The wagon's shaking, too." She didn't stop.

Matil laid her hand on Khelya's. Khelya's large eyes opened and she looked pitifully at Matil. Her shaking calmed down some, however. Then, Dask put his hand on Khelya's, too, and she appeared to have been shocked into stillness.

Hide. Fade. Matil shut her eyes and mentally drew her surroundings closer.

"Are you sure you don't want a bite?" the agent said, the barest hint of anxiety entering his voice.

"I'm on duty, I'd better not waste time. Though it is right kind of you to offer."

The tarp closing the back of the wagon made a soft noise as the guard pulled it aside and stepped in.

"Hmm."

Whap! That was likely the guard pulling the canvas from a crate stack.

Whap! Another.

"That one," he said suspiciously, "now, that one looks a bit lumpy to be crates."

Whap! A breeze whipped past Matil as the canvas came off. Hopefully the dark would hold…

To her dismay, she could see the light of the Sangriga's wings through her eyelids. It would drive away the darkness covering them and they'd be seen!

"Nothing," the guard muttered.

Matil inched one eye open and saw, to her surprise, that the three of them simultaneously blended into the dim surroundings and repulsed the guard's light. Wild relief filled her, but she fought it down and stayed motionless. Just a moment more and he would be gone.

The guard sniffed. "Smells like a soggy chipmunk. What do you keep in here? And why's there all this space in the middle?"

Matil yelped as he jabbed her in the shoulder. She whimpered as the darkness receded and they were revealed.

"*What—*"

Matil was pushed aside and bounced hard against the side of the wagon. There were two loud thunks and then silence.

With a groan, she turned around to see the hooded agent staring into the wagon, jaw hanging open, and Khelya standing over the guard with her fists out.

"Good shot," Dask said weakly.

* * *

"I ain't never punched a Sangriga before," Khelya said between sobs. "We're allies an' now I'm a real criminal an' I was gonna be a *farmer!*" She buried her face in her hands.

She was currently slumped against the wall of the wagon. The agent had gone up to the driver's seat to do something and Dask was pacing and flapping his wings agitatedly. The guard was still on the floor in a senseless heap.

Matil stroked Khelya's arm comfortingly. "It's all right, Khelya, it- it was only that one guard." She looked out at the peaceful road behind them. Lights glimmered in the distance, wreathing a few graceful buildings whose windows were dark. The cover of night calmed her and she tried to pass that wordlessly to Khelya.

"Yeah, we're going out of Tyrlis and Obrigi for a bit," Dask said. "We can lay low for a while."

"I'll bet you know a lot about lying low, you dirty… dirty…" Khelya burst into a fresh round of tears.

He put his hands up. "Just trying to make you feel better."

"Listen, you three." The agent came around the side of the wagon with a beetle shuffling behind him. "I'm going back to Corwyna with this poor devil."

"But aren't you supposed to take us to the border?" Matil asked.

"Plans change, especially when one of your deliveries drops a guard. Miss Khelya's taking you to the border now.

If she buys a cloak or a hat or somethin', she should be able to keep from being recognized. Word won't get out for a while yet. You nightskins stay outta sight. Get to Quarrytown, ditch the wagon, and go all the way through the abandoned quarries, keeping east. After that, you know 'ow to get to where you need to be?"

"Yeah," Dask said.

"Good. Keep to the shadows."

"Hm. Didn't think I'd ever hear a Sangriga say something like that."

"What will you do?" Matil asked the agent.

"I'll leave the guard off at the gates with a story about finding 'im nearby. I can add in some misdirections, too."

"What if the guard wakes up?" Dask said contemplatively. "Or runs into you later by chance?"

"Eh, he won't stay awake for long. As to meeting 'im... it's dark and I've been wearin' my hood low this whole time. Our guard shouldn't be able to tell me apart from the King himself."

Dask laughed. "I think you belong in Ecker's Brug."

"It's by necessity, mate. Can't let any Council business find my family. Now gimme a hand with this lump."

Khelya climbed out of the wagon and heaved the guard onto the beetle, which chittered in a disgruntled way. The agent mounted the beetle.

"Wait," Matil said. "Why are your wings so dark? I haven't seen a Sangriga yet with wings like yours."

"Oh, any Sangriga can do this with practice." He narrowed his eyes. His wings flared with light, then dimmed again. "Most just don't."

They all quietly said farewell and the beetle carried the agent and the guard back up the road. Khelya wiped her eyes, sniffed, and closed the wagon's doors. The wagon squeaked as Khelya sat in the driver's seat, and then lurched to a start.

Dask was throwing the canvases back on the crates. Matil moved to help.

"You should get some sleep," he said, handing her a canvas. "This'll be a good blanket. I'll do the same once I'm done."

"Thanks." Matil smiled and curled up on the floor in the canvas. It seemed like she was always tired.

17

Sleep In

"Is Mother okay? When can I go in and see the baby?"

"Hush, my rose. You can go in when it's time."

"But when will it be time?"

Matil sat in the dirt outside of their home. Women occasionally fluttered in and out the door, carrying buckets and towels and things.

Father was next to her, his arm around her and his fingers tapping quickly on her shoulder. "It's time when the midwife comes out and says, 'Bridev is past, vanath triumphs." He bent his head. "Dyndal's wings. I hope—" He cut himself off.

Matil kicked her feet on the ground impatiently. "How long has it been already?"

"Not even long enough for bread to rise. It'll take some time, rose, be patient. I believe your friend Arla's birth took a day."

"I'm going to have to sit here for a whole day? I don't think it's worth all this trouble to have a little sister."

"It will be worth it, believe me." Father gave her an amused look. "And how do you know the baby is a sister?"

"Because I know it. I named her Meskie and she's going to marry Bric."

Father raised his eyebrows. "Who's Bric?"

"One of the mean boys who lives near Crell. Meskie's going to marry him and turn him nice. And then he won't throw things at us."

"What if Meskie doesn't want to marry Bric?"

"Oh. Well, she has to do what I say because I'm older."

"You can't decide who she's going to marry. Besides, that's a choice to be made a long way into the future." He nodded once. "A very long way. Same for you, little rose." He poked her nose.

Matil's surroundings changed. They stood next to Mother's bed. Everyone looked tired and happy.

She climbed up on the bed. "Can I see the baby?"

Mother smiled and brought the gurgling bundle of cloth closer to Matil.

"Hello, baby Meskie."

"It's Bechel," Mother said with quiet warmth.

Matil wrinkled her nose. "That's a boy's name."

"He *is* a boy."

"But I wanted a sister!"

"Hush, you'll scare him. Isn't he precious, olrin?"

Matil looked down at his pudgy brown face and sleepy, ruby-colored eyes. "I guess. Maybe he can marry Arla." She gasped. "And then *we'd* be sisters!"

* * *

The wagon jolted and Matil woke painfully. She lifted her head.

The rattling wagon, the tromping beetles, and the singing of the birds outside were the only sounds. Dask was a mass of feathers and canvas in the back corner of the wagon. His face had disappeared somewhere in the piles.

Matil wished that she could go out and talk with Khelya, but she'd probably be seen. Her stomach growled. She remembered the agent opening the side of one of these crates and putting things in it.

Not this crate.

Nor that one.

No inconspicuous compartments on this—

Wait, there it was.

She fumbled with the roughly-carved door and managed to pull it open, breaking one of her fingernails in the process. With annoyance, she looked down at her hand. Her nails were caked with dirt. She cringed. When was the last time they had been able to bathe? Before the Obrigi camp, certainly. It felt like so long ago.

The supplies weren't nearly as plentiful as she had hoped, but there was enough dried meat and dense bread for a good, if dull, breakfast. The joys of travel food.

"Any chance you could leave some for me?" came a crackly, groggy voice. Bright green eyes stared out of the Dask-pile.

Matil squeaked in startlement and began choking on the bread she had been chewing.

Dask threw off his canvas. "Are you okay?"

"Yeah—" She coughed. "Sorry."

He relaxed and crawled over to the supply crate.

Matil abruptly remembered her dream. It had been so lifelike.

"You know," she said, "I had a dream where I was sitting outside with my father while my mother gave birth in the house."

Dask looked up, eyebrows raised. "Your parents? Like your actual parents? You remember them?"

"I don't know. When I'm awake, it seems like they were made up in my head, but I think I've seen my father in a different dream. I don't remember it very well."

"Is there any more to the dream?"

"Yeah. I was really young. I told Father that the baby would be a girl and I even named her. The baby turned out to be a boy named Bechel." Matil smiled. The dream had been so warm.

"That sounds…normal. Too normal." He put a chunk of meat in his mouth.

"What do you mean?"

"Dreams are weird. At least mine are."

"Oh."

"Like last night, I dreamed that Khelya wanted to shake my hand because it would heal her broken arm. Except her hand was so big that she kept knocking me over accidentally and then we got swarmed by a bunch of angry Ranycht. And then I woke up in my old flat in the Brug and had breakfast in bed. Served by a rabbit. The food was really tasty."

Matil looked blankly at him.

"Weird, right?"

"Yes."

"See, your dream made sense."

A flare of hope lit within Matil. "A couple of days ago, I was thinking that…maybe my dreams are memories. And if my dreams are memories, that means I have parents! And a brother! And…" she remembered now, "Arla and Crell! They were my best friends." Things fell into place. What she had just said was true. She *remembered* something. There was so much still missing, however. Her mind grasped at her faded past and came up empty.

"Memories, huh? We should just make you sleep all the time until you remember everything."

Matil laughed and rubbed her eyes. "I wouldn't mind that."

"Here, go ahead and sleep until Khelya stops."

"I might not be able to."

"Just try. We've been traveling so much that we're all worn out. I'll sleep, too, and I bet I'll drop off the moment my head hits the floor."

"Khelya's going to need sleep sometime, even more than we do. She's been up all night."

"True. Maybe we can find a good place to hide when we get to the Quarries."

Matil settled back down, but didn't get to sleep right away. She lay awake thinking about her family and friends. They must be out there somewhere. Those thoughts turned into vague dreams where faces from her past rose out of the mist and faded back in.

"S'time, guys," Khelya said. She yawned deeply.

Matil opened her eyes with a start and sat up. She yawned, too. "I'm glad we made it." She smiled.

"Not yet, we haven't. Still have the quarries to go through."

"They're abandoned, though, so it should be easy going, right?"

"Abandoned by normal Obrigi, yes, but there are a lotta things that ain't 'normal Obrigi'."

"Oh."

Dask zipped out past Matil and stretched his wings out completely, something that hadn't been possible in the wagon. He put a hand on the top of his right wing where the bandage was still wrapped. "Talrach," he said with a frown. "That hurts."

Matil climbed out and looked around. The sky was warm and uncomfortably bright, but that didn't seem to matter to the dreary gray hills in which she found herself. The grass was thin and scraggly and gravel covered the ground. To the distant north, Matil's left, crags drastically overshadowed the foothills. She realized that they were mountains, even stronger, older, and more massive than the buildings of Corwyna.

Ahead of the group were the geometrically cut cliff walls of the quarry. She walked to the edge and looked down. Ramps had been dug out of the side, going down. The quarry's rough floor stretched into the distance. She turned back to see Khelya consulting the map and Dask flapping his wings experimentally.

"Well," Khelya said, "the quarry doesn't split off for a couple greatlengths yet. Let's move on." She rubbed her eyes.

"How safe are we right now?" Matil said.

"That depends. Right now we *might* be seen by someone from the closest village. So it's not too bad."

"We still want to move soon," Dask said. "The Sangriga might not get on our trail for a while, but we should be long gone by the time they find our wagon."

"You'd know best about that kinda thing, wouldn't you? Now, it's hard to tell how safe we'll be in the quarries. I've never been here." Khelya grimaced. "But I've heard *stories*."

Matil looked worriedly at the wide, empty quarry floor.

Khelya strode over to the wagon where the beetle was stamping and moving its head around slowly. She unhitched it and slapped its shell, prompting it to wander off. "Help me hide this thing, 'kay?"

18

Quarry and Prey

After Khelya had packed some rolled-up canvas sheets in the supply bag, they pushed the wagon into a thick bush and started down the ramp. Dask kept twitching and complaining about how visible they were.

"Remember, talk quietly," Khelya said. "If we're loud, every livin' thing in this quarry and the next will hear us."

Matil decided to ask a question to take Dask's mind off of their visibility. "What are these Massacres everybody keeps mentioning?"

Dask's eyes widened and he looked down.

His reaction made Matil uneasy. Maybe that would take his mind off of visibility a bit too capably.

"It's something that happened a long time ago," Khelya said, "when I was just a kid. See, some Sangriga went crazy and snuck into Nychtfal. They burned down a few villages and that's it. The Ranycht get pretty—"

"*That's it?*" Dask sputtered, struggling to keep his voice low. "*No*, that is not *it!*"

"That's what happened, right?"

Dask looked like his head was going to explode. "*No!*"

"Oh, yeah? Tell us what *did* happen, teacher-man."

"They murdered entire towns! They left behind huge numbers of Ranycht orphans! And it wasn't just 'some crazy Sangriga'. Do you call ten thousand Sangriga '*some*'?"

"Ten thousand's an exaggeration."

"Almost seven thousand were arrested by the Ranycht and a bunch more got away!"

"Aren't you a little biased, you know, being a Ranycht an' all?"

"Where did you learn about the Massacres?"

Khelya rolled her eyes. "I s'pose I must've been in First School back then."

"And who's in control of the Accord's schools?"

"The Corwyna Council."

"Would the Council want the Obrigi to know that ten thousand Sangriga had gone on a killing spree? Don't you think the Obrigi might re-evaluate their treaty with the Sangriga? I mean, if the Ranycht are fair game, maybe the Obrigi aren't worth much either—"

"Shut your stupid face!" The word 'face' echoed faintly and Khelya switched to a whisper. "The Sangriga have always helped us!"

"And what happens when the Obrigi have built all that they need? What if the Sangriga suddenly ran out of uses for the Obrigi?"

"It was just those crazy Sangriga, nothing more!"

"Yeah, well, those nothing more did horrible things! I say you Obrigi should just lose the Sangriga. Oh wait, Obrigi are too stupid to think for themselves."

"*You* won't be able to think for *your*self when I'm through with you!"

"Please, stop it!" Matil's ears drooped. "I didn't know bringing that up would make you so mad. I'm sorry."

Dask closed his eyes. "It's fine," he said. He didn't look fine, but he opened his eyes and gave her what was probably meant to be a reassuring smile. It looked more painful than anything. He bent his head and shuffled his wings.

Khelya blew out a long breath. "*I'm* sorry. I…" She sneaked a look at Dask. "I'm not a Ranycht."

"Whaddaya mean by that?" he said venomously.

She glared at him. "It just means that maybe I don't know as much as you do. About the Massacres. Maybe. *Okay?*"

"Oh." Dask looked confused. "Uh…okay."

Matil was too scared to bring up another topic. They continued in silence, probably for the best. Out of the corner of her eye, she thought she saw something dash across the quarry floor. Then it looked like something had climbed up the wall. Squirrels? Birds? Spiders? Rats? Even Khelya was biting her lip and wincing at every sound.

A single harsh call rang out, echoing through the quarry. Matil's insides seized up. The call was joined by others, and she realized that it was something she'd heard only a little bit before. Khelya and Dask had explained that it was the cawing of crows. But where Matil had heard one or two lonely cries, it sounded now as if there was an entire army.

"Hide," Dask said.

"Wall," Khelya said at the same time.

They flattened themselves against the quarry wall. Matil did the same, pressing herself into the stone. It was just past noon, so there wasn't much shadow to hide in. With the cawing filling her ears and echoing around the quarry, she could completely understand Dask's worry about being visible.

The first crows flew into view above. Matil desperately gathered the small amount of shadow around her and watched, relieved, as her body became darker and began to fade. She grabbed Khelya's hand and the fading spread.

Some of the crows swarmed down into the quarry and came back up with limp, gray-furred shapes. Matil shrank back as much as she could, imagining – but trying hard not to – those black claws digging into her.

She gave a sharp intake of breath as one of the crows landed on the edge of the ramp, a little way down from where they currently stood. The crow's head darted around. Its dark, glittering eyes took in everything – of that Matil was sure. But somehow it hadn't spotted them yet.

As she strained to hide she remembered the last time, when Dask's and her powers had failed them. This time Khelya wouldn't be able to save them with a quick punch to the beak. The other crows would notice the movement and then…

Matil looked up at Khelya. Oh, no. Her light face and hair were too visible. Another peek at the crow confirmed the worst. It was moving toward them in a wary sideways shuffle that would have been funny under any other circumstance.

Khelya met Matil's eyes, then looked down at her semi-transparent body. For some reason she closed her eyes and screwed up her face, as if she were lifting a great weight. Her cheeks and forehead turned red from the effort and then, to Matil's shock, nearly disappeared into the background of the murky quarry wall.

The crow let out a sharp cry. It hopped closer.

Matil closed her own eyes reluctantly and forced her exhausted mind and body to make one final pull at the shadows. She didn't even open them to see if it worked. She stayed absolutely still.

Her arms and legs began to tremble and her heart pounded loudly. If the crow didn't go soon, she wouldn't be able to keep it up.

But none of them had been executed, she realized. Had her request to Thosten been answered? Would they have been saved anyway? Either way, if they'd survived that, they couldn't die now. She had to find out who she was, they had to recover the Book of Myrkhar, and Khelya and Dask had lives ahead of them.

They *must* keep going.

Wind battered Matil's sweating form. She flinched, ready to feel stabbing pain and nothing but air beneath her.

Instead, she remained where she was. Khelya's hand stayed tightly clasped around hers. There were no screams or yells or panicked voices. Only the busy chatter of the crows as they searched for food.

Unable to bear blindness for any longer, Matil opened a squinting eye. The crow had left them. Her heart soared. The other crows flew around, coming dangerously close, but Matil felt giddy and light-headed.

For now, *they were alive*.

19

What Friends Share

The cawing grew fainter and the military-like crow formations departed further east against the hopeful blue sky.

Matil, Khelya, and Dask waited until they were out of sight for certain, and then collapsed.

"I…" Dask gasped. "I leave one dangerous job…where I find myself in scrapes at least twice weekly…and get a new one where the day isn't complete without," he slid all the way onto his wings, "possible death."

"At least back at home I had scarecrows and a bow," Khelya groaned. She sat up straighter with a dreamy look on her face. "And the scarecrows were real beauties, too, with mechanical scythe arms copied off schematics passed down through my family. I heard they were from the ancient times."

"Yay." Dask twirled his hand in the air and let it drop on his stomach.

"Khelya?" Matil said.

"Yeah?"

"What was that…thing you did?"

"Hm?"

"Back when we were hiding. I think you made yourself blend in."

"I did." Khelya seemed just as surprised. "It was Dask's idea, he told me to 'use the magic' or something weird like that, but even weirder was it actually worked."

Dask propped himself up with his arm, then rolled into a cross-legged sitting position, rubbing his elbow and wincing. "Wasn't my idea, actually. Kerl was talking about it once. He used to tell me stories he'd heard about history. This one time he said that in the past alva could sorta share each other's magic. I didn't think it was a big deal at first. You two probably don't know, but Ranycht combine their powers a lot when they need to. That's what we've been doing, Matil, when we've hidden Khelya.

"Kerl said that was only the start of it. Different kinds of alva worked together in the past, sharing magic. I thought it was gross back then, but now that I'm traveling with an Obrigi…" He shrugged. "Anything can happen. Anyway, apparently Obrigi were especially good at channeling others' magic because they didn't have their own to get in the way."

"Huh." Khelya was staring at her hands in awe.

"So Khelya used our magic to cover the rest of her?" Matil said.

Khelya wiggled her fingers. "Yeah. An' it felt *strange*. All tingly. Not bad, though. Hate to say it, but, uh, thanks, Dask."

"'Hate to say it'?" he muttered. Out loud he said, "Sure."

Matil smiled. "Thank you, both of you." And Thosten.

Dask glanced up at her. "No problem. Um, why?"

"Without you two I wouldn't have gotten nearly this far. Thank you so much."

"I've gotta say, thanks for being my friend." Khelya heaved herself off the ground and swiped the gravel from her clothes. "I…never mind. Just thanks and no prob… well, there *was* a problem, plenty of problems, but you're welcome and I'm grateful, all the same."

"Hey," Dask said in a teasing voice, "am I your friend, *too*?"

"Aw, shut up. You're not my friend yet."

He gasped. "Yet? So what do I have to do to become a part of that very special club? Bring you ten squirrel hides?"

Khelya was facing Matil and not Dask, so Matil could see the corners of her mouth turn down. Not in anger, but in the way that it does when one is trying not to laugh. "No, you've just gotta sacrifice yourself to save my life while shouting about your undying love for the Obrigi. Then I'll consider it."

Dask clapped. "Reasonable terms, fair lady. I'll keep that in mind when I'm throwing dungbasks across the border."

Matil chuckled, the stress rolling off of her. Looking up, she remembered a thought she'd had. "That was a crows one."

Khelya and Dask stared at her blankly.

"A crows one," she repeated, feeling awkward. "Get it? Close—"

"Ooooh. Nice." Dask broke out in a grin and he took her hands, twirled her in a circle, then let go and walked ahead.

Khelya frowned. "But that doesn't make any...*ohhh*." She laughed and patted Matil on the back. "That's just horrible."

As they walked along the bottom of the quarry, Dask looked around restively and shuffled his wings. He didn't say anything, but Matil understood. She felt the same.

They were trying to stay out-of-sight as much as possible, walking next to the walls and boulders that lay scattered around. Even so, Matil couldn't shake the feeling of being seen. The cold quarry floor was so barren that they surely stood out. And, a little while after the crows left, the seldom-seen creatures began to skitter about again. What if they got hungry?

A rock fell nearby and everyone tensed and looked up. Whatever had jostled the rock was gone.

Thankfully, there were no more incidents for the rest of the day. The quarry was dark and the western sky was glowing by the time Khelya stumbled and Matil proposed that they stop.

"This time I'll keep watch." Dask peered into a crevice between some boulders, and then jumped back. "Snake," he said. "Let's find somewhere farther along."

As they walked, Matil spoke up. "I'm not very tired yet. I could keep watch."

"I'm afraid you might fall asleep."

"…Maybe. How about I stay up with you until I get tired?"

"Oh." Dask appeared to consider. "Yeah."

They found a hollow, rotting log that had fallen from the edge of the quarry to the floor some time ago. Khelya could stand up comfortably inside of it.

"Yech, doesn't smell too good," she said.

Dask crossed his arms. "So grateful."

"I can handle it fine. It'll do."

They spread out the canvas sheets, ate a small dinner, and Khelya quickly dropped off to sleep, lying lengthwise down the log. The night air had a cool nip to it, so Matil bundled up. She and Dask sat across from each other with their backs – and Dask's wings – against the inside of the log.

"So I know I have a family," Matil said quietly. "Or at least I think I do. What about your family, Dask? What are they like?"

For a long time, Dask didn't say anything.

Matil opened her mouth to take the question back.

"Nice," he said. "They were nice."

"I…" Matil rubbed her nose. The rot in the log smelled sharp and unhealthy. "What do you do to stay awake on a watch?"

Dask looked startled. He ran a hand through his hair, moved his feet around, and gave her a sheepish smile. "I play games, you know, counting stuff. I work out my arms a little bit." He curled one arm. "If it's cold out, like tonight, that helps me stay alert. A lot of times I tell myself stories."

"What kind of stories?"

"They're about, uh, stuff. You know, dumb adventures and maybe being the leader of the gang and what life would be like if things were different. Stuff."

"We're sort of on an adventure right now, aren't we?"

"Heh, yeah. But I don't think it's dumb," he said quickly. "I meant that the ones in my head were dumb."

"Oh, I know what you meant. And I'm sure they weren't as dumb as you think."

"Yes, they were."

"Pfft. Hey, why don't we tell stories? I'll tell you one and then you tell me one. If it would be too distracting, though, when we're supposed to be watching…"

"It'll work, as long as we're quiet and we stay alert. Go ahead."

"All right. Um. There was an old man named, uhhh… *Frask*, who fought…bears."

Dask covered his mouth and snickered.

Matil blushed. "It's not bad, is it?"

"No, no, it's perfect. Keep going."

"If you say so."

20

Outsider

Crell was older. She was older.

Should she show herself? Nerves harried her. How long had it been? Four years? What if he was angry with her? What should she say?

Since she'd left, she learned a lot about improvisation and confidence. She told herself to wait for Crell's reaction before making a move.

Matil flew out of cover, leaving the shadow and embracing moonlight, and landed in front of Crell. He looked up from chopping a branch into smaller pieces. No recognition. Expressionless, he straightened up.

He'd gotten even taller. Still not a sign that he knew her. Until he met her eyes.

His own eyes opened wide until they looked like orange-and-white lily pads. His lips moved – was he mouthing her name?

"You-you're here?" he said. His voice had become deeper, as well. He shook his head and looked at her again. "You came back."

"I suppose I did."

He dropped his axe at once and swept her up in a huge hug. Just as quickly, he let go and watched her with a stricken look on his face. "Are...are you still mad at me?"

"Me? No, I don't think so. I'm just glad to see you again. I'm sorry I ran off. I mean, I know sorry won't help, but I—"

"I'm the one who's sorry," Crell said miserably. "I should have agreed with you in the first place. You were right, they don't deserve to live, and I'm so, so sorry."

Matil was taken aback. This would make things much easier. "Don't be, you were just saying what you thought was right. Now I'm back and we can move on."

"What happened while you were away?"

"A lot of very important things. You remember what my plan was?"

Crell nodded slowly.

"I know it sounded crazy, but I'm still working on it. I've gotten further. I have contacts now, and an idea of where to get the power needed for something like this. But I realized I needed help. I need your help."

"Anything you need, I can do it," he said immediately.

"Thanks, Crell. I've missed you." Old memories washed over Matil in a bittersweet wave of nostalgia. She had hated him so much when she left, but now...now they could be friends again and things would come together. She began walking and gestured for him to join her. "You've, um, heard of Myrkhar, of course."

Crell put his hand over his heart protectively.

Matil had forgotten about that superstitious gesture. "Myrkhar has power," she said carefully. "He can help us bring our 'friends' to justice."

"But- but he's…*Myrkhar!* The bringer of *in*justice."

She spoke in a gentle, reassuring tone. "He does have unsavory associations, but most of what you know is a mere bedtale. I've met with some of his followers and it's not like they're murderous freaks. They're like you and me, and a lot of them are rich. I'm not saying we should join their cult, I just think that speaking with one of his spirits – the followers have ways of summoning them – would be worth our while."

Crell looked up at the trees. "I agree." He gave her a bright smile.

* * *

It was no use; she wasn't going back to sleep. Matil reluctantly opened her eyes.

The quarry was dim and shady. Peering through a hole in the log, she could see crystal clear sunlight falling on the lip of the quarry. She looked away and tried blinking to get rid of the bright spots that had burned into her vision.

The spots dimmed and she found that she was looking at Dask.

He was rubbing his arms and looking out the ends of the log. Matil hadn't noticed the night before, but his stubble was now nearly a beard. Looking at the dark, drooping skin around his eyes gave her a guilty feeling. She should have stayed awake.

"Good morning," she said. She pulled the blankets closer to keep out the chill air.

"Sleep well?"

"I dreamed again. About Crell. We hadn't seen each other in years and I was asking him for help."

"What did you need him for?"

"I don't really remember. I think it had to do with…" Matil hesitated. "I was talking about going to Myrkhar's followers."

Dask's face clouded. "Why would you want to go to *them?*"

"I don't…oh."

"Hm?"

"I had a dream a few days ago where I was in some kind of summoning ritual, but instead of just a spirit, Myrkhar appeared."

Dask stared at her with his mouth hanging open.

"I don't exactly know why I would do something like that and I'm worried."

"You should be! I don't think Myrkhar exists—"

"But I saw him."

"It must've been a spirit who'd convinced the idiots it was Myrkhar. I've heard they're slippery like that."

"It really, *really* seemed like it, though."

"Anyway, I don't think he exists, but spirits and rituals are things you just don't want to mess with. Whatever was going on with you must have been serious."

"I think you're right." Matil's resolve to find out who she was wavered a bit. What if forgetting everything had been a blessing? The more she learned…

Her eyebrows drew together. Even if something bad lurked in her past, she needed to know the truth. She would find her family and friends and get her life back. She rubbed her eyes. "When did I fall asleep?"

"A little bit before the sun came up."

"Aw, I was so close."

"Forget about it. Let's get Khelya."

A few flicks to Khelya's arm were all she needed to wake up, complaining at Dask. They ate a quick meal and cautiously left the log. The quarry seemed as empty as ever, but Matil could still hear and sometimes see things moving all around. The group stole away to the southern wall, for extra safety, and followed it further east.

Eventually, the sun rose to the highest point in the sky. The three of them were now going single file to fit in the shade next to the wall. Matil couldn't even bear to look to her left. The sun glared at her anyway, reflected by the quarry's bright stone floor.

Soon they reached the end of the quarry and began to walk up and up and up the exit ramp. At the top, the ground was covered in grayish, sparse grass and the occasional knobby tree. Nearly a greatlength farther south, toward the Eventyr border, it became more forested again. Dask immediately made a beeline for the trees and Matil and Khelya followed him.

"That's better," he said when they had reached the beckoning branches.

"I don't know, all these trees are kinda close together. What's wrong with wide open spaces?" Khelya asked.

"You weren't worried about being seen when we were in the quarry?"

"All right, I did feel like a woodlouse in a barrel. Still, we're goin' back into Nychtfal and it's kinda nice to be out where the sun can see me."

Dask and Matil shuddered.

"There's an idea! When we find out who Matil is, you two are coming with me to Obrigi in broad shinin' daylight to see a proper Round-the-Ring game."

"That sounds fun," Matil said. "In daylight, though…"

Dask nodded. "Ranycht invented Round-the-Ring, you know."

"Yeah," Khelya said, "but all you Ranycht are so small and skinny, the game isn't any fun. You gotta watch it with players whose bones won't break at the drop of a hat."

"Our bones do not break at the drop of a—okay, listen, we have to be quiet. Stealthy."

She shrugged. "You're right."

Dask gave Khelya a shocked look. "Thank you."

"Oh, stop it."

"Wow, I mean, you just said I was right." He made a low whistle. "That is a big step for all of Ranychtkind. My goodness."

"Thought you said we had to be *quiet*?"

"Of course." Dask grinned.

They continued on under the leafy boughs. It wasn't like Nychtfal, though Matil knew the forest would eventually be thicker and its foliage would darken, but even a little bit of cover, shade, and softer dirt was a welcome change from the stark, gravelly flatness of the quarry.

She looked to her right, the south. Just more trees and plants as far as she could see. "What's past the border of Eventyr?" she asked.

Dask followed her gaze. "Nobody really knows."

"Alva say there's a whole 'nother world out there, filled with humans," Khelya said.

"What are humans?"

"Big creatures that look like us, but sort of don't, too. They're almost like myths, but Mr. Korsen is one and he once said that there are more."

"Mr. Korsen doesn't exist," Dask said.

"Yes, he does. Sometimes he talks with us."

"I know a lot of alva. If Korsen exists, why haven't I heard of any living alva who's met him?"

"I never said he talked *much*. Sometimes whole generations grow up without seeing him, but he always shows himself again."

Dask sighed and rubbed his eyes. "Sounds like someone never grew out of their bedtales."

Matil eyed Khelya's increasingly red face. "Dask, let's talk about this later. Khelya, please, *please* calm down."

"Mr. Korsen is a made-up story, just like the rest of the Elders," said Dask. "Conversation over."

"*Ha.*" The deep syllable resonated through the forest.

Cold terror gripped Matil. Dask took a step back and Khelya sucked in her breath.

"What was that?" Matil said in the smallest voice she could manage.

Khelya tilted her head toward the border. "Look."

Something was out there, just a greatlength or so from them. There was a whoosh, a rustle, and a quiet but deep reverberation in the ground. It was moving. Matil reluctantly raised her eyes higher and higher.

Peeking out from behind the trunk of a tree was a huge face. Matil could only see part of it, a watery blue eye, a gray eyebrow, and its wrinkled forehead, but that was quite enough. She hid her own face and tried to turn invisible.

"If we go slowly enough, it might not see us," Dask whispered.

Khelya grabbed both of them by their arms. "Wait," she said. "He won't hurt us." An excited smile grew on her face.

"Are you insane? Big animals – *bigger than big* animals – are *dangerous!*"

"He's not an animal! Don't you see? Didn't you hear him laugh?"

"Him?"

Matil looked up in awe. "You mean…Is that…?"

"Mr. Korsen," Khelya breathed. "I never thought *I'd* see him, ever. I mean, it'd crossed my mind a couple times when I moved south last year. My house is, uh, was close to the border, but I never expected…"

"That's not Mr. Korsen, now let me go!" Dask flapped his wings and tugged his arm. "Ow! Come on! If you're not going to leave, then at least let me and Matil leave. We're not about to get eaten by a bear!"

"He's not a bear, you idiot!"

"Dask, look at his face. Look at his eyes," Matil said.

"Yeah, I have. So?"

"They're the eyes of an alva."

"A human," Khelya said.

"Even if he is a human, it's safer to assume he's dangerous than to stick around here. We're leaving."

As he spoke, the ground vibrated again, making more of a booming feeling than a sound. The face vanished. Soon, the forest was still.

"Too late." Khelya let go of their arms.

"Don't *ever* do that again," Dask said angrily.

"I just wanted you two to see—"

"What if it hadn't been a human, or whatever that thing was? What if it had been something that wanted us dead, huh? What if you were under some kind of spell?"

"But I knew he wouldn't hurt us!"

Matil put a hand on Khelya's arm. "Dask's making sense."

"It…" Khelya deflated. "Sorry."

He looked a little surprised. "You are?"

"Yes, I *am*, thank you very much." She looked at her feet. "I shouldn't've done that. But," she said, looking up again earnestly, "you did see that it was Mr. Korsen, right?"

Matil nodded, remembering the face. She couldn't figure out if it had been frightening or kindly.

Dask rubbed his shoulder. "I saw something, but whether it was Mr. Korsen or another human or something else entirely, I don't know. I'm tired, we're all tired. Maybe what we think we saw isn't the same as what was actually there?" He glanced up at Khelya's face. "I don't want to get into it right now. Let's go." He marched off and Matil and Khelya followed.

"Why didn't Mr. Korsen come talk to us?" Matil said quietly to Khelya.

"For one thing, there's the Wall."

"I didn't see a wall there."

"No, most alva can't see the Wall. It's right on the border. It pretty much *is* the border."

"I've always heard it called the Barrier," Dask said.

"If you can't see it, what does it do?"

Khelya twisted her face in thought. "No one ever gets through it. It's some kind of magic that keeps us from leaving and keeps outsiders – like Mr. Korsen – from getting in."

"That's too bad," said Matil.

"Well, it might be for the best that it's there. If everyone outside of Eventyr is as big as Mr. Korsen, we'd be at their mercy."

"But what if the humans are good?"

"Not every alva does good, an' I'm guessing that it's just so with humans."

21

Love Is a Punch to the Face

An early dinner was eaten in the relative safety of the trees, and then they moved on. Not much later, the forest ended. They came upon another empty quarry. A smaller one than the last, Khelya promised when she checked the map. It was nearing dusk and Dask mumbled something about stopping for the night.

Khelya eyed the quarry. "We could make it to the other side long before midnight. Why don't we keep goin'?"

"He's exhausted," Matil said. "I could keep going, but I'm tired, too."

"Oh, all right. But...if you *could* keep on, I can carry Dask while he sleeps so we don't have to lose any time." She looked at both of them, smiling enthusiastically.

"Maybe. If Dask wants to," Matil said.

Dask cringed.

Khelya crossed her arms and frowned. "What's that supposed to mean?"

"It's just...you know..."

"It's just, you know, *what?* It's just 'cause I'm a smelly Obrigi? Is that it?"

"Could be."

"Dask?" Matil said mournfully.

"Okay, okay, I'll let her carry me."

"What if I don't want to carry him anymore?"

"Dask's sorry. Aren't you, Dask?"

"Yeah."

Matil and Khelya looked at him.

He cleared his throat. "Yeah, sorry."

Khelya's eyebrows drew together.

"I, um, I *am* sorry. It was stupid. What I said. I wasn't thinking. *Okay?*"

"Okay." Khelya walked over and scooped Dask up into her arms.

"Ah—hey—whoa—watch my wings, will ya?"

"There you go, all snug like a slug."

"What does that even mean?"

"Nobody knows. Just gooo to sleep," Khelya said in an attempt at a soothing voice. She started walking toward the quarry. Dask stirred and twitched uncomfortably. Peering up at him, Matil tried not to laugh.

By the time they reached the bottom of the quarry's ramp, Dask had grown still.

"Aw," Khelya whispered, "he's just like a little baby."

Dask opened his eyes, scowling. "I'm not asleep yet."

* * *

The quarry was very similar to the first one, but it was narrower and rougher. Matil and Khelya often had to skirt squarish outcroppings of rock. After many quiet conversations, they made it to the ramp on the other end of the quarry. The fat sliver of moon was high in the sky.

Matil thought about her family and the rosebush. Sparks fluttered in her stomach and she grinned with anticipation. She would find them, get back her memories, and everything would be perfect. She turned to look at Khelya. The Obrigi must have a life far beyond her friendship with Matil. Thinking about that, Matil felt a little sad. Though it wasn't a sad thing. She should be happy for Khelya.

Hmm. Khelya had only talked about her family in passing. Maybe Matil should find out about them. "What's your family like?"

Khelya lowered her head reflectively. "They're fine. They don't have much to do with me these days, seein' how I live so far sou—oof." She had tripped over a rock, but managed to keep a hold on Dask. "Anyway, I've got my pa, my ma, my two older brothers, a younger brother, and my one sister. She's the youngest. My siblings an' me, we didn't care for each other much growing up, though."

"Really?"

"I didn't get along with most alva back then. Whoa." She narrowly avoided a large stone. "Still don't."

"Why not?"

"I don't know…" She looked vaguely irritated, though whether it was with the ground, Matil, Khelya's family, or herself, Matil couldn't tell. "I always made it hard on my teachers, and I get into arguments that other Obrigi don't take kindly to, I s'pose. It didn't help that alva made fun of me being short. My parents didn't really know what to do with me. *I* didn't know what to do with me. But my telvogir was always so kind. Taught me about building and about the beauty we Obrigi used to be able to create. *Ow.*" Khelya limped for a few steps, having accidentally kicked a rock. "He passed away when I really needed him."

"I'm sorry."

They made it to the top of the ramp and left the quarry. Now they wove through the tall, gently-waving grass.

"It's okay. I was mixed up inside for a little bit, but things got better. Pa suggested I become a farmer, and that's what happened. Or, well, that's what sort of happened." She winked at Matil.

Matil bit her lip. "Right…" They began walking by a bush and she checked to see if it might be a good place to stop for the night. It was more forested up ahead, so she decided against mentioning it.

Khelya gently nudged Matil's head with her elbow. "You know I'm over it now. And even with all the possibly treasonous things we've been doin', I'm glad to have met you. We—*aaah!*" she yelled.

Shooting into the air, she dropped Dask and knocked over Matil.

"*Ah!*" Dask jumped to his feet and staggered around.

Matil looked up in dismay.

Hanging by her foot from a swaying bush was Khelya. She flailed in panic. "What happened?! Are we bein' attacked? *Why's the world gone upsy-down?*"

A leaf fell next to Matil.

"What happened?" Dask said blearily.

She shook her head. "We were walking along and then Khelya went up—"

"Oh, talrach," Dask muttered. He flew up to Khelya with his knife already out. "Try not to land on your head."

"What? What are you doin'?"

"Cutting you down."

"Am I gonna *fall?*"

"Yes, now be quiet before—"

They all froze as voices boomed from nearby.

"This prey of ours is awful chattersome."

"That mean what I think it do?"

"I b'lieve it do, my friend."

Around the bush swaggered two Obrigi men wearing patchy clothes. One of them had ropes and nets of all sorts hanging from various belts he wore around his waist and across his chest. The other held a wide, swooping sword that looked big enough to halve Matil in one blow. She swallowed and barely noticed as she started disappearing.

"And we just got here," the sword-wielding Obrigi chided. He reached for Matil more quickly than she expected he could.

She stumbled backward, but he wrapped her in his iron grip and threw her over his shoulder. With desperation, she thought to herself that she might have been able to escape if only she had wings.

"Matil!" Dask yelled. He dropped lower to avoid a net weighted by four whirling rocks.

The Obrigi who had thrown the net cursed and ran to pick up the fallen device.

"Matil?!" Khelya said. She had drifted around to face away from the fighting and was now swinging herself, trying to spin back around. "What happened to Matil?"

Matil struggled, but her captor just clamped down more tightly. From somewhere, he produced a length of thin rope and tied Matil's hands up with one hand and his teeth, using the other arm to hold onto her. She wrinkled her nose at the Obrigi's hot breath on her hands, and jabbed her knee at his back, to no avail. He swung her back down and plunked her into a big, loosely-woven bag. The top closed and Matil curled up grumpily.

"Ow!" the Obrigi said. "Bloodsuckin' Ranny."

Excited, Matil put her eye down to one of the larger gaps in the rough cloth of the bag. She could just barely see through. A flash of black wings…

"Git 'im!"

"Agh!" That was Dask.

The Obrigi's chuckles boomed above Matil. "Good throw, Klem."

Sounding a bit strained, the other one said, "Aw, thank ya kindly. Falgar's fangs, this one's a dirty fighter. There we go, off to sleep now."

Matil tried to see out of the bag, but it kept moving around and she couldn't tell what she was looking at.

The bag opened and in tumbled an unconscious Dask. Matil caught a flash of the sky, and then the bag was cinched shut. She scooted over to make room for him.

"Get your filthy hands off me, you rotten, muddy slug-eater!" Khelya said.

"Hey," Klem said, "I like me a feisty girl, but you'd best mind your mouth if'n you don't want your stay with us to be perticklerly discomfortable."

"I'll show you *discomfortable!* Let me dow—mmf!"

"Pretty thing like you shouldn't be wastin' time sayin' such hateful things. Jist hang on."

After swaying and waiting for a while, the bag swung around until Matil felt ill. The Obrigi holding the bag seemed to have begun walking. Muffled yelling came closer. Had Khelya been gagged?

"Weird haul, innit?" he said. "One of these Ranychts don't have wings."

"That's weird, all right. And this little lady goin' along with 'em. My, my, Tobb, someone's gonna pay us good for this catch, I'm sure." Klem made a dreadful noise. Matil cringed as she heard his spit hit the ground.

"Yeah, I reckon they will!" Tobb said. "Smart thinkin', Klem."

They walked for a bit longer, then Tobb set the bag down. Matil felt the warmth and heard the crackling of a large fire. Her stomach seized up. A memory…shouts, screams, sickening heat. The feeling passed and she shuddered.

Hopefully the bag wouldn't catch fire.

To her surprise, the bag opened again and Tobb reached in. He hefted her out with both hands, grinning, turned her upside-down, and shook her vigorously. Matil yelped.

"Got any coin on ya?" he said.

"I don't, I promise!" She bit her tongue. "*Ow…*"

"Huh." Tobb shoved her back into the bag and pulled out Dask.

Matil grimaced at the metallic taste in her mouth. Again, Dask was none-too-gently crammed in the bag and the top was closed tightly.

"Gimme that," Tobb said from somewhere nearby.

"Mmph!"

Klem laughed. "Sit down, girly."

"When d'you think Berten's gonna be back? I'm starved."

"I dunno."

"He'd better hurry it up. Cooee, the lady was carryin' *useful* stuff!"

Oh no, now they had the supplies.

The two Obrigi continued talking, but a noise from Dask caught Matil's attention.

He stirred and groaned. Then he sat up quickly and groaned some more, holding his head. "Where are we? Where's Khelya?"

"Hmuh," came Khelya's voice right next to them.

Matil pointed in that direction. "Khelya's there. How are you feeling?"

"Terrible. Why wasn't she watching where she was going? That was a trap meant for animals, she should've been able to avoid it no problem!"

"Hmf," Khelya mumbled.

"It was my fault, Dask—"

"Don't say that."

"It *was*. I'm closer to the ground and I can see in the dark. We were talking, distracted. Anyway, right now it doesn't matter whose fault it was," Matil said urgently. She lowered her voice. "We need to get out of here."

"Yeah, okay. What's been going on?"

"They took us to their camp and searched us."

"Did they take what Khelya was carrying?"

"Yes…"

"Talrach. Okay, um, let's—wait, shh!"

"Whatcha have there, boys?" a new voice said.

"Cooee, Berten, we catched ourselves two swoopies an' a lady!" Tobb said.

"Do they got any valyables?"

"Nope, checked 'em already. Just some food 'n maps 'n stuff."

"Mebbe we can fetch a good price with 'em. I hear there's a demand for slaves up north!"

"Well, they're a funny bunch, an' Klem was sayin' there might be someone lookin' for 'em. Someone with money."

"Yeah, maybe! I'll check the boards in Gherdan's Place tomorrow."

"What brings you back here so soon?" Klem said.

"Catched a mouse."

"Ooh."

"Nice."

"Yep. I need more rope, though, I wasn't expecting more'n a beetle."

"Rope? Here ya go."

"Great. See you boys later!"

"See ya."

"See ya!"

They quieted down. A cricket began chirping loudly behind Matil.

Klem's voice drifted over. "You don't look to be enjoyin' that gag."

"*Hm*," Khelya said.

"Promise ya won't holler an' I'll see what I can do for you."

"Hm-*hmmm*."

"Is that a yes? Ain't you a sweet thing."

"Careful," Tobb said. "She's with Ranycht. They coulda teached her their sneaky ways."

"Don't you worry, one scream from her and the gag goes back on. 'Sides, there's no one 'round to hear."

"If ya say so."

For a moment, Matil could only hear stomping, shuffling, and the cricket.

"You're welcome," Klem said curtly.

Once again it was quiet, interrupted occasionally by Klem and Tobb's chatter.

"Khelya, are you all right?" Matil said.

"Yeah."

"It sounds like someone has an admirer," Dask whispered.

"Oh, you shut up."

"Listen, be nice. Make him like you."

"*No*," Khelya said under her breath.

"Trust me, okay?"

She grumbled. Then she spoke out loud. "Um, 'scuse me?"

"What is it?" Tobb said.

"I just gotta say, uh, thanks."

"What for?" Klem said with curiosity.

"These Ranycht took me prisoner and made me carry all their things. You two rescued me."

There was a pause. "Where're all them poison words you was spittin' earlier?"

"I...was afraid. I ain't never seen a guy so...uhh... handsome...as you."

Dask put a hand over his mouth and stifled a laugh. Matil attempted to keep from smiling out of respect for Khelya.

"Cooee, ya hear that, Tobb? Told you ladies couldn't keep their eyes off a man with a beard."

"I still say that pelt on your face is nasty."

"Oh, not at all," Khelya said. "No, it's really… somethin'."

"Now that just touches my heart, girly. Tobb, I think I've found *her*."

"Huh?"

"The woman worthy of bein' my wife."

"Brush the beard," Dask whispered.

"What?" Khelya sounded very confused. Matil didn't blame her.

"I understand if you're not ready just yet," Klem said. "But I think we could get to know each other in time for a Vana wedding."

"Um…"

"*He'll untie you if you brush his beard,*" Dask said.

"What…?" Now she sounded a little queasy. She took a deep breath. "Mr. Bandit?"

"You can call me Klem, bumblebee."

"Klem, uh, your beard really…shows how…tough you are."

"See? What a lady."

"But it needs a little tiny bit of…order."

"What're you sayin'?" he said in a dangerous tone.

191

"W-what I think is truly *amazing* is a beard that's been brushed out."

"Huh. Tobb, think you could get out that fancy brush we got last week?"

"Fine," Tobb said, "but then I'm gonna go find Berten. This is too mushy."

Klem guffawed. "You ain't never been in love, my friend! You'll feel the same as I do now when we nab the girl for you."

There was a rustling noise and Tobb said, "There. See ya."

"Yeah. So, how should I go about this brushin' business?"

"I think I should do it," Khelya said quickly.

"Why?"

"Because…I know what it's gonna take to make it look amazing."

"I guess you're right about that."

"'Course, you'd need to—"

"Not so obvious," Dask whispered.

"—I can't really do it right now, can I?" Khelya gave a high-pitched laugh.

"No. Not unless I untie you." Klem cleared his throat. "I don't mean to brag or nothin', but I'm a pretty good judge of alva. And you look to be someone I can trust."

"Oh, uh, I'm glad."

"Good. To prove how prepared I am to marry you, I'll let you brush my beard."

"That's…lovely."

Matil moved to the side of the bag and again put her eye up to a gap. Beside her, Dask did the same.

Not much could be seen, just the vague shape of Klem walking over and cutting the ropes off of Khelya.

Khelya stood, wobbling uncertainly. "Oh thiffen, oh thiffen, oh thiffen," she muttered. She leaned toward Klem.

"What's that you're sayi—*mm? Mm. Mwha—*"

"This knife," Khelya said breathlessly, "goes into your gut if you so much as move."

"But…bumblebee, we were gonna be married!"

"Not anymore."

The bag opened. Dask grabbed Matil's hand and hopped out.

"Why're you lettin' 'em free?" Klem cried.

"Oh, right, uh, I'm sorry, I lied about them capturing me, I'm really sorry—"

"Quiet, Khelya, let's go!" Dask said.

Klem stared at Khelya. His eyebrows came down in a furious scowl. "Stal *curse* you! *Fellas! The prisoners're escapin'!*"

Dask was disappearing. Matil closed her eyes and instinctively backed away from the fire and toward the darkness. They held onto Khelya's fingers, and, when Matil opened her eyes again, she saw that they were all blending in with the forest.

"Git back here!" Klem leaped forward.

To get out of the way in time, the three of them began running. Matil lost her concentration and had become visible along with the others. Outrunning Klem would be very tough. If they couldn't stay unseen…

"We need to stop him," Matil shouted.

Klem laughed. "Right, like you little flies could—*owww!*"

Dask was above, flying around and kicking at Klem's head. The Obrigi's arms swiped through the air. One arm hit Dask, and he dropped out of the sky.

"Dask!"

"Don't come over here!" Dask said. He struggled to his feet, but Klem kicked him in the side. "*Oof!*"

Matil looked up at Khelya, who didn't seem to know what to do. "I'll distract him, you get him, okay?"

"Okay."

Matil ran in, wailing at the top of her lungs. She tenaciously clung to Klem's leg, even though he began shaking it violently.

"Git off, stupid little—"

She was thrown off, landing hard on the ground. Her ears twitched as she heard the painful sound of a large fist connecting with a larger face.

"Come on!" Khelya said, lifting Matil and Dask into her arms and heaving them away. "Do your magic stuff!"

Dask moaned, clutching his stomach. He didn't look ready to do anything.

"Hide behind something, Khelya," Matil said.

Khelya ran around a tree and stood with her back to it, catching her breath.

Matil closed her eyes and felt the shadow around them. She opened her eyes to see Khelya, eyes tightly shut, becoming indistinguishable from the tree. A moment later, Dask faded.

Matil slouched with relief.

"You can set us down now," Dask said wheezed.

Trembling, Khelya bent down and released Matil and Dask.

"We did it!" Matil whispered. She wrapped Dask in a hug, and then attempted the same with Khelya, though stretching her arms around Khelya was a bit more difficult. Khelya leaned over and patted Matil on the back.

Dask cleared his throat. "We haven't really finished *yet*. We've gotta get away first."

He was right. Matil noticed the voices of the bandits approaching.

"Slowly," he said. "Quietly."

They slipped away from the tree, all holding hands to keep Khelya concealed. The bandits eventually fell out of earshot and the forest was once again quiet, relatively speaking. Bats still chittered and flapped through the air and crickets continued chirping. Matil, Khelya, and Dask had traveled mainly near inhabited areas, but in this part of the forest, deep growls drifted out from unexpected places.

To her knowledge, Matil had never seen a badger, a fox, or a wolf. From what she'd heard she probably didn't want to.

The three of them stopped so that Dask could fly above the tree canopy and check their direction against the stars, and then they went on traveling eastbound. They didn't speak for a long time. The breezy night air swept past, bringing with it the fresh fragrances of things growing, and

Matil realized how much more she loved the forest than the scrubby rockscapes of the quarries or the wide meadowlands she had seen in Obrigi and Tyrlis. She was overwhelmed by the sense of getting closer to the place she belonged.

"How long until we get to Nychtfal?" she dared to ask.

"We should be there in a few greatlengths at the most. You two crossed the easternmost quarry when I was sleeping, and the border isn't far from it." Dask looked up at the sky.

"My house is right there," Khelya said softly. "Right near the border."

Matil squeezed Khelya's hand. "Do you…want to go and visit it?" Secretly she hoped that they could just hurry on to Nychtfal, but she was responsible for Khelya's homelessness.

"Naw, I don't wanna see it yet."

Matil heard the sadness in Khelya's voice and wasn't sure what to say.

Dask saved her the trouble. "You know, knocking a Sangriga flat is one thing, but an Obrigi guy? Not bad."

"Well, Matil was keepin' him occupied."

"Where'd you learn how?"

"You just assume it don't come natural?" Khelya said in mock offense. "Heh. One of my brothers was in this boxing group, and I thought it looked fun. So we made a deal: I do all his chores for a week, he teaches me how to box. He didn't go easy on me, though. I finally gave up after a while. But I learned how to punch pretty hard, and building a house kept me strong."

Dask led them toward the base of a small tree. "Let's stop here for the night. All of us this time."

"Okay." Matil *really* wanted to keep going.

Dask separated, staying concealed, and scouted out a deep indent in the ground next to the tree's trunk. He revealed himself and beckoned them over. "They took our blankets, didn't they?"

Khelya's shoulders slumped. "Yeah."

"Don't worry, I'll buy us stuff in the next town."

"You have money?"

"Not with me right now, no, but I've got a few humble stashes elsewhere." Dask grinned. "Tonight, we'll sleep in these decaying leaves. How about it, huh? Like a palace."

Matil looked dubiously at the soft, grimy pile of…stuff that filled the bottom of the indent.

Khelya squinted blindly; it was too dark under the tree's cover for her to see properly.

"We should get rid of the bugs first. Don't wanna wake up to crawlers crawling around us." Dask wiggled his fingers.

Matil gulped. To momentarily distract herself from the thought of many-legged creatures, she turned to Khelya. "How did you get the knife away from Klem?"

Khelya wiped her mouth on her arm. "Ughh. I kissed 'im and grabbed his knife. Thiffen, that beard really *was* awful. I don't think he's washed it in weeks." She stuck out her tongue. "Months."

"You thought pretty fast for an Obrigi," Dask said casually. "I mean, your performance wasn't perfect, but it was a lot better than I expected."

"Oh, thank you, Dask," she said in a mockingly breathy voice, "you know I can't live without you tellin' me I did good."

"Naturally. What did you think of my beard plan?"

"It was, uh…interesting," Matil said.

"Just looking outside the egg for a solution. It's one of those things I picked up in the Brug." He kicked some of the leaf bits. "Hey, Khel, you became the object of a man's affections and then broke his heart, bam. Congratulations."

Khelya shuddered.

22

Building Borders

"Isn't rain pretty, Bechel?" Matil said to the red-eyed toddler beside her.

"Pitty." Bechel scooted forward, pulled his fingers out of his mouth, and pressed his hand against the window. "Mmnibpa," he whispered. He turned to Matil with a huge grin. "Nibpa!"

Matil laughed. "Tell me when you can say it right." She turned back to look out through the round, thick pane, where Bechel's saliva hand print almost glowed against the cold glass. Outside, rain dripped from plant to plant as each drop found its way to the forest floor. It was enough water to extinguish any fire.

* * *

Cold. Cold and damp.

A warm hand settled on Matil's arm and shook it gently. "Time to get up."

The hand left and Matil pried open her eyes. "Morning," she croaked. At least, that's what she tried to say. It might have come out as "muhh."

Dask was crouched in between her and Khelya, rubbing his arms rapidly. "I got us some breakfast. Help yourself."

Matil sat up, stretching and cracking her joints uncomfortably. She rubbed her ears, which were freezing, and wrung out her dew-soaked hair. A shiver ran through her. Catching sight of a pile of blackberries leaking juice, she climbed up, grabbed one, and slid back down to the warmish spot where she had been sleeping. "Mm, thanks." To her surprise, she found a grubby shirt shoved at her.

"You can use this to dry your hair, if you want." Over his torso, Dask wore only his vest. He must have taken it off to get the shirt and then put it back on. "I mean, I know it's kinda dirty, but I thought you might feel better with your hair less wet."

"My hair's not much better than your shirt at this point," Matil said. "I couldn't take it, though. You must be as cold as I am."

"I've been flying around, so I'm warm for now. Besides, I'll get us new clothes when I can."

"Really? Thank you!" Matil took the shirt and set down the blackberry.

Dask looked closely at the underside of one of his boots. "No problem."

She began rubbing her hair with the shirt, which, admittedly, was smelly. It did the trick, however, and soon her hair was somewhat dryer and she had worked up warmth from the action. Afterward, she shook out the shirt as best she could and handed it back to Dask.

He accepted it and glanced at the berry pile. With a flap of his wings, he scrambled to the pile and picked up a dark ant, gripping it by the midsection with both hands. Its legs, antennae, and mandibles twitched and waggled. "No," Dask said to the ant, "this is *our* food." He walked farther away and heaved it off into the forest.

Matil slowly picked up the blackberry. The ant unpleasantly reminded her of the Skorgon that had attacked them. Now they were going back into Nychtfal to track down whoever summoned the creatures. Matil's enthusiasm to move on was dimmed by that thought. She popped a drupelet off of the blackberry and bit into it. The flowery, slightly sour flavor filled her mouth.

"And now for the adventure of waking up Khelya," Dask said.

He clapped his hands together above Khelya's snoring face. "Come on, get up!"

Khelya flung her arm out and rolled over, toppling Dask.

"Oof—hey!" Dask jumped up, dusting himself off. "I still have bruises from last night, ya know! How would you like being kicked by someone twice your size?"

"Snails eat lard," Khelya mumbled.

"Up, up, up, Princess Khelya. Your carriage awaits."

Khelya yawned loudly and dragged herself into a sitting position. Her blonde hair, darkened by the damp, hung down messily. She stood up and stomped around. "Thiffen, it's like Thrual." Her arms curled over her head for warmth.

Dask had been so kind earlier. Matil smiled. "Would it be all right if Khelya used your shirt to dry her hair, too?"

He sighed. "Of course." He threw it at Khelya.

"Huh," Khelya said. "Thanks."

* * *

Walking briskly, they managed to warm up. Paired with the sun climbing higher and shining down through the leaves in full force, they became dry and hot.

"Dask," Matil panted, "when will we cross over into Nychtfal?" Beyond the echoing birdsong and the rustling of animals, there were some new, faint noises. Voices? Sawing and pounding?

"Right now." Dask dropped into a crouch. "Everyone, hide."

"What?"

"Shh!" He grabbed Khelya's hand.

Matil worriedly did the same and let Dask pull them under a bush, where the thick leaves concealed them. They faded. Safe. Except for that spider, smoothly spinning a web, that Matil had just noticed dangling alarmingly close to her head. She shuffled away. At least they were hidden from whatever it was Dask had seen. What *had* he seen? Matil peered out through the bush's leaves. Oh.

"What's wrong?" Khelya said.

"Heh, it's kind of funny," Dask answered. "You know how nobody's ever sure exactly where the border is?"

"Yes we do, it's on every map."

"When you lived down here, did you really know where the border was?"

"…I s'pose not."

"Yeah, I think they're trying to fix that." He pushed Khelya so that she could see out of the bush.

"I don't see—oh!"

Running northwest, as far as they could see, was a huge wooden wall. The incomplete end of the wall had beams sticking out of it like a hedgehog's bristles, and beyond that, there were markers tied with bright cloths that had been placed to show where the wall would continue. Teeming around the place were Obrigi workers calling out in harsh voices, a few Sangriga floating nearby, and on the Nychtfal side, a group of armed Ranycht watching the progress. The wall was nearly twice as tall as the Obrigi working on it.

Such a wall would be impassable for Matil, or even Khelya, but… "How is that going to keep out the Ranycht?" Matil said.

Dask pulled a leaf aside. "See those Ranycht soldiers? Their presence means the construction has been agreed to. They don't mind the Accord putting up a barrier, because it means an end to pesky border disputes, at least for now. Both sides will probably guard the wall. It'll be pretty secure against both walking and flying alva."

"I see."

"Maybe this'll keep war from starting," Khelya said.

Dask laughed. "Or it could be the start of a war."

"Don't be a downer."

"Why would we need a wall in peace?" The question hung in the air. Dask looked back at the construction. "Obrigi work fast."

"Yes we do," Khelya said proudly.

"You don't have to sound so happy about it."

"Why shouldn't I be? Sneaky *Ranycht* sneakin' over the border all the time. That wall can put a stop to it."

"But it's bad for business! Uh, not that I'm…part of that business anymore. Anyway, once we're in Nychtfal, you won't be able to get back, not without a lot of fuss."

"Right. Huh."

Khelya had a job to do, and a family. Realization dawned on Matil and her heart sank. "Stay here," she said, finding it hard to speak. "Stay in Obrigi."

"Matil—"

"You can rebuild your house and keep farming. It'll be just like before I messed everything up."

"Oh, hush, you silly birdface. I'm going with you."

"You are?" Matil tried to squash the hope that rose inside her. Khelya had a life. "What about your family?"

"I should really let them know what's been goin' on. That'll be hard to do when I'm in Nychtfal."

Dask put a hand on Matil's shoulder. "I'll get a message across for her sometime. Don't worry."

"How is she going to keep from being seen? I don't want

her to be captured or anything."

"Eventyr has a lot of secret places. We'll find a way to keep Khelya safe."

"Really?"

"Yeah. *Don't worry.*"

* * *

Matil's ears twitched as she heard the soft flap of wings. She held a hand up to quiet Khelya. A face appeared at the entrance of the tiny wood niche they had squeezed into. Her heart jumped in fright. To her relief, she recognized Dask's long nose, shaggy hair, and uneven beard.

"Hey," he said with a smile. "Mind helping me out with this stuff?" He looked from side to side, then up and down. "It's safe."

Matil climbed out easily. "How did it go?"

"Great. Well, there was this one old lady. I don't think she liked grimy strangers roaming around *her* town. She even called it that. *Her* town. I couldn't find a map either."

Khelya had more trouble prying herself from where she had been leaning. The niche, set into the base of a tree, was coated with sap. Once Khelya was out, she put her hand on her back and made a face as her shirt stuck to it. "I need new clothes. Wish I'd saved some from the fire."

"You any good with sewing?"

"I wouldn't say good, but I'm not bad. Why?"

"Because not only did I get some clothes for me and Matil, I looked into cloth. I knew we needed some blankets and the cloth wasn't too expensive. Might not be comfortable, but you can use as much as you want. I'm feeling generous." Dask clasped his hands and smiled condescendingly.

"I almost wanted to thank you," Khelya said. "Good job."

He snickered.

Matil knelt down next to the coarse sacks of supplies that Dask bought. Like he said, there were piles of cloth complete with a small kit of thread, needle, and shears. Another bag held some food: dry biscuits, dried seasoned meat, and a glass jar filled with something red and transparent.

"What's this?" she said.

Dask looked over. "You'll like that. It's crab apple jelly. I thought the biscuits would be pretty boring on their own and—"

"I told you, he got mighty suspicious friends!" shrieked a hoarse voice.

Dask sighed. "Oh, thiffen. It's her."

"*Ma'am*, please keep your voice down," someone else said.

Matil turned with wide eyes.

An old woman with scraggly wings and a man wearing a patchy guard uniform were watching them from a thick clump of grass. The guard stepped out and drew his bow, pointing an arrow at Khelya.

"Stay completely still," he yelled, voice cracking at the end. "If you don't surrender, I'll shoot."

"Okay," Dask said. "Hold on a moment." He lowered his voice. "You know what to do. Khelya, can you take our bags?"

"Sure thing." She picked everything up – about six bags – and cradled them in her arms. "Will we be able to make it?"

"Hurry up!" the guard said.

"He's obviously new. We can make it."

Matil looked at the guard. He seemed scared. "Poor man."

"Shoot the lily-barked giant already!" the old woman screeched.

Matil and Dask grabbed Khelya's pant legs and pulled her backward, disappearing against the tree as they did so.

"Sh-show yourselves! Now!" The guard loosed an arrow. It grazed the far side of the tree and fell to the ground. "Thiffen! How did the Obrigi do that?"

"You let 'em get away, boy!"

"Ma'am, please!"

The three of them crept away, staying faded. It was slow going, however, and Dask gradually came back into sight, releasing Khelya.

Matil dropped her hand, too, and in her mind unwrapped the dark shroud around herself. "Khelya? Where are you?"

"Hm? Oh, I'm still…" Khelya reappeared next to Matil. "I didn't know I had to think about it. Usually it stops when you two aren't touching me." She reached around the bags to itch her arms.

"Everybody ready?" Dask said. "Let's keep going."

23

The River Alva

A few days later, Khelya wore new, roughly-sewn garments and a large cloak that she used as her blanket. Dask wore his purchases, too. For Matil, he had gotten pants, cheap boots, and a knee-length dress. Though they were too big, she delightedly wore them and used her old, moldy belt to keep the pants up. Bits of moss stuffed in the boots served to keep them on her feet.

The crab apple jelly, dripped onto the biscuits, *was* good. It tasted fresh and a little tart. Matil tried pacing herself, but by now the jar was less than half-full.

As they journeyed, Matil's dreams took a turn for the dark. The swirl of anxiety, fear of the sun, and inexplicable anger with which she awakened made her glad that she couldn't remember these dreams.

Dask had briefly slipped into Lowen, only to come back out empty-handed and worried. "They've posted my portrait all over the place, along with a reward and descriptions of an Obrigi and a wingless girl," he said. "*And* the place is crawling with guards. The portrait's really accurate, aside from the beard, but I'm not surprised. I'll bet my old buddies tipped the guards off. They must think I'll go visit Kerl."

From then on they kept more and more out of sight. They went deeper into Nychtfal than Matil had been before. She loved it. The trees grew thickly together, screening the sky until a green dimness was the only source of light, something that lowered Khelya's vision along with her spirits. Roots and rocks shaped the ground into fanciful hills that were hard to traverse but beautiful to look at. The birds here were quieter and the mushrooms were taller and more colorful. The cold creeks and streams were good to wash in, though removing dirt from their clothes was difficult.

Occasionally, Matil would see round, nest-like houses perched in the trees, and more than once they walked underneath vast wooden trays hanging from the branches. Those were farms and gardens, Dask said.

Now they reached a part of the forest that was inhabited more by animals than by alva – although the line between the two was blurring. Matil once saw a robin, sitting in a bush, who winked at her. Another Kyndelin? She pulled the bag she carried closer to herself.

All was peaceful until Matil noticed a faint, constant noise. She looked this way and that, trying to catch the sound. It was very familiar. A waterfall? "What's that?"

Dask's expression brightened. "Something I've been waiting for."

"What're you two talkin' about?" Khelya said grumpily.

"I'm sure you'll be able to hear it in a little bit," Matil said.

Khelya muttered something about "ears" and continued her cautious and frustrated shuffle. A short time later, she picked up her head. "Hey, I *can* hear it. Is it a, uh, river?"

Matil perked up. A river! She couldn't wait to see it.

"Of course it is," Dask said. "Ever seen a map?"

"Yeah, I have, but I don't look at maps for fun, you little know-all."

"You should. You might learn something. Oh, thiffen, what am I thinking? Of course you can't learn something, that's your greatest weakness."

"I'll have you know that I do like learning. But not learning from snotty Ranycht. What can they teach besides how to get on the wrong side of the law?"

"A lot, when whiny Obrigi are being nice and quiet."

The three of them were now climbing up a fungus-dotted ridge as the river roared ahead of them. Matil held her nose at the musty smell and wondered if she should interrupt Dask and Khelya's latest 'discussion'. No matter what she said, though, a day later they'd be arguing again.

"Remember," Dask was saying, "if you kill me, you might never get out of Nychtfal. I'm very useful."

"I'll give you that, you're useful like my feet are useful. *And* smelly and weird-lookin' like my feet."

Dask pouted. "I'm not weird-looking. I—"

At the top of the ridge, they pushed past a fern and froze.

Down below and some ways ahead of them rushed a roiling monster of a river. Matil hadn't yet seen so much water. Slick boulders that rose up from the riverbed were perpetually battered by the frothy current. Falling in would be a nightmare. Even with that frightening thought, she was filled with wonder. Where the water wasn't capped with white, it had a deep green tinge. The trees here were big enough to arch over the river, leaving only a sliver of blue sky in between.

"Asta River." Dask shook his head. "I'll never get used to that."

Khelya shuffled backward. "Wow," she said, almost too quietly to hear. Or was the river really loud enough to drown her out?

Matil watched the leaping fields of water in amazement, but a worrying thought nagged at her. "How will we cross?"

"We don't have to worry about that yet," Dask said. "This is where we find our contact, and he could already have something worked out for us."

Khelya rubbed her arms and looked up. "Where exactly is this contact?"

"There's a village nearby. He should be there. Or in the Asta."

She went white. "*In* the Asta? What is he, a Nervoda?"

"He might be. Look, some are swimming out there."

Something in the river caught Matil's eye. She squinted and tilted her head to the side. Lithe figures played above and below the surface. They blended in, and at this distance she hadn't noticed them. They wore clothes in muddy browns, greens, and blues. Their motion matched the flow of the river so well that it almost looked like they were a part of it.

"Those are Nervoda?" Matil said. "The water alva?"

"Yeah. Their village is called Asta Polaras."

She watched, fascinated. "They don't have any wings."

"No, but they can fly when they're near water. Weird, right?"

"I'll say," Khelya said. She looked at the Asta nervously. "I'm gonna stay back. Back there." She gestured at the ridge they had come from.

The river was lovely, though. Matil's eyes were glued to the deep swell and the darting Nervoda. "Couldn't we have lunch here?"

"Would that be a good idea?" Khelya scuffed at the ground with her boots. "I mean, we're probably way behind. We should move on. Move faster."

"Khelya, are you all right?"

"*I'm fine!*"

Matil and Dask stared at her.

Her shoulders fell. "I just, you know, I don't much like water."

Dask whistled. "You're in trouble, then. I'm not sure if you noticed, but that's what we drink to stay alive."

"You know what I mean! I don't…like being near something that I could drown in."

Matil looked down. "Oh. You can wait for us, then, while we find the contact."

Khelya nodded, thin-lipped.

"See you," Matil said. She smiled and took a step toward the river.

"Okay. Just wait by that tree, Khel, and don't move. Keep outta sight." Dask pointed at a tree they had passed.

Khelya hurried back over the ridge.

Matil watched her go and felt a pang of regret. "Should I stay with her? Will she be all right?"

"You worry too much about her," Dask said. "She was on her own before we met."

"I suppose."

They picked their way through the stony riverbank. At the edge of the river, Dask lifted off and called out to the Nervoda. "Do any of you know Jindi?"

A boy with long, shiny, black hair and pale skin floated out of the river. Fine mist surrounded him. Unlike the Sangriga, the Ranycht, or the Obrigi, this alva's ears slanted downward as if they couldn't be bothered to stick up properly. "I'm Jindi," he said indifferently. "Who're you?"

Dask flew closer and said something too quietly to hear from where Matil stood. She knew he would be saying the code words. What were they again? 'Lost gravy'? He and Jindi flew down and landed next to her.

The boy raised an eyebrow at Matil. "Never seen a Ranycht without wings. Does that make her an Obrigi?"

"Definitely not," Dask said.

"How'd she—"

"Long story."

"I got time."

"We don't."

"Sheesh." Jindi turned around. "This way." He went further downstream along the riverside, jumping from slippery rock to slippery rock. The beginning of each jump was normal, but when he fell, he didn't really fall. He just drifted slowly down like a feather. The mist around him glittered.

Matil stepped carefully, hoping she wouldn't fall into the river. Jindi's comment only made her yearn even more for wings. Dask didn't have to brave the rocks, but he walked beside her anyway.

They arrived at a split in the Asta and followed the smaller stream, down which the water flowed more gently. Shortly after the split, a sprawling mess of skinny buildings came into view. Matil was confused at first; the town appeared to be floating. Then she realized that it was built on columns and stilts that went down below the water and fastened the buildings in place. Rafts and small boats were tied everywhere, bristling out and making the town look like a giant centipede. Waterwheels could be seen over the rooftops, turning and turning.

"I've been here twice," Dask said. "Pretty rinky-dink, huh? It's probably worse than Lowen. I mean, at least Loweners work."

"Alva in Asta Polaras don't work?"

"Okay, they do work. Just enough to survive, though. They like to have as much free time as possible. Nervoda are like that almost everywhere. Hey, kid, wait for us," he yelled.

Jindi stopped hopping and turned around. When Matil and Dask had caught up to him, he shrugged. "Slack up."

"They're always doing that, too," Dask said, irritated. "Telling me to 'slack up', or 'take a load off', or 'relax'."

Jindi stuck his tongue out at Dask.

Dask ineffectively kicked a pebble at the boy.

There were no signs in the little town, nor even proper streets. The houses were ramshackle and piled on top of each other. Pasty-skinned, dark-haired Nervoda lounged around Asta Polaras, chatting, fishing, or simply staring at the river. Even though Dask had been complaining about it, Matil couldn't help feeling relaxed. How nice it would be to stop and forget her search for a while.

No. No, she couldn't forget. She needed to know. Her tired legs urged her to sit down somewhere and start a trivial conversation with one of these amiable-looking alva, but she kept her eyes on Jindi.

The boy led them onto a dock, at the end of which draped a gangly old man wearing a wide-brimmed hat made of leaves. In his hand was a fishing pole.

Jindi tapped him on the shoulder. "I got 'em, Haros. They said the words."

"Good job, boy." Haros turned around slowly.

Jindi held out his hand.

"Right, yeah." Haros patted his unbuttoned vest and reached in one of the pockets. He pulled out a coin and gave it to Jindi. Jindi grinned and dove into the water. Weaving in and out, he swam back upstream.

"Catch anything?" Dask said.

Haros glanced nonchalantly at the fishing rod. "No. You said the words, yeah? Say 'em again."

"Loose grain."

Oh, that's what it was.

"Good. Here's what you do: Head up north to Goska. Just after nightfall, you're to stand at the well in the market and meet two alva. One in a red hat and one very tall. You say, 'The fish with wings ate a field mouse.' They'll say, 'It tastes so good, he has another.'"

"Fish, wings, field mouse," Dask said. "Okay."

Haros turned back to the river.

Dask waited. "Is that all?"

"That's all, yeah. Bye."

They wound between the buildings that they had passed just a moment before.

Dask repeated Haros's instructions a few times.

"Where is Goska?" Matil said.

"North of the bend in this river. Let's get Khel and have lunch, then we'll be walking for another day or so before we hit it."

She beamed. They were so close. It was exciting.

* * *

Mother disapprovingly watched Matil nibble away at a honey cake.

Matil looked up. "What?"

"What do you say when you're given something?"

"Mother," sighed Matil, "Arla said nobody does please-and-thank-you."

"Arla said that, did she?" Mother crossed her arms. "Without giving other alva the proper recognition for doing things for you, it's almost as if you're stealing from them."

"But- but if nobody does it, that means *everyone* is stealing from *everyone*. That's not fair."

"Thosten wants us to be good alva, and being good isn't always easy or fair, my olrin. Sometimes it seems like no one else is being good. Even so, you always, *always* need to follow the Chivishi. And follow courtesy, which means saying 'please' and 'thank you'." Mother winked.

"So I have to do it even though none of my friends are?" Matil pouted. "That's dumb."

"Listen closely and you *will* hear others do it. It can be hard to hear over the sound of Arla telling you it doesn't matter, but they are there. Please," she said in a high-pitched whisper. "Thank youuu…"

Matil giggled. "Thank you for the cake, Mother."

The room grew brighter, too bright. "Listen closely," Mother said again, but she was disappearing. As her image faded, so did her voice. Other voices floated up to obscure her last echoes.

"Need."

"Take."

"Steal."

"Thief!"

"Steal."

"Need."

"Want."

"Take."

"Stop!"

"*Take.*"

"*Stop, thief!*"

"I can help you," Myrkhar breathed in her ear.

* * *

Matil wrenched her eyes open. Her heart pounded and her chest heaved with shaking breaths.

It was still dark out. She supposed she would stay up. Keep watch with Khelya.

24

Even the Trees Have Spies

Khelya's foot found her next hiding spot. It brought her crashing, face-first, to the ground.

Aghast, Matil held her arms straight out in front of her as if that would save her Obrigi friend.

"Good eye," Dask said. "That's where you're staying tonight."

Khelya groaned and rolled onto her back, away from the hole that had tripped her. Matil rushed over.

Dask turned his face to the forest ceiling, through which the cloudy sky's light sneaked. "It'll be sunset in a while. Let's check out this burrow."

He slipped down the hole and surfaced a moment later. "Quiet, move slowly. We'll have to go past a nest of shrews."

"Shrews? Won't they be angry if we go right past them?" Matil said.

"The Kyndelin worked out a deal a while back with the Ranycht and the Sun Accord. Their magicians can sort of…influence animals. Their side of the deal is to keep the animals from hurting us so long as we don't hurt them. They even get the really humongous animals to stay in Deep Valdingfal. Accidents do happen, but," he said, seeing Matil's face, "not very often. We just have to get past, like I said, and Khelya can stay farther in."

"Shouldn't we fade?"

"In there, no. The shrews can smell us and they might not take it well if they can't see us."

Matil swallowed and nodded. "Okay."

"Remember, Khel, *quiet*."

Khelya pouted. "I can be *quiet*."

"Yeah, yeah."

Dask and Matil went in the hole, and then Khelya squeezed through.

Matil's eyes quickly adjusted to the thick darkness, but Khelya, kneeling to fit in the small space, moved her eyes around the burrow blindly. She squeaked when she finally noticed the shrews. Only a couple of lengths away was a twitchy, long-nosed creature, hunched up and fur bristling. It bared its teeth at them. A brood of baby shrews huddled together in their nest. Little roots clumped with dirt hung down from the ceiling. Beyond the shrews were a few tunnels.

Dask moved smoothly along the wall to the nearest tunnel. He gestured with his head for them to follow him.

Khelya had to get down and crawl through the cramped tunnel. When they found themselves in a little cave with another tunnel leading out, Matil relaxed.

Khelya went over to the far wall, sat against it, and pulled her blanket up to her shoulders. Matil and Dask put their bags next to her.

"Hey," Khelya said, "can you put one of those behind my head?"

Matil took a bag and did as she was asked. "How's that?"

"It's better than the wall, at least. Thanks."

"Okay, Khel, we might be gone for a short time or a long time," Dask said.

"We'll try to get back as soon as possible," added Matil.

"Make yourself comfortable. If you fall asleep, don't snore."

Khelya looked peeved. "I can't not snore. Snoring is just something that happens."

"Try sleeping on your side for once. That might help. Now, stay here and hold the magic for as long as possible. We can't risk you being found by anyone."

"Is that a good idea? I mean, it's been feelin' strange when I disappear lately—"

"Stop complaining. You'll be fine if you do as I say. Are you ready?"

"I s'pose."

Dask put his hand on Khelya's arm.

Doing the same, Matil shut her eyes and pulled the darkness of the burrow around them like a cloak. They stood like that for a few moments.

"Got it?" Dask said.

Matil opened her eyes. There was a big empty space in the middle of their circle of bags. Inside, she saw the outline of Khelya.

"Yeah, it's workin'," Khelya said, sounding strained.

"Don't try so hard. It'll just make you uncomfortable."

A long exhale stirred Matil's and Dask's hair.

"Not in my face," Dask said crabbily.

Matil gave a little wave, though it felt strange to wave at a ghost. "Stay safe."

"You too."

Dask nodded once at Khelya. "See you. I'll help you with the cloak, Matil."

He took some fabric, piled it up on her shoulders and back, and tied it down. Matil put on the leftover fabric that they had fashioned into a sort of cloak. It wasn't a very pleasant arrangement, but at least it looked like she might have wings underneath her cloak. Afterward, they headed for Goska.

Matil didn't realize until they were nearly to the town that they hadn't eaten food since their small lunch earlier. It would be a distraction, though, to mention how hungry she was. They needed to find the spies.

"When will we get there?" Matil asked.

"The town's center and the market are about a greatlength from here, on the ground. But we've been in Goska for a little while now."

"We have?"

"Look up."

Above them, dotting the tree trunks, were houses perched on platforms. It was like the little villages Matil had seen before, but there were many more buildings here. Rope bridges connected many of the houses and some were clustered together like a beehive. A man sleepily stepped out of his house and glided to the ground somewhere ahead of them.

Dask smiled at all the homes. "Alva are busy all the time in Ecker's Brug. Here, though, it's…peaceful, right?"

"Yes, peaceful."

"Yeah…reminds me of something. I—" He frowned and shook his head. "Never mind."

They entered the town center, which included a short bell tower, a main square built around a large well, and shops spreading out into the forest and up in the trees. A single guard acknowledged their presence with a nod and peered at Matil's cloak-covered back.

Dask strolled casually toward the well and leaned against it. "Now we wait," he said.

"Red hat, tall alva," Matil said. "Red hat, tall—"

"Don't say it out loud," he whispered. He put two fingers across his lips in a shushing gesture.

"Oh, sorry."

In the dimness of twilight, yawning Ranycht unlocked shops and set out wares on stalls. Matil got a few strange looks, but she tried to look friendly. Stall-tenders called for them to come over and shop. These Ranycht were darker-skinned than she had seen before, just as this part of the forest was darker.

"You hungry?" Dask said.

"A little."

"All right, I'll get you something to eat."

"Do you have enough money?"

"I have a small stash in this area. I could fly out and grab some."

Delicious smells floated around them as pots full of food began boiling and frying. Matil's stomach rumbled. Her eye settled on one stall that offered little cups made of pastry, drizzled with honey and filled with tiny fruit chunks and nut shavings. "I wonder what that tastes like," she said longingly.

"It's really good. You wanna take me up on that offer?"

"We still have food with Khelya. I don't want you to spend a lot just because I'm hungry."

"Trust me, it's no big deal."

"All right," she said, warming to the idea. "But is it, um, stolen money?"

"I don't know where it came from originally, but I earned it and I'm going to use it to buy us breakfast."

If he didn't know, there was no use worrying about it. She still couldn't help feeling guilty that the clothes she wore had been paid for by Dask's illegal activities. "Thanks."

"You stay here and scout for them. I'll come back soon. Remember the phrase?"

Matil opened her mouth and Dask quickly put his fingers to his lips again. She nodded, blushing.

"Good. See you!" Dask took off.

Matil looked around and suddenly felt agitated. More alva were trickling into the square. What if she didn't see the spies? No, there was no way she could miss them. She took a deep breath and kept watching. Sweat broke out on her forehead. What was the phrase again? She couldn't remember. It had something to do with…with…*fish*, right, okay.

It would be fine, she would see the spies, and everything would be all right. Night was falling.

Time passed and no red hat appeared.

With great relief, Matil spotted a short man strolling across the square in a red pointed cap alongside another man who greatly resembled the short one. The other man wasn't exactly tall, but maybe the instructions just meant tall in comparison.

Matil approached them. "Sir?"

"Hm?" The short man looked at her.

"It's going to have to wait, sweetie," the taller man said sourly.

"I'm sure we have enough time…" He began wringing his hands. "Oh, but we're probably late."

"We would've been there by now if *you* hadn't been pushing this snail's pace on us."

"I wanted to enjoy the night."

"Too bad, now we have to make up for it by rushing, and I don't like to rush. Tell the girl we can't talk."

"But it could be something important."

"It is," Matil said.

The taller man's face creased. "Ugh. You can go ahead and be late, but I'm getting there now."

"Oh, okay…"

"Grandma'll kill us if you don't hurry." He flew away.

The man in the red hat turned to Matil. "Yes?"

She cleared her throat. "The fish with, um, wings eats a field mouse."

"Excuse me?"

"The fish with—uh, are you the—"

"Loger, I apologize!" came a voice behind Matil. "This is my little cousin. She likes saying weird things to alva, just for the fun of it."

The man squinted. "Oh, hi there, Ulia."

Matil turned around and her stomach sank to her feet. Under a floppy, red, short-brimmed hat was a woman with deep golden eyes and strands of gray in her dark hair. Beside her stood a tall young man whose eyes were a lighter shade of gold.

Were *these* the spies? With Dask gone, Matil was already ruining things.

"Well, y'know, I'll just take the girl home," the woman said. "Sorry if she caused you trouble."

"Oh, no tr—"

"Stech and I'll see you at the Trinns' party."

"Oh, yes, see you—"

"Don't forget to tell Grandma Tillie I said hello."

"Of cour—"

"Have a great night!"

"Oh, you too—"

The woman grabbed Matil's arm and pulled her away. "Now," she said as they marched around the market square at a brisk pace, "do you have something to say to me?"

"The…the fish with wings eats a field mouse."

"It tastes so good, he has another."

"I'm sorry," Matil cried.

"Keep your voice down."

Matil's ears drooped.

"And don't feel too bad. I was late and it's just bad luck Loger decided to wear a red hat tonight. Although, he wasn't with a tall man."

"There was another man who left just before you came."

"Oh, his brother. His brother's not tall. But Loger *is* pretty short, compared." The woman looked around. "Let's go somewhere secure before we talk further."

"Please, I came with a friend."

"I suppose you want us to wait, then?"

"Could we?"

"Go stand next to the well again. I'll be right there when your friend gets back."

"Thank you!"

Matil bumped her way through the crowd, apologizing as she went. She reached the well and looked around. A little bit later, Dask landed next to her, carrying a few greasy, leaf-wrapped parcels that smelled delicious.

"Hey," he whispered. "Have—"

Matil couldn't help herself. "What did you buy?"

He handed her two of the parcels, one of which held the pastry bowl she had seen earlier. "Heh, this is called a loolookap, and the other one," the other parcel contained a hearty sausage with salted, shiny-crusted bread woven around it, "that's called gotenskamp."

"Thank you so much." Matil took a bite out of the gotenskamp. It was very juicy and tasted like squirrel meat. The bread was a little tough, but it was sweet and salty. "Mmm."

"I guess our friends haven't shown up yet."

"Guess again," came another voice.

Matil inhaled some of the sausage in surprise, but managed to swallow without too much choking.

The red-hatted woman stood next to her. "Sorry about that, dear. Let's go."

They went quickly, all of them on foot. Ranycht would call out to the woman and she responded energetically, gesturing at Matil and Dask and saying they were cousins in town on an unexpected visit. The man next to her was quiet and spent most of the walk looking up at the sky dreamily. Occasionally he stumbled, and sometimes he glanced at Matil and Dask.

Matil continued eating. After she finished the sausage, she started in on the loolookap. It was sweet and spiced and fruity, and tasted just as good as it had looked. Maybe even better.

When they had left the more crowded part of town, the woman spoke quietly to them. "Call me Brenna. And this silent fella is my son, who'll go by Nat."

"But," Matil said, confused, "isn't your name Ul—"

"Not to you, it isn't. And I'll have you know that neither of them are my real name, so don't go getting any ideas."

Dask pointed at himself. "Dask."

"I'm Matil."

"That's your name?" Brenna said with a hint of disgust.

"Not exactly…"

Brenna shot a strange look at Matil, but didn't press further. "Here we are," she said. At the foot of a tree, she stopped. "Nat can carry the girl up."

Matil looked up. They would get to go in one of those tree-houses? She was feeling better and better.

"I can do it," Dask said.

"I don't mean to be rude, dear, but you might not be able to make it. I can tell you're used to flying, not lifting."

"Hey, I'm not weak or anything!"

"Go ahead, then. I won't stop you."

Dask looked at Matil, and then eyed the distance up to the platform in the tree. He made a face. "Hm. I can help, at least."

"Nat doesn't need any help." She proudly patted Nat's muscular arm. He looked at the ground with an expression that suggested he didn't want to be there.

Dask grumbled under his breath.

Brenna pushed Nat forward. He nodded at Matil without meeting her eyes. She almost fell over as he put one arm around her back, the other behind her legs, and lifted her up in a jerky motion. He crouched down and pushed off from the ground, flapping his wings powerfully. Brenna's platform was very high up, above most of the other ones, and the flight took just enough time to be too much. It didn't help that Matil could see Dask flying beside them, watching with an uneasy look.

Nat landed on the platform and attempted to set Matil down gently. Her belt got caught on his sleeve and he fumbled, trying to get it off as Matil nearly fell a few more times. At last he succeeded.

"Um, thanks," Matil said with a smile once she had recovered.

It was hard to catch what Nat said, but after thinking it over, Matil realized that he had mumbled, "You're welcome."

Brenna flew up as well, and was now unlocking her door. "Come on in," she said.

Matil ran a hand over the twig-covered exterior of the building as she followed Brenna and Nat through the doorway.

The inside of the squat house was cozy in a strange way. Everything, from the chairs and tables to the quilts hanging all over the place, was as clean as it could be and placed in a way that looked casual yet calculated and near-perfect. Groans and creaks whispered in the walls and floor, making

Matil aware that the house swayed with the branch it was built upon.

The main room was filled with an eclectic collection of furniture. A short table with skinny legs was surrounded by a couple of fat blue armchairs, a polished wood stump, a couch with a red crisscross pattern, and a few rickety wooden chairs. Thin curtains covered the windows. The chaotic furniture, combined with the low ceiling, took the edge off of the super-cleanliness and made it homey.

On the wall was a familiar unrolled scroll bearing the word 'Chivishi'. It looked exactly like the one in Khelya's house. Maybe a lot of homes had this scroll.

Brenna locked the door, pulled off her hat, and set it on a stand that looked like a little trec with hats instead of leaves. "Go on, hang up your cloak. I admit, I want to see the 'girl without wings' for myself."

Matil looked at Dask, and he nodded. She pulled off the cloak and untied the cloth from herself.

"My, my," Brenna said in fascination. "It's true. You're like a short Obrigi." Her nostrils flared as if she had smelled something foul.

"Maybe it's not her fault," Nat mumbled at Brenna.

"Whatever," she said with an edge in her voice. "I'll go make the tea. I left the water simmering while we were gone, so it shouldn't be too long."

Nat followed her through a door, but Brenna pushed him back out gently. "Entertain our guests, please," she said.

He stood in the front room as if he wanted to move but couldn't.

"Nice place," Dask said. He sprawled on one of the blue chairs.

Nat fidgeted and turned to Matil. "You can sit…if you want to."

Matil chose a spot on the couch, trying not to get it dirty. Nonstop travel through the forest had left her clothes dingy.

Nat huddled on the shiny stump and examined the floor carefully. Humming floated out from behind the door.

"Huh," Dask said, standing up and going over to an interesting set of objects. "This is Climb, isn't it?"

Climb? It looked like a board covered in many book-shaped wooden blocks of different sizes stacked on top of each other like some kind of jagged staircase. Small, colored cubes were lined up at the foot of the blocks.

Nat looked up. "Uh, yes. It is."

"I used to play this all the time."

"Really?"

"Yeah."

"I play, too."

"What's Climb?" Matil said.

"You've…never heard of it?"

"I lost my memory." She shrugged. "I think Dask mentioned it once, but I don't know what it is."

"…Oh. It's a…game." Nat blushed. "You have these little playing pieces and you move them up. But you roll the dice first…and you have to stop the other pieces…um…"

"The goal is to get your alva – the cubes – to the top of the mountain, right here, see?" Dask tapped the top block. "So you roll the dice," he pointed out two little pyramids with numbers on them, "to find out how many spaces your first alva, the leader, can move. And you do the same with the rest. You have to move every turn. But you can move them to any spot on the mountain, even backward, although the leader can only go forward or side-to-side. So when you move your alva, you try to block the other team from getting up. First team to get all their pieces up wins."

Matil had been listening intently. "That sounds fun."

Dask shot a smug smile at Nat. Nat just rubbed the back of his neck, very clearly ill-at-ease. Matil wasn't sure what was going on, but she didn't want Nat to be uncomfortable. "Maybe you two could play Climb with me?" she said, hoping that would get their spirits up.

"Only two players," Nat said.

"One of you could be on my team, then."

"I'll have you winning in no time," Dask said with a grin.

Nat looked irritated. "You should let her decide."

"Okay, okay. Matil?"

Matil's ears drooped. "I really don't know…"

"Enough talking about games," Brenna said, bustling out of the kitchen with a delicate cart that carried cups and pitchers of various shapes. One pitcher even had a long spout. "We have serious business to discuss."

She distributed the little clay cups on little clay plates to each alva, then poured a steaming liquid out of the long-spouted pitcher into each cup.

Matil lifted hers up with great interest. The liquid was pale red and the steam warmed her face. She sipped.

"No, Matil—"

"You might not want—"

Pain seared the inside of Matil's mouth and she let the liquid spill back out into her cup.

Brenna, nodding sagely, handed her a napkin. "Blow on the tea some."

Matil wiped her mouth with the napkin and panted to cool down her burned tongue.

"I was told," Brenna said, passing a bowl of sugar to Dask, "to provide you with a guide and, when you return, to send back the information you gather. There *are* three of you, aren't there?"

"Yes, Khelya couldn't come into town because—"

"She's an Obrigi," Brenna finished curtly.

"How did you know?"

"If I hadn't already been briefed, her name would tell me right away." Brenna pursed her lips. "That explains your name, too. Toast and string, I can't believe you brought an *Obrigi* into *Nychtfal*. Out of all the bad ideas in Eventyr, that one has to be the third-worst."

"She's my friend," Matil said.

"How could a Ranycht be friends with an Obrigi? It's not right."

"I don't know," Dask said. "We've kinda gotten attached to her. I figured we could go fast and quietly enough through Nychtfal that she wouldn't really be noticed. You gotta admit, the south's pretty laid back. And we discovered a very interesting thing about Obrigi. They really can use other alva's powers."

"*You let her use Ranycht magic?*" Brenna said, her ears angling back in hostility. Nat put a hand on her shoulder.

"Whoa." Dask raised his eyebrows. "It's not so bad."

"Not so bad?" Brenna raised her eyes to the ceiling. "Obrigi," she muttered. "Fine. I don't care, so long as I don't have to see the giant. Anyway, woodsmen are in short stock in these parts, so you'll have to wait until maybe…next week at the soonest, when the trappers get here to trade. We'll find at least one who can guide you."

"Next week?" Matil said, discouraged.

"At the soonest. It depends, so you may have to wait longer."

Weeks and weeks of nothing but the increasingly bad memory dreams to tie her to her past…Matil bit her lip. She needed to know who she was. She didn't want to wait, not even until next week. "Maybe we could go by ourselves. We've done pretty well so far."

"…Aside from getting in trouble with the Sangriga *and* the Ranycht," Dask said. "Matil has a point, though. We could find Olsta on our own. Otherwise she might leave this area, and then there would be no point in waiting for a guide."

"We'll know when she's planning on leaving," Brenna said.

"You will?"

"You betcha. So far as we can tell, her current location is where she'll stay for several weeks."

"How do you know?"

"We're spies. Pretty good at sneaking around and hearing things others don't want us to hear. Unfortunately we haven't been able to see much, so we can't confirm whether Olsta has the Book or not. Our employer seems to think you'll do better."

"Maybe you could guide us," Matil said. "Please?"

"We can't risk it. We're the ones who have to get the information to our employer when this is all done."

"*You* can't risk it."

Everyone looked at Nat.

Brenna forced a smile. "What are you saying, dear?"

"I want to…" He shuffled his wings and said in an even quieter voice, "I want to go."

"No."

"Why not?"

"You know very well why not."

Nat rubbed his hands on the knees of his pants. "I know this part of Nychtfal better than most. I can- can get them in and get them out. And you always tell me to do whatever I do best to fight bad things. We both know Nychta Olsta is doing bad things. Even a few days extra could give her a huge advantage."

"You're right," Brenna said. "You still shouldn't go."

For the first time, Nat smiled. "I'll be fine. I can take care of myself. And when I come back, you'll see that it was all worth it."

She took a long sip of her tea and set it down, arranging the cup directly in the center of its plate.

"You're a man now," she said eventually. "You can choose for yourself."

25

Bedtale

After Matil thanked Brenna and Nat profusely, they decided what was to happen. In a bit, Matil and Dask would sleep while Brenna and Nat went about their business and prepared for the trip into the forest. Nat would also get some sleep in preparation. Before daybreak, they would all be awakened.

"We won't forget Khelya, right?" Matil asked.

"Yeah, we'll check up on her," Dask said. "But, um...I think we should leave her behind until we get back."

Matil felt hurt. "Why would we leave her behind?"

"He's absolutely right," Brenna said. "Too big and loud, y'know, lacking in common sense. She'd just ruin everything."

"Uh." Dask shot a glance at Brenna. "I wouldn't put it that way, but Khelya is definitely not cut out for spying."

"I understand." Matil's ears drooped.

"Hey, we're going to see her in the morning. Everything'll be all right."

Brenna stood up. "I've got to be off now. Matil can take my room and Dask can take Nat's."

"Where are you going?" Nat said curiously.

"I'm having lunch with Olie today."

"Again?

"She's been lonely since her husband died."

"Oh. See you, then."

Brenna left and Matil finally picked up her tea cup. Just to be safe, she had waited until the tea was room temperature. Now she drank some. It was very watery, with only a faint berry flavor to it. Not bad, but not exactly good. She continued drinking it anyway.

Without Brenna, the room became quiet again. What had they been talking about before the tea? Right! "I have an idea!" Matil said brightly. "Is there time for two games of Climb?"

"If we play with the fast rules," Dask said.

"Great. How about you two play the first game of Climb while I watch, and then I'll play against whoever wins?"

Dask eyed Nat. "All right."

Nat gave Dask a dark look. "Okay."

* * *

Matil awoke to her shoulder being shaken. Reluctantly, she opened her itchy eyes. Above her stood Brenna.

"Follow me, dear," the woman said. She put two fingers to her lips.

Matil forced herself out of the warm, soft bed. What time was it? She quickly pulled aside the curtain. It was still night. Perhaps she hadn't been sleeping for long.

She followed Brenna through the house, sneaking across the front room, and into a steep stairwell made completely of dried plant stalks woven together. It shifted with the tree even more than the house did. They climbed and climbed. Brenna came to a sudden stop and Matil heard the whisper of a hinge gliding open. Brenna's long skirt and wings whipped upward and disappeared. In her place was a large, square opening, through which Matil saw a swirl of stars on the deep blue sky.

When Matil made her way out of the passage, she stood up and panted. She and Brenna were near the top of the tree, on a deck made of the same plants as the stairs. Some branches had been sawed away to afford a better view.

The swaying deck made Matil feel unsafe; it had nothing around the edges to keep an alva from falling. Only their own wings or a branch in the way would save them from the ground many lengths below. Looking up, she tried to ignore her wobbly legs and focus on her surroundings. It worked.

Spread out around them were treetops forming a rolling, never-ending meadow of leaves. Matil's breath seemed to freeze in her throat. The moon was just beginning to wane, and it glossed everything in a pale, cold light that didn't bother her eyes. Behind her lay her shadow, as sharp as if it had been cut from a cloth. Far, far in the distance Matil could see massive dark ridges that rose up above the forest.

What was it? Some titanic beast that slept, curling itself around Eventyr?

"Have you ever seen the mountains before?" Brenna said.

Matil looked at her and quickly returned to gazing at the ridges. "I've seen mountains, but they're hills compared to these."

Brenna gestured to the closest mountain. "That's Brotinnfjol, over there. To my knowledge, no one's ever gotten to the peak – well, what's left of the peak."

Brotinnfjol reached a great height like the other mountains, but instead of being pointed at the summit, it appeared as though someone had sliced the peak off. A sloping edge remained.

"Why does it look like that?" Matil said.

"A long time ago, before the Mekydra Age, things were different in Eventyr. One of these things was the Brandur, alva with fire for hair. The stories say that Myrkhar tainted the Brandur and used them to destroy relentlessly. The Brandur had destroyed before, but always together with the Eletsol so that new life could spring from the flames. Now, they ended life indiscriminately."

Matil's tired mind could only understand half of what Brenna was saying, and Brenna's hushed tones lulled her.

"So many died or lost their families that the alva called out to the Heilar. In answer, Calo gathered together some of his strongest Elders to capture the Brandur. They set traps all over the forest and caged the crazed alva. It took all of their power, and Jalt, Elder of the mountains, knew they couldn't keep the Brandur locked up forever. He proposed to seal them away in his own home, the great mountain Jalt-Hym, and offered to guard it himself." Brenna sat down on the deck.

With relief, Matil knelt, rubbing her cold hands together and blowing on them.

Brenna continued, "After arguing until they were spent, the Heilar agreed to his plan. Jalt destroyed the crown of Jalt-Hym so that the Brandur would fit through. Once the prisoners were inside, he closed the mountain's top. The Heilar, exhausted and glad, each went away to patrol their own domains.

"But," Brenna said, raising a finger and an eyebrow, "the Brandur had the fury of Myrkhar driving them. They pushed out, destroying the seal and spilling over the side of the mountain. When Jalt saw what was happening, he picked up the escaping Brandur, flung them back in, and exploded in a cloud of smoke. The Heilar returned and cleared the smoke. There was no trace of Jalt, but instead of a hole in the mountain they found a crater, and the Brandur were, for once, quiet.

"In the center of Jalt-Hym's crater was a stone inscribed with a message: 'I hold back the fire unto death. Colthal, my friends.' Calo and the Heilar understood that Jalt was not dead, but he would never come back to them. He had become the seal that kept the Brandur imprisoned."

Matil stared at Brenna, then looked at Brotinnfjol. "Brotinnfjol is Jalt-Hym?"

"Supposedly."

"Does that mean the Brad—um, Brandur are still inside?"

"There are a lot of stories about the Mekydra Age. Who's to say if any of them are true? Only Thosten knows."

"And the Elders. Right?"

"I don't believe the Elders were really…Elders. Oh sure, maybe they were heroes, but they were probably only normal alva whose deeds were made a few barrels bigger over the years."

Matil's brow furrowed. "What about Mr. Korsen?"

"A bedtale. I don't even think the original Mr. Korsen story had anything to do with the Elders. They must have just got lumped together as time went on. Anyway, what did you think of the story?"

Matil wanted to say that she *saw* Mr. Korsen, but had she really? Maybe it was a bear all along, like Dask said. "I liked it. It had a sad ending, though."

"That story was one of Am…Nat's favorites, when he was younger." Brenna smiled, eyes wrinkling at the corners. After a moment, she dropped the smile and looked at Matil piercingly. "He's not a boy anymore, and he can do what he wants. But I sure would prefer it if what he wanted to do was safer and closer to home. I'd like you to stay in Goska and forget about this mission of yours."

Had Matil heard that right? "What?"

"He already likes you. If he has a good reason to stay behind, he will."

"*Likes*...me?" Matil was having difficulty forming proper sentences even in her head.

Brenna scowled. "Oh, get over it. You're a sweet girl. I suppose I wouldn't mind having you as a daughter. All you have to do is make yourself charming and suddenly realize that you're happier here than flouncing around in the wild." She took in Matil's startled-rabbit expression. "Take time to think about it."

"No, it's not—no!" Matil swallowed to moisten her dry throat. How could Brenna tell? Was *that* why Nat had been acting so nervous and quiet? Or was he always like that?

"What's the downside, dear?"

"I-if Nat and I..." Matil stopped and tried to get the words together. "I can't stay in Goska. I can't. I'll never stop looking for my family, even if it takes me all over Eventyr. I won't stop until I find them and my name."

Brenna looked down at her hands. "This'll probably sound harsh, but it's something to consider. By now, your family probably thinks of you as dead. Why don't you take a new name and stay here, where you'd have a family?"

"It won't leave me alone," Matil said. "Whenever I'm not moving, I want to be moving. I need to find them. Nychta Olsta will lead me to them somehow."

Brenna held Matil's gaze again. "If they're connected to that evil woman, don'tcha suppose there's a reason you left?"

Matil shook her head firmly. "They're good alva, all of them, I know it. I've seen them in dreams."

"Dreams?"

"Some of my memories come to me while I sleep."

"You *are* an oddball." Brenna shrugged. "Maybe you're right. Maybe you're wrong. I can see I won't convince you."

"Dask and Khelya are wonderful, Brenna. We'll all work together to stay safe."

"I'm sure you will. I…apologize, dear. I've lost one man and I don't want to lose the other."

"Oh." Matil hesitated, then reached over and held Brenna's hand.

Brenna looked up. "Thank you." They sat in silence briefly, and then Brenna stood. She helped Matil to her feet. "You're probably dead tired. Let's head back down."

Matil's mind whirled as they descended. She went sluggishly, yawning the whole way down. Finally, she found herself in the warmth of the house. Across the floor, into the bedroom. She went to close the door, but stopped before it shut completely. Her ears twitched. Was that Nat?

"…shouldn't have said that to Matil," he was whispering angrily.

Matil was embarrassed. Had he been listening when they were on the platform?

She shut the door without a sound. Poor Nat. He *was* nice. Matil got into bed and pulled the covers up around her. Maybe after she found her family she could come back and play more Climb with him and maybe…

* * *

The man's scarred face twisted with rage. Behind him, the gloomy sky threatened rain. "Give it back, ya little *nit!*"

"Help!" Matil screamed. She backed into the empty barrels that filled the end of the narrow alley.

"Wastin' ya words," said another man, this one painfully thin. He sneered at her. "Hand over the dagger and the necklace, and we'll give you a shiny coin. Ya wanna coin?"

Matil's chin trembled. In her sweaty fist she clasped a thin dagger with a round guard. She held it in front of her in a reverse grip, like Etsel taught her. Safe in her pocket was an amulet etched with an odd round symbol. It gave off an unceasing feeling of rotting. She looked around the alley.

Nowhere to go but up. She sniffed, feeling her throat tighten. She'd never make it.

But what if she had a distraction?

She screwed up her face and sobbed, lowering the dagger. "I'm sorry! Don't hurt me and I promise I-I'll never steal from you again."

"See, buddy? A little persuasion and the brat's as sweet as a sugar beet!" the skinny man said.

The scarred man grimaced. "Ugly as a sugar beet, ya mean. Let's get this over wi—"

Matil shoved a barrel at the thugs and launched herself into the air, flapping as hard as she could.

"Hey! *Get her!*"

The men shot up at her. Their wings grazed the alley walls as they fought for space.

"Outta my way," the scarred man yelled. He pushed the skinny man aside and reached out for Matil.

She snapped her wings shut and dropped back down. Just before reaching the cobblestone ground she opened her wings, slowing the descent but straining her muscles painfully, and then pushed off with her bare feet. Back up she went, grabbing hold of the corner of a building and swinging out of the alley. She searched the dark, empty street frantically.

A balcony!

Matil hopped over the low railing. Dusty crates and old furniture littered the balcony, leading inside the building through a gaping door. She pushed the door closed, making sure to slam it, and hid behind a stack of rickety chairs on the balcony. With a great effort, she imagined pulling her surroundings closer and closer until she couldn't be seen.

"I heard the door, she's in the building!"

The balcony wobbled as the two men landed.

Matil glanced down at herself. She was barely visible. Hopefully they wouldn't notice.

Stomp, stomp, stomp, stomp.

"We ain't gonna hurt ya!" the skinny man shouted. Matil winced at the sudden loudness. "Just come out and give us what we want! Ya know there's no way outta there, don't ya?"

They opened the door and walked right past the chairs.

"Come on, brat, give us the necklace!"

She waited until it sounded like they were far enough in the building, then quietly leaped off the balcony. As she unfurled her wings, pain stabbed through her shoulders and chest. A whimper escaped her mouth. Couldn't stop, though. Had to get to the drop-off.

Magistrate Gerig was an awful old man, and Matil didn't want to know what he'd do with the creepy amulet she carried. But he could tell her what she did want to know, which made this trade worth it.

When she had everything figured out, she would go back and show Crell the good she'd done. The good that she had made happen while he did nothing.

26

Unseen

For the second time, Matil was awoken by Brenna shaking her. The heavenly aroma of sizzling sausage filled the air.

"Time for your breakfast, dear. And my dinner." Brenna left the room.

The door shut softly and Matil sat up. She was still tired, and the unsettling dream was fresh in her mind, but that must have been the best night of sleep she had ever experienced. Proper pillows and blankets and a soft *mattress*. She wished that Khelya were a Ranycht, so all three of them could have slept comfortably.

Matil yawned. The sun hadn't even risen yet.

Instead of her dress, she put on a short tunic over her undershirt and pants. The tunic was a gift from Brenna, who had insisted on Matil wearing something better suited to stealth. She went through the hall and into the front room, where Brenna sat her down with a plate of sausage and fried mushroom. Before long, Nat joined them at the table.

"Where's Dask?" Matil said.

Nat speared a sausage on his fork. "Shaving." He avoided looking at her.

Matil's face turned warm as she remembered Brenna's talk last night.

A smooth-faced, short-haired stranger entered the room. Matil stared until she realized that it was *Dask*.

She burst out laughing. "I'm sorry," she gasped. "I can't help it."

"What's wrong? Do I look funny?" Dask frowned.

"No, no, it's just different! I haven't seen you without a beard in a long time."

"I guess not."

Matil forced herself to stop smiling and picked up her cup. "It looks nice." Just in time, she remembered to cool the tea before drinking. This one was a little tastier than the last.

"It does?" Dask rubbed his chin. "Huh. Thanks." He sat down and dug into the plate that Brenna had prepared for him.

"You cut your hair, too?"

"Yeah. I didn't want the beard, but I had to do something to change myself a little. The portraits the guards put up show me with longer hair. With a hat, I doubt alva will look twice at me."

After breakfast, Nat showed Matil and Dask to a small room. Racks hung on the walls, covered in bows and a few swords. In the corner were quivers full of arrows. Wooden boxes were stacked against the far wall.

Nat turned to Matil. "Do you know how to use a weapon?" he said.

"I…do." Matil hadn't done much real fighting with her dagger before it was taken in Obrigi, but she knew the proper way to use one like she knew the proper way to eat. "If you have a dagger, I could use it."

"We have some." Nat took a box from the top of a stack and opened it. Nestled inside were several different daggers. "Go ahead and pick."

"Ooh," Dask said, looking over Matil's shoulder. "Can I have one? Actually, can I have two? Wait, wait." He held up his hands. "I think four would be good. Extras, you know?"

"You can borrow as many as two," Nat growled. "When we come back after the mission, they'll be *returned*. To this box."

"Uh-huh, sounds fantastic." Dask scooped up a few daggers and slid one out of its sheath. "Nah." He tossed it back into the box and looked at another. "Mm. Nice."

Matil looked over the daggers. A skinny, three-sided stiletto caught her eye. She took it out and weighed it in her hand. Facing away from Nat and Dask, she made a few test stabs. It would do well if needed.

Her mood clouded over as she put the dagger back in its sheath. The dagger brought her thoughts back to that strange city scene. Wings, those thugs, an amulet. Why had her dreams become nightmares? She wanted the simple peace of waking up with Bechel's grinning face fresh in her mind. *Maybe there's a reason you left.* She wished Brenna hadn't said that.

Matil shook her head to clear it and attached the dagger to her belt. She also picked a longer dagger, one she could slash with, just in case. "Thanks for letting us use these," she said. "And thank you so much for coming along with us."

Nat reddened. "It's no trouble." Then he smiled. "You've said that a few times now."

"I know. I just like saying thanks."

He chose a sturdy bow and a short sword. Dask took twin dirks. After they left the little room, Dask helped Matil put on her lumpy cloak again, while he and Nat wore cloaks that fit around their wings. Brenna had gone earlier to pick up some food for their day-long journey to Olsta's camp. Now they would meet her in the town square and then be off.

With all the cloaks and weapons they were wearing, Nat was even clumsier during the flight to the ground than last time. He must have been thinking what Matil often thought: *If only she had wings.* But she laughed it off, telling him it was all right, and they went on to the town square.

As the sky became lighter and the town's bell rang, the shops and stalls closed, though some Ranycht still strolled around. Matil, Dask, and Nat tried to avoid notice and found a shady place in the square.

They waited, yawning and rubbing their eyes.

A smooth, delicate voice carried to Matil's ears. She tilted her head and focused on it. It sounded familiar.

"…as I was saying, you have a very lovely town, sir Mayor. I'm considering staying here permanently."

"You are? That's great! We'd all welcome you, I'm sure. My secretary told me you were asking about an advisory position, and I'm pleased to offer such a thing up to you, if you do stay."

Matil searched the square and saw where the voices came from. Just outside of a neat little building sat two men on a bench, talking. Their wings hung off the bench behind them. The second voice came from a rotund, mustachioed man. If he weren't so involved in the conversation, he'd be looking directly at her. The first voice must be coming from the other man, of whom Matil could only see fine clothes. For some reason, she was glad for that. She didn't want him to see her either.

"Who is he?" she said to Nat.

"You might not want to do that." Nat tapped on her arm, which was pointing at the man.

She bit her lip. "Sorry."

Out of the corner of his eyes, he took a quick, curious look at where she had been pointing. "Him? He's a rich newcomer, Tren Yinder. Alva here love him because of all the gifts and compliments he gives. My mother's a little worried about him. We haven't found anything on him yet, but we have someone returning from a trip to Yinder's home city. Then, hopefully, we'll know—"

"Chatty, aren't we?" Dask said.

Nat flushed.

"Thank you for telling me," Matil said.

He gave her a small smile. "Why did you ask about Yinder?"

"I don't know. It seems like...I've met him before."

Brenna met them in the square. She carried a bag, which she gave to Nat. He put it in his own pack, which was strapped across his body and hung at his side.

"Keep yourselves alive," Brenna said. "Bring back that information."

Dask nodded confidently. "We will."

Brenna and Nat looked at each other, and then he pulled her into a hug. "Bye," he said.

"Thosten fly with you."

The group left Goska and headed back to find Khelya. Once they were in the burrow, they crept past the shrews. Matil avoided looking at the mother shrew's sharp teeth. It would be good to get Khelya out of here. If she were even still safe.

They entered the little chamber where they had left her. The bags were strewn across the ground.

"Khelya?" Matil whispered. "We're back."

Dask stepped closer, wings twitching open. "Khelya?"

A groan responded.

"Khelya, where are you? Are you all right?" Matil's voice rose.

"Muh-tuh...?" There was an odd snorting noise.

"Khelya, what's wrong?" Matil said, panicked.

Dask put a calming hand on her arm. "Shh." He crept forward slowly and reached out. He touched something solid, and Matil began to see a faint, wavery shape lying in the corner.

To her surprise and horror, Dask lifted up his foot and shoved the shape with it.

"*Hey!*" Khelya's voice said. The shape clambered into a standing position. "Ain't no call for that!"

"Khelya, is that you?" Dask squinted at the shape.

"What do you mean 'is that me'? 'Course I'm me, I—" She stopped dead. "I feel kinda funny, I—" The shape moved around a lot now, making it slightly easier to see. Matil thought she saw Khelya's face up near the burrow's roof.

"Great Falgar," Khelya finally said. "I'm still invisible."

27

On the Trail Again

Dask tapped his chin. "I really thought it would wear off when you slept, but you managed to keep it going. Hm. You can stop it now."

"That's…just…it," Khelya said through gritted teeth. "I can't."

Matil looked at Dask and Nat's flabbergasted faces. "You can't stop being invisible?" she said.

"Nope," Khelya squeaked. "What do I *do?*" It sounded as though she were losing it.

Dask held up his hands. "Stay calm, relax, sit down, we'll, uh, we'll figure this out."

Khelya's shape sat down immediately. Matil knelt next to her. Even up close, Khelya's concealment tricked Matil's eyes so that it was almost like looking through her.

"Khelya, that's our guide, Nat," she said, gesturing to Nat.

"Best hurry," he said. "The sun's flying quickly."

"The sun is flying exactly as fast as it always does, which is *not quickly*. We have plenty of time!" Dask ran a hand through his hair.

"Who's the guide? You or me?"

"Please," Matil said, "let's help Khelya."

"Oh, right. Right." Nat nodded.

Dask threw a scowl Nat's way. "Yeah. Khelya, you said you felt funny? Precisely how funny? Hilarious or just amusing?"

"Dask," Khelya said warningly.

"Heheheh. Seriously, how do you feel?"

"All tingly, like my whole body fell asleep, but I'm not numb. Every time you two hid me, it's felt like this, only not as bad. But it *had* been getting worse. Hey, I told you that earlier, didn't I? You said I'd be fine! Told me to stop complainin'!"

"I did, okay, but that's not important right now. Just relax. I'm gonna think about this."

Khelya settled back against the sloping burrow wall and grumbled.

"How was your sleep?" Matil said.

"Rough. But I did sleep."

Matil remembered the warm night she spent in a real bed. She bit her lip. Then she forced a smile onto her face. "When this is over and I know who I am, we'll all get a good rest. Indoors."

"About that..." Khelya said quietly. "You won't, um, you won't forget me or anything, right?"

"Why would I do that?"

"You'll want to spend time with your family once you find them, right? Most alva like doing that. Spending time with their families."

"That won't make me forget you. Don't be silly."

"A-all right—"

"So, this is weird," Dask said. Everyone looked at him. "I think I've got it, though. Khelya's been using our magic a lot, and we've both been powering her up. It's simple counting. We must've used too much magic on her in a short amount of time. And then it sort of...broke."

"Oh, great, I'm broken. Got any big ideas on how to fix me?"

"None at all. But it's pretty useful. We never have to use our magic on you again."

"I'll be invisible forever," Khelya moaned.

Nat looked contemplative. "Might wear off."

"What?"

"He said it might wear off," Matil said excitedly. "Maybe he's right, maybe it'll go away."

"I hope so."

"Wait," Dask said, "we could try one thing before we leave."

"Yeah?"

"Matil and I could try pulling the magic out! See, just like we were doing before," Dask put his hands on Khelya's shoulder, "only this time we *pull* the magic. Like pulling a splinter!"

That sounded simple. Matil held Khelya's hand and, eyes closed, imagined magic fizzing around in Khelya, then pictured the magic swirling back into her own hand.

Matil opened her eyes. Did Khelya look more real? It was hard to tell. Her outline did seem stronger. "Do you feel better?"

"There's not so much tingling. What do I look like?"

Dask stood back. "It worked."

"It did?!"

"A little bit. Still faded."

"Thiffen!"

"Hey, you know what? This means we can take you with us. A sort-of-invisible Obrigi could be a real advantage."

"Y-you were going to leave me here?"

Nat looked Khelya over, ignoring her words. "As long as it doesn't wear off too soon…"

"Really?" Matil said excitedly.

Nat smiled at her. "Sure. We have a long way to go, so hurry up, Obrigi. Find a stick for hitting things. We want to go unseen, but we may have to fight."

Khelya took some food, and then, with difficulty, they tied the bags to her back. The longer the bags touched her, the more transparent they became until they were part of her shadowy outline. To help Matil's maneuverability, they took off her fake wings cloak and stuffed it in one of the bags. She immediately felt more balanced.

They passed through the burrow one last time. Once outside, Khelya scavenged the ground for a good-sized stick and picked it up. It vanished like the bags. With that done, they began the journey. Matil's heart and feet felt light.

As they went farther away from Goska, however, it became apparent to her that something wasn't right. She tilted her head every which way, trying to catch a sound. No luck. For some reason, the birds didn't sing and the animals didn't scamper and crawl. The forest was unusually subdued aside from Khelya's crunching footfalls. She mentioned it to Nat.

"There've been Skorgon scouting the area for the past week and a half," Nat said in a low voice. "Ever since the bugs got here, the animals keep to themselves."

Dask looked disquieted. "Animals shouldn't be afraid of Skorgon."

"Who says...who says it's the Skorgon they're afraid of?"

A deep pang troubled Matil's heart as she thought of one thing that could frighten them this much.

The Book of Myrkhar.

That idea somehow made the forest's silence even more ominous. Well, finding the Book *was* their goal. Perhaps they should take the warning.

Matil steeled herself. This wasn't the time to doubt and ponder.

The group trod carefully through the greenery – except Khelya. The invisible Obrigi couldn't see her feet, which gave her difficulty in figuring out where to put them. This, on top of the darkness of the forest, made her a stumbling nuisance.

After she finally fell to the ground, Nat and Dask shared a look.

"Khelya," Dask said.

Her shape moved in a familiar way; she was pushing up her headband. "I'm sorry. I s'pose I should hide again."

"That…would be best," Nat said with an apologetic glance at Matil.

They were right. "Please, just a little longer?" Matil said. "I'll help her. If she keeps quiet, can she come along?"

Dask tried to focus on Khelya, who now seemed to be standing up. "Maybe."

Matil went over and managed to grip part of Khelya's hand with her own slender fingers.

"Thanks Matil, but I shouldn't." She gently pulled her hand back.

"Do you want to?"

"I don't know…"

Matil looked down. "That's fine if you don't want to come. But if you do, hold my hand. I'll keep you from falling."

There was a moment of hesitation before Khelya's hand wrapped around hers. "All right."

Dask and Nat started moving again, following shadows across the forest floor.

Matil pulled Khelya along behind her, going around things that could trip them up and murmuring suggestions. It didn't stop Khelya from accidentally kicking Matil, but she eventually improved her stride.

Matil also felt steadier. Holding Khelya's hand seemed to help her as much as it helped Khelya. She hadn't realized how jittery she'd been.

The day wore on. Matil kept getting the urge to talk and ask questions, but they had to be quiet. It was like an itch that couldn't be scratched.

Now that she was thinking about itches…she noticed a tugging sensation. It was faint, but it pulled her in a different direction than the one they were heading. Strange, but easy enough to ignore. On through the quiet forest they trudged.

Over time, the tugging grew more irritating. It *wanted* her to follow its call. Matil tried harder to pay it no attention. She was on a mission and this weird feeling wasn't going to interfere.

Eventually, Nat beckoned everyone over. "We're getting close. Let's stop for a break and food."

They all sat down and took out the food, which consisted of oatcakes and roast beetle. There was only enough for the three Ranycht. Khelya ate the last of the dried meat in the bags.

"Mother told me to ask if you could sense the Book," Nat said.

Sense the Book? What did he mean by that? Oh, perhaps the tugging was the Book calling out to her! "I *have* been feeling something. It's leading me that way." She pointed off to the left.

"That's where Olsta's camp is. You really do sense it."

"Why are we walking this way, then?"

"We thought we'd see if you were connected to the Book like our employer said. And it's true! We might even be able to secure the Book, if we're careful enough. Ready to go?"

They resumed their arduous march in the direction of the tugging. Flecks of blue sky in the tree canopy above were darkening with the oncoming dusk. Matil started counting the trees they passed. She had reached eleven when Dask told them all to stop.

"I thought I heard something," he said.

Each of them looked around edgily.

A low buzzing noise made Matil's ears prick up and her stomach fill with dread. That sounded familiar.

"*Go!*" a powerful voice shouted.

The buzzing immediately became deafening.

Matil looked up to see a cloud of Skorgon descending from the trees.

"Run," urged Nat.

Dask seized Matil's hand and pulled her along, almost causing her to lose hold of Khelya. "Run run *run!*"

Matil noticed Khelya keeping up well. Now that the Obrigi wasn't concerned with being quiet, she found surer footing as they ran. Fear of the Skorgon catching them gave Matil speed, but it didn't last long. Her legs felt like they were made of wood, tired from the day of walking. She had the fleeting thought of giving herself up so the others could make it. If she did, what would happen to her? The question spurred her onward. They might have a chance if they could lose the swarm and then fade.

Several Skorgon dropped to the ground in front of them and brandished their claws.

Nat's head whipped from side to side. More skorgon landed all around, walling them in. "Thiffen." He readied his bow and nocked an arrow. "Fight!"

Dask unsheathed his dirks and Matil took out her stiletto. Khelya let go of Matil's hand. Her silhouette hefted the stick she had found.

The Skorgon rushed upon them. Matil rubbed the dagger's pommel with her thumb. A Skorgon reached for her and she danced clumsily out of the way. Weaving and dodging the Skorgon that launched themselves at her, she watched for chances to strike. She stabbed. Ducked, jabbed. Her heart pounded and her breathing became labored. She couldn't see her friends anymore and desperately hoped that they were doing well. A few Skorgon fell back bleeding light green liquid.

The swarm lessened. Were they beating the Skorgon? They were! Matil's mind cleared enough that she noticed cuts all over herself and an awful stitch in her side. Where were the others? The fight had taken her away from them. Her hair began to blow about in a buffeting wind.

Whump.

A large, imposing Ranycht man landed before her. Looking at her, his dark orange eyes grew wide.

As Matil recognized him, her heart soared. "Crell?" she gasped.

Crell stood still, his mouth frozen open. "Your- your eyes are…"

"My eyes?"

"No!" he yelled, covering his face, and she stepped back in startlement. "No, you're not her…you're a…a fake."

Things were making even less sense than usual. "What are you talking about? It's me! I know you. You know me." Her eyebrows rose and she smiled. "Hey, you know me! Crell, who am I? Please tell me!"

Crell stood up straight and glared at Matil. "Shut up."

"But—"

His eyes moved slightly, looking at something behind her, and she realized too late that she hadn't been watching her back. He nodded.

Matil whirled around, dagger at the ready. Pain lashed through her head and she blacked out.

* * *

Khelya bashed two Skorgon in a single sweep of her stick. Her headband slipped over her eyes. Pushing it back up, she caught a glimpse of something strange through the scattered swarm.

A Ranycht man stood, holding a small figure. He removed a dagger from its belt and threw it onto the ground. What was going on?

Was that *Matil* in the Ranycht's arms? Was…was she…?

"*Matil!*" Khelya cried. The Skorgon kept smacking into her as she tried to run through them, slowing her down.

The Ranycht looked in her direction, grew puzzled, then launched into the air with Matil. "*Back!*" he yelled.

Khelya screamed and hit as many of the Skorgon as she could, but soon found herself hitting only air. The trees echoed with fainter and fainter buzzing. Khelya, Dask, and Nat were left alone with the slain Skorgon, breathing heavily and splattered with both Skorgon blood and some of their own.

"They got her," Khelya said, panicked.

"They *what?*" Dask scanned the area.

"Matil," he and Nat called out. They shot each other a look.

"Khelya," Dask said, "what—"

"Some guy took her!" Khelya threw down her stick.

"*What?* You didn't try to stop him?"

She took a frustrated step toward Dask. "I couldn't get to 'im!"

"What did he look like?" Nat said.

"I dunno! He- he was kinda bulky for a Ranycht. That's all I could tell! There was stupid Skorgon buzzin' all over!"

"That might be Olsta's second-in-command. I saw him once, flying through here. That means Matil is probably at their camp. Which is in a tree, I'm afraid." He looked meaningfully at Khelya.

"You can't come with us, then," said Dask. "You did a really good job here, though."

"I let Matil get stolen."

"We all did."

Khelya shrugged despondently. She walked to the spot where the Ranycht had departed. Two daggers – Matil's borrowed weapons – lay in the dirt. She picked the little things up. They became partially concealed when she held them.

Wheels started turning in her brain. "Hey, hey, wait!"

Dask and Nat looked toward her.

She ran to the nearest tree and stabbed it with both daggers. She pulled one out with some strain, and then tried the other one. They would do. Whirling around, she pointed at Nat. "You! Do you have rope?"

"Yes…"

"And you, Dask, you have two knives?"

"You've finally gone insane, haven't you?" Dask said.

"I know a way to get up a tree," she sang. "Help me tie these daggers to my hands and feet, and get these bags off me."

"Will it work? You won't fall or anything?"

"Aw, lookit you worrying."

"I'm not worrying," he grumbled.

"Listen, it might not be perfect but it *will* work. I've done it before with my brothers. We're Obrigi. We make things work."

* * *

Trees and cold wind flew past Matil.

No, *she* was flying past *them*. She could feel her muscles working, the large wings flapping behind her, and her feathers whipping through the night air. Bugs whizzed by and bats chirped. A river rushed somewhere below. Every sense seemed sharper.

This was life.

Nestled in the branches of a nearby tree was a cluster of rough brown and black tents. Matil glided ahead eagerly. Could it be true? She told herself not to be so excited. These past few weeks had been a strange mixture of disappointment and victory, and she didn't like to get her hopes up only to have them dashed.

However, this time there was something different. Something faint pulling her forward.

She alighted on a branch.

* * *

Her eyes opened with a start.

All around her it was dark, but she could see, if a bit blearily. She was in some kind of tent. The walls were flimsy canvas draped around a frame of curving green sticks.

Matil groaned. She *really* didn't like being knocked unconscious.

Wait, where were Dask, Khelya, and Nat? Where was Crell? She tried to move, but her arms started tingling and she realized that she was tied to a chair close to the tent's back wall. And half of her body had fallen asleep.

Matil could hear breathing just outside the tent's entrance. Somebody walked up briskly with a thunk-thunk-thunk noise.

"Report," a woman said right outside the tent.

"We have retrieved her from two Ranycht who escaped our grasp," said a thin and choppy voice. That was probably a Skorgon. "She awaits you inside."

"Are you sure of it this time?"

"Completely."

That woman's voice…it was so familiar, but strange. It sounded like somebody she knew.

The woman paused. "I'll believe it when I see her with my own eyes."

It almost sounded like Matil. It sounded *very much* like her.

Oh, no. No.

Crell. The dream she just had. Her own voice.

"Of course, Lady Nychta," the Skorgon said.

Matil's stomach sank.

Footsteps thunked outside, moving toward the tent. A brown hand pulled aside the canvas in the entrance. As Olsta stepped in, Matil forced herself to look.

28

The Woman Who Shouldn't Be

Same hair, same skin, same face, same ears.

Nychta Olsta and Matil were the same.

The only differences between the two alva were Nychta's dark leather armor, sparrow-like brown wings on her back, and a pale film that lightened her purple irises and reminded Matil of frost.

Nychta blinked, startled, but quickly recovered and settled her expression into one of curiosity.

"Do you know who I am?" she said.

"…Nychta Olsta."

"Do you know who you are?"

Matil dropped her gaze.

"That's *right*." Nychta's voice held amusement. "You're Nychta Olsta, too."

"But how?" Matil cried, looking up. "How is that even possible? There can't be two of the same alva!"

"There can be and there are. Still, you're not whole." Nychta eyed Matil. "The Book said that you wouldn't have all this," she tapped the side of her head, "and that you might not have all your limbs either. You're lucky it wasn't something like your legs or arms, but…" Her wings opened slightly and she smiled unpleasantly. "You're missing something pretty important, I see. Too bad. I shouldn't be surprised that my lesser half is nothing better than a tiny Obrigi."

Matil felt a pang in her heart. "Why don't I have wings or my memory? Who am I?"

"It's not a question of who you are. It's *what* you are."

"Then what am I?"

"You're my weakness. The ropes that tether me to the ground. You're part of a ritual, nothing more."

"What?" Matil's breathing quickened with apprehension. The sound of a desperate incantation rose out of her memory, and then faded away. "Why? What kind of ritual?"

Nychta pulled out her dagger. "You exist because I didn't kill you when I should have." She stroked the blade. It was the same stiletto Matil had been carrying when she met Khelya and Dask.

"I don't understand, you're not explaining at all!"

"I don't need to explain. You'll be gone in a moment." Nychta looked at Matil with disdain. "The Book was right. I should've waited until it was safe to begin the spell. But here you are now. No time for regrets."

Nychta walked toward Matil, raising her dagger, then cocked her head thoughtfully.

Matil could feel the pull in the back of her mind growing stronger. It made her dizzy.

"Do you feel that?" Nychta said.

Matil groaned. "Yes."

"Interesting." Nychta reached out, and, as if she were touching something disgusting, poked Matil's head.

Suddenly, everything changed around them with a loud rushing noise, a sound like a waterfall. They stood in a black place, staring at each other, and then Matil was once again flying through the forest at night.

Branches flashed like lightning in front of her. Just as fast, she swerved and dodged them. She was exhausted; her wings felt like falling off.

A deep, icy voice echoed in her head. *Power. Revenge. The Sangriga will fall at your feet. Their blood will paint the forest red. I give you my strength.*

Desire and energy welled up in her. Justice at last.

She was standing, holding a book in her hands. It was warm and slimy, as if it had been bound in a living toad. A circular metal symbol was nailed to the cover. Crell was there, looking at it with dread in his eyes. Matil had misgivings. If Crell was afraid, shouldn't she be afraid?

No. He didn't understand what she had to do.

She forced down her repulsion and opened the book. Strange words in another language floated up and swallowed her whole and she was falling a very long way…

CONCENTRATE! the voice roared.

She snapped back into focus. Yes, *there* was the spell that needed to be cast. With her stiletto, she drew the symbol from the book's cover in the dirt. The Heart of Myrkhar. She stood in the inner circle of the Heart and read from the book.

"Hurach. Sliva." She doubled over and cried out. Pain tore through her entire body.

Continue.

"Lancruv," she choked out. She was burning alive, she was dying.

Continue!

"Hol, amysdir…ol!" Light was blossoming from the book. It seared her eyes. "Lancruv!"

"It's the thieves!"

She looked up with tears blurring her vision. Hateful Sangriga with blindingly bright wings flew toward her. Crell rose up to fight.

Finish it!

A Sangriga threw a bolt of light at her and she stumbled out of the way. She smeared the lines on the ground but it was too late to fix them.

"*Hurach!*"

It was as if the sun had exploded. The light blinded her. Water seemed to crash in her ears. The spell was incomplete, she needed to say the last word. What was it again? Couldn't see the Book…

The world slowly grew dim and quiet. She collapsed.

She was lying on her own bed. Panic gripped her and she sat up. Where was the Book?

Oh, it was on a nearby table. She relaxed. Her entire body ached.

Pursue your revenge however you see fit, but it will not be complete.

"Nychta, are you all right?" Crell was frowning. He looked pitifully worried.

He put a hand on her shoulder and she shook it off. She grabbed the Book and flipped it open. Every word was as clear and sharp as a thorn.

Not until you have summoned and harnessed the full power of Myrkhar and the Saikyr.

Power. Revenge.

She felt free. No doubts plagued her, no worry that she might not be doing the right thing.

But something twitched steadily in the back of her mind. She was not whole. The Book spoke harshly, assailing her with insults. The spell had been butchered.

Her double was loose in Eventyr. Who knew what it could do? She had to find it and kill it.

This is only the beginning.

The tent came back into view and Nychta jerked her hand away from Matil as if she had been bitten. She lifted her chin, sneering down at Matil.

"I don't know what you saw and I don't care," she said, "but what *I* saw was pathetic. You're not only so useless that I had to get rid of you, you're a helpless baby. Just as useless to your 'friends'. You can't do anything on your own. It would be funny if it weren't so sad."

Matil felt like the bottom had dropped out of her stomach. Useless? Helpless?

She was, wasn't she?

"Now that that's over with…" Nychta raised her dagger. "Sliva," she whispered. The cold blade sparked.

An arrow ripped through the canvas wall and speared Nychta's shoulder. She staggered back in shock. Then, tearing into the tent was a sword. It slid down to the floor, making a rip through which a tall Ranycht stepped.

"Nat!" Matil said, immensely relieved.

He seemed just as glad. "You're here! Thank Thosten." Looking over at Nychta, who had fallen to her knees, he swallowed. "Better make sure." He held his sword over her.

Matil averted her eyes, wincing at Nychta's feeble cry of pain. When Nat came over and began to slice away her bindings, she glimpsed Nychta on the floor, the arrow in her shoulder and a ragged hole in her leather jerkin. Her own stomach hurt just looking at it.

"So that's Nychta?" Nat said. He frowned. "She looks just like you. Do you know what's going on?"

"I…she's…Where are the others?" Matil focused on Nat's face. She felt that hysteria might overwhelm her if she even saw Nychta out of the corner of her eye.

"Making a distraction and looking for the Book." He brushed away the last of the bindings and helped Matil to her feet. "We're in a tree, and the Obrigi climbed up."

"How did she do that?"

"She…found a way."

"It must have been quite a way."

"It was. Obrigi aren't as bad as Mother always said. At least—*aagh!*" He cringed with pain and feebly moved his hand toward his chest. A rose-red spot bloomed on his tunic.

A wavering phantom behind Nat resolved itself into Nychta, gripping his shoulder as she appeared out of her fade. She lifted up her dagger, coated with blood – *Nat's blood* – and smiled triumphantly. Another stab and she let him crumple to the floor.

Matil couldn't move or speak. How was Nychta alive?

Nychta pointed the dagger at Matil and kicked her in the shin. "Back in the chair."

Whimpering half with pain and half with terror, Matil collapsed onto the chair.

Nychta narrowed her eyes. "You always have to get someone else to do things for you, don't you?" She chuckled. "You're wondering why I'm not dead, right? The Book explained it, but I didn't really believe until now. It's the simplest thing. When I performed the ritual, it also gave my mortality to you. Killing you will make *me* unkillable!"

"Matil," Nat gasped. "Run…"

"Shut up, you." Nychta shoved him with her foot.

Matil looked at him. He mustn't die. She couldn't let it happen again.

Again?

As she stared, a memory replaced him. And she knew the man in the memory. This must be a dream. A nightmare.

Sprawled face-down across the branch in Nat's place was a lean Ranycht, hair tied in a short tail. His back shook as he tried to breathe.

"Etsel!" Matil screamed. "Don't go, I won't survive!" Everything was a blur except for Etsel on the ground. Or was it Nat?

"What?" Nychta said sharply. "How do you know that name? Etsel's not here anymore, wretch." She followed Matil's desperate gaze to Nat. "Oh. You mean him." Nychta nearly turned away, but something caught her. The scornful look changed to something else. "It does make me think of…of Etsel. When he was—" Her eyes lost their brightness and even – little by little – darkened to their natural color. "When he…" Nychta dropped to her knees beside Nat. "Etsel, what did I do? How did I fail? *Stay alive!* I still need your help!"

Matil clutched the chair's seat as if it were driftwood and she were drowning. Her head was clearing, but everything still swam before her.

Nat watched her through half-lidded eyes. He mouthed the word again. *Run.*

Jarred to her senses, she jumped from the chair and bolted out through the rip Nat had made in the tent.

Stumbling across the thick branch, she yelled in a broken voice, "Dask! Khelya!" Her ears picked up the swish of wings behind her, and she dropped in time for Nychta to sail over.

Nychta landed and turned quickly, her eyes pale again. She stabbed with her dagger. Matil crawled backward to avoid it and sprang her feet hard into the other's stomach. Nychta gave Matil's leg a shallow slice right before the impact, then nearly dropped her weapon, winded, and clutched at her midsection.

Matil struggled to her feet. Her leg throbbed. "*Help!*"

Breathing hard, Nychta threw herself at Matil and stabbed again.

Matil caught her arm, the dagger two finger-lengths from her face. They kicked and shuffled and pushed, but the stiletto's cruel, bloody point hardly moved. Matil's mind had no room for anything but the dagger.

The metal glinted with an orange light, and they both looked for its source. On the next branch over, a tent was burning. Nychta's mouth opened with a small gasp. Her grip slackened for just a flicker.

Matil punched her in the jaw and the woman buckled with a sharp cry.

Instinct took over Matil's mind. She wrestled the dagger out of Nychta's hand, slammed the pommel on her skull, and shoved her off the branch. For a few heartbeats, Matil watched her fall through the leaves. She felt numb, breathless relief.

The sound of wingbeats made her spin around, ready to fight.

It was Dask. He had landed on the slope of the branch. "I can't believe you fought her off! If we're lucky, she won't wake up. Let's get to a lower branch and hide. Try to fade while we go."

At the sight of him, a lump grew in her throat and she didn't trust herself to speak. The stiletto slipped from her hand and off the branch without her noticing. She made a faltering step toward Dask. He grabbed her around the middle and dropped from the branch, flapping to slow the descent. Matil drew upon the deep night around them for her fade. The air rushed by, carrying the scent of smoke. An empty nest was wedged in the crook of a branch, and Matil thought she could feel the twisted presence that had driven away the birds.

With a grunt, Dask landed on a broad branch and shook out his arms. He faded. "What happened? Is Nat still over there?"

"Nat." It all came back to her. "Yes," she managed.

"Should we get him?"

"We can't."

"Can't?"

She shook her head, though he couldn't see her do it. "He won't m-make it out."

"You mean he's…dead?" Dask sucked in his breath. "I'm sorry. Two of us should've gone for you."

"You didn't know."

"Then maybe if I went instead, I'd have done better."

"No." Matil sniffed. "Ny-Nychta can't die. Nat killed her, but she- she got back up and…"

"Nat didn't kill her, then. A corpse doesn't get up and repay the favor."

"I saw it, Dask."

"…If you're right, that's really, really bad. Let's get outta here fast." He cupped his hands around his mouth. "Khelya! *Khelya!*"

Above and around them on almost every branch, tents were going up in flames. Skorgon threw themselves on the fires in attempts to smother them, only succeeding in joining the tents with a whoosh, pop, and crackle. Matil took an involuntary step backward, even though they were far from the nearest tent.

The fire flickered mischievously as if inviting her to dance while holding a knife behind its back. Cold sweat broke out all over her skin and her heart felt like it was about to burst. Everything was turning…gray…

Why couldn't she feel her legs…?

"Oof! Matil, what's wrong?"

She blinked spots from her eyes. Now she was lying down. "Did I faint?"

"Yeah." He searched her face worriedly.

"Sorry." She fought her rubbery arms and sat up. "The fire…"

Dask chewed on his little finger's nail. "I don't like it either. It was the best we could do, though. Where *is* Khelya?"

"Don't do that, you idiots, we need water!" Nychta's voice drifted over to them. "Crell, get over here!"

"That's her? She sounds like she could be your sister." Dask's brow furrowed. "Did she just say Crell?"

Matil gripped her tunic in her fists. *Don't think about it.*

The branch thunked hollowly. She looked up to see Khelya's tenuous silhouette.

"I'm here," Khelya said.

"Take Matil and get to the ground. You need to carry her on your back or something. If anyone comes after us, I'll distract them."

"Thank Thosten, you're okay! You're okay, right?"

Matil gave a weak shrug.

"I see." She knelt down. "Climb on my back and hold on."

Matil climbed up and put her arms around Khelya's neck.

Khelya stood. "Where did that other fella go?"

"Nychta got him," Dask said. "He's gone."

She was very still. "Thosten save him."

"Didn't you hear me? He's dead. Gone."

"My telvogir told me that no one's ever gone."

"Then he lied to you. Go!" Dask zipped away in a swish of air.

Khelya made a frustrated noise. "You ready?"

"Yes." Matil swallowed. No one is ever gone? What did Khelya mean? And how was she going to get down the tree? If Matil had wings, she could do it herself and not burden her friend.

Burden.

Nychta was right.

Khelya ran down the branch to the trunk.

Whick. Whock. Whick. Whick.

It was as if she were hitting and kicking the tree. Matil squinted. Khelya somehow stuck her hands and feet to the tree's bark. Alternating, she yanked them out and put them back in. She was using daggers to hold herself up! They crawled like that around the tree and then went down.

Whock. Whick. Whick. Whick.

Though her arms were already getting tired and Khelya was constantly jolting from pulling the daggers out, Matil did her best to hold on. Nat's face stayed at the front of her mind. Over and over again he told her to run. She tried fading, but it was difficult to concentrate.

"*Aharjen!*"

Something crashed through the branches high above Matil. The smell of singed feathers wafted into her face.

"Talrach, she's definitely got the Book!" Dask cried. He flapped around them and went back up.

Confused sounds rang out from the tree. Nychta's shouts overrode them all, but Mail couldn't make out what she was saying. Skorgon buzzed all over the camp. Thankfully, Khelya had gotten low enough that they didn't notice Matil appearing to float down the side of the tree.

"Over here!" Dask yelled. "Now I'm over here! Come on, come get me!"

"Aharjen!"

A crash and a sizzle.

"*Ahahaha!* You missed!"

"Tell me where she is or I'll kill you!"

"No thanks!"

"*Aharjen! Aharjen!* Ahar…"

"Nychta!" Crell shouted.

What was going on? Was Dask still there? Matil couldn't hear his voice anymore.

At last Khelya pulled herself from the tree and stepped down.

Matil jumped in surprise as Dask barreled past them and slid across the ground. "Dask! Are you all right?" If he were dead, too…

To her relief, he sat up. "I'm great." He winced and held his arm. "Another burn for my collection. Did you *see* those fireballs she was throwing?" He hopped to his feet. "I think she collapsed, so now would be a good time to scram."

"Wait," Matil said. "Remember how we thought I was sensing the Book? It's Nychta that I sensed. She can sense me, too, but it's not as strong. It could still be enough for her to track us down."

Dask watched Matil sharply. "She kinda looks like you, if you had wings. What happened up there?"

Matil squeezed her eyes shut, then opened them. "I'll tell you later, when we're safe."

"Okay. Let's run…that way to start with. It should misdirect them. Khelya, can you carry Matil? We'll be able to go faster if I'm flying and you're running."

Khelya took off the climbing daggers, sheathed them, and handed them to Dask. "Yeah. Come on up."

Matil's ears drooped and she let Khelya lift her up.

As the Obrigi ran, Dask disappeared into the forest.

283

29

The Burden of Truth

Khelya jogged tirelessly, switching directions when Dask flew down and told her where to go. She stumbled and tripped but never fell. Sometimes they heard buzzing and they stopped to hide. The noise always moved on.

With relief, Matil felt the pull gradually lessen. She wanted to be far away from Nychta's presence. This whole night confused her, made her feel like sleeping forever. Had the mission been a success or a failure? She knew who she was, but…where was her family and where was Arla? Why had Nychta and Crell been so ruthless?

What changed them?

Dawn's light softened the forest's darkness, and Matil closed her eyes. She couldn't feel the pull any longer. Without it there, she questioned the reality of the night's events. What if they were on their way to Goska now for the first time? Nat and Brenna could have been imagined.

Matil might not be *Nychta*. It was all a dream. It had to be. It just couldn't be real. It wasn't fair.

Unbidden, the name Myrkhar sprang to mind. It was his Book that whispered to Nychta and gave her power. It needed to be destroyed. Matil couldn't imagine why it hadn't been before.

"Matil," came Dask's breathless voice. "Do you still sense Nychta?"

She opened her eyes. "No."

"Good. We should stop for a rest and find out where we are later this morning."

A quick search revealed a sheltered area between the twisting roots of a tree. Khelya immediately set Matil down and flopped onto the ground. She combed through the dirt with her ghostly fingers to make it softer. "Ooooh, I could just about sleep like a bear right now."

Matil found her own spot in the very corner; not too far from her friends, but not too close. "You ran all that way. And Dask *flew* all that way."

"Yeah," Dask groaned. "I won't be flying that much for a long time." He lay down face first and let his wings fall at his sides.

Matil glowered at the dirt around her feet. "Thanks. For saving me. For risking your lives. For everything."

"Don't mention it," Dask said.

"Mm." Khelya looked up from her blank staring. "You're welcome. Thank Thosten we got away together."

There was something Matil needed to know. "Khelya?"

"Yes?"

"If Nat's not gone, where is he?"

"Hopefully in Betha. Home."

"Home? But he's- he's dead. How can he be home, too?"

"It's kinda like…well, Betha is our *home* home. The one we always have. When we die, if we've done good, it's where our spirit goes. To be with Thosten in Betha."

"Stop," Dask said. "You'll ruin her. Don't give her hope that doesn't exist. It's not right. Matil…" He looked at her almost pleadingly. "Nat is dead. Just dead. It'll be the same way when we're dead. This is the only 'home' that there is, so we do the best we can, right? We make the most of it."

Khelya scowled. "You sound like my brothers."

"They must be smart Obrigi, then!"

"I don't know what happens," Matil said with a touch of grumpiness, and then she sighed and spoke more gently, "but I like the sound of going home when it's all over."

Dask rolled onto his side and curled up. "Good luck with that."

"She *will* have good luck with it." A loud intake of breath indicated another yawn from Khelya. "I'll teach 'er…what my…" she laid an arm across her eyes, "telvogir…taught…" A snore rose from her.

Maybe sleeping was a good idea. Now that Matil was thinking of it, her eyes and body felt heavy, as if the earth itself were calling to them. Wait. Shouldn't they set a watch?

Too late. Matil was already in the land between lands where sense was nonsense.

* * *

Matil could hear someone flying behind her. Too close. Too close. If she didn't go faster, Nychta would catch her.

She went on until her breath wore ragged and her lungs couldn't get enough air. Still the wings flapped. This was too much. Matil wouldn't make it. It was time to stop. She sank to the cold forest floor.

At the same time, her pursuer fell silent.

Matil waited for the final blow. Mist floated around her as she sat and caught her breath. Finally, she couldn't stand it any longer. She slowly turned her head.

Brown feathers filled her vision.

Wings.

Nychta's wings. But here they were, on Matil's back.

Or was it Nychta's back?

Panic rose in Matil's chest and she breathed faster and faster. She tried to scream – needed to scream – but only a small, hoarse noise made it out of her parched throat. The mist caged her in and drifted closer. Couldn't scream, couldn't see, Nychta, Nychta, she was—

"My olrin, what's wrong?"

Air filled Matil's lungs. She breathed deeply, refreshingly. "I'm having a nightmare, Mother."

"Tsk, we can't have that. Come here."

Arms lifted Matil into a lap and she realized that she was a child again, taking comfort in the baking-bread smell that always surrounded Mother. Her thin voice sniffed and whimpered.

"Hush, hush." Mother kissed her forehead and brushed away her tears. "It was just a dream." She began to sing softly.

"Do you hear the day-bell? Loo-ai, loo-el.
Still all your quickness and turmoil quell.

"Where did your dreams stray? Loo-lai, too-ro-lay.
You journeyed so long, they were lost on the way.

"Sweet rest to pursue, ai-loo, ah-loo.
I found some good dreams and I'll give them to you.

"Till moon shines again, lor-el, ah-loo-en,
sleep long, my little love, sleep sweet until then."

* * *

At first, Matil didn't know what woke her. Then she felt it again. An itch? Or a tug? Something like that. What did it mean? She rubbed her eyes and froze as she came to a realization.

"Dask, Khelya," she said in a low voice. "*Dask. Khelya.*"

"Mm?" Dask asked.

"They're looking for us."

"Looking...?" Dask's eyes drifted open. "Looking for us."

"Yes."

In a mighty shuffle of wings and limbs, he jumped up and promptly groaned. "Rach, my wings are sore."

Matil found Khelya's still, transparent form and shook her, though it didn't have an effect. She looked up. Weak golden light found its way through the leaves. Still day, then. "Khelya, come on, we have to go!"

"Lemme sleep…"

"Allow me," Dask said.

For once Matil didn't complain, though she winced as he enthusiastically kicked Khelya's arm.

"Ow!" Khelya shoved Dask away and sat up. "Listen here, bird-wing, I do *not* need to be woken up that way."

"In this case, I think you did. Matil?"

"Sorry about that," Matil said. "I sense Nychta, and it might not be long until she senses me. We have to leave."

Her ears twitched and her heart skipped a beat as a buzzing noise pierced through the echoing sounds of the forest.

She and Dask shrank back into the shadows, fading quickly.

Khelya frowned. "What's wrong?"

Dask pulled Khelya back with them.

Two Skorgon streaked past and Matil felt Khelya jump with surprise. The Skorgon were soon gone.

"That was too close," Dask said uneasily. "When we sleep again, we'll need to keep watch."

"Where to?" Khelya said.

They both looked at Matil. She bit her lip. "We should go back to Goska and…and let Brenna know what happened."

"Only if we're quick. Leaving Valdingfal seems like the best thing to do." Dask narrowed his eyes. "What *did* happen?"

Matil's mouth hung open as she tried to think of what to say. "I'll tell you later." She would. When she was ready.

He looked dubious. "Okay."

Soon, they were creeping, faded, through the brush. The pull haunted Matil, tugging at the very edge of her senses. She hoped its faintness meant Nychta couldn't sense her.

They heard the telltale buzzing a few more times. Skorgon or just bugs?

A village appeared among the trees and Dask, pleased, flew over to the village square. He returned with directions from someone who was awake. Goska was to the south.

After a while of tense traveling, Dask directed them to a bush where Khelya could hide.

"So you're meeting his ma?" Khelya said.

"Yes," Matil said softly.

"Hold on. Can I have a knife?"

Dask fidgeted. "We have to go, Khelya."

"Please. I'm serious."

"Fine." He gave her a dagger.

Immediately, she used it to cut out a flattish chunk of the bush's branch, and then carved something into the chunk. "His name was Nat?"

"That wasn't his real name."

"Oh. Tell his ma to write his real name down on this." She handed the dagger to Dask and held the chunk out to Matil.

Matil took it and turned it around to read the characters Khelya had written. She didn't know the word. "What is it?"

"It's a labeta. We Obrigi make them to respect those we've lost. Each one says 'Labet'. 'The day's work has been done well,' it means. I thought I might…make one for our hero. Would you please give it to his ma?"

"I will."

They left Khelya behind. The forest had darkened into night and the hoot of an owl made Matil jump. She had the sudden urge to flee. To flee everything. It wouldn't matter which way she ran.

Somehow she kept herself moving forward.

Her ears pricked up at the sound of laughing and shouting. Up around the houses, children flew and passed a leather ball to each other. Matil stopped. They would notice her. She faded away instinctively.

"Matil? Where did you—right. No wings." Dask's gaze searched. "You're still here?"

"Yes." She must seem pretty skittish for him to ask that.

"I'll get Brenna. And don't worry. Things'll be okay."

"Thanks."

He stayed for a moment longer, looking as if he wanted to say more, and then took off.

Things wouldn't be okay. Not for Nat, not for Brenna, not for Matil or Khelya or even Dask. And, remembering the terrible voice in her vision, Matil realized that things might not be okay for anyone in Eventyr.

…it will not be complete. Not until you have summoned the full power of Myrkhar…

This was Nychta's doing, and Matil was Nychta.

It was Matil's fault.

Dask and Brenna landed in front of her. Reluctantly, she stepped away from the tree, becoming visible as she did so.

Brenna's eyes snapped around. Her hand went to her throat. "Where's Nat?"

Dask went to stand next to Matil. "He didn't make it," he said quietly.

"I'm so sorry." Matil blinked back tears. "Nychta has the Book. Nat saved my life and killed Nychta. But she got back up and killed him and she's not dead and I-I-I'm...sorry." She avoided meeting Brenna's eyes.

Brenna's lined face was frozen with shock. "No. You're lying. *You're lying.*" She leaned heavily on the tree, then sank to the ground and shook her head over and over again. "He wasn't supposed to leave," she cried. "He wasn't supposed to leave me alone."

"Ma'am," Dask said, "uh...sometimes alva leave you alone. You just have to...keep living and be with others."

"You don't understand. He was everything."

"I do understand, Ma'am." He knelt down. From his pockets and belt he produced the four borrowed daggers. "These are yours."

Brenna frowned at the daggers, took them, and put them aside. "How could you understand?"

"The same way I ended up an orphan in the city."

Brenna's eyebrows lifted over her tearful eyes.

"Just, um, remember him," Dask said. "And keep living."

Recalling the labeta in her hands, Matil sat. "Our Obrigi friend made this to honor Nat." She laid it on the ground in front of Brenna.

Dask nodded. "It means that he did good work. If you want, you can write his name on it."

Brenna watched it like it was a wasp about to sting. A long moment passed before she moved, cautiously gripping the labeta's sides. She ran a thumb over one of the hastily-carved characters and began to speak in a low, weary voice. "Olsta has the Book and she killed my son. Stal's claws, he was right. She must be fought. You'll do that, won't you? You'll fight?"

Dask twitched and looked to Matil.

The question made something strong grow in her heart. "Of course," she said.

"Good." Brenna's voice wavered.

Dask glanced behind them. "Olsta will be searching for us."

"Go, then."

Matil and Dask stood up, unsure.

"Go."

Matil bowed her head to Brenna and thought about Nat being home. "Colthal."

"Colthal," Dask said.

"Thosten fly with you." Brenna looked back down at the labeta. In the blank space above the word, she traced something out with her finger. "His real name was Amacht."

* * *

Matil, Dask, and Khelya were together again, traveling furtively to the west. The presence, Nychta's presence, seemed to hang on Matil's shoulders like a haunting spirit.

"My stomach is asking for a feast."

Matil jumped at Khelya's voice and tried to calm down.

"We can't stop, Matil still senses Olsta," Dask said.

"I know, but I keep thinkin' about juicy roast quail and pear tarts. Or treacle cookies. Or bread pudding full of figs!"

"That's not helping."

"No," Khelya said longingly. "It's not."

Matil herself was yearning for the good food she had eaten in Goska. Khelya's bags were gone, discarded when they went to rescue Matil, so they didn't have anything on hand to eat.

Dask looked at Matil. "Are you going to tell us what happened with Olsta before we got there?"

Surprised, she stumbled with a squeak over a small root that poked out of the ground. "What? I mean, um, we should probably wait until it's a good time, right?"

"Now's a good time."

"Yeah, I wouldn't mind." Khelya bent lower as she walked so that she could hear better.

Matil paused. "I don't want to."

"Why not?"

"You wouldn't want to stay with me anymore."

"Slug spit. We'll stick with you no matter what. Just tell us."

"We just need to know what we've gotten into, Matil. Why can you and Olsta sense each other?"

Matil rubbed her arm. "Nychta and I have a connection."

"Connection?" Dask prodded.

"Something happened and…we could see each other's memories. I saw what happened on the night the Book was stolen. The Book was talking to Nychta."

Both of them stared at her.

Matil continued unsteadily. "It told her something about summoning Myrkhar and the Saikyr."

"The Book was talking and you could see Olsta's memories," Dask said. "Matil, are you all right? Maybe you didn't get enough sleep."

"Shut up, Dask," Khelya said. "Nychta wants to wake up the Saikyr. This is serious."

"The Saikyr aren't real."

"Now isn't the time to disbelieve!"

"Now is the perfect time to disbelieve! If we take this stuff seriously, we're going to end up panicking and thinking the world's going to end!"

"The world might not end *but our lives will—*"

"The Book created me," Matil said.

Khelya and Dask slowly turned back to her.

"I…am…" She gritted her teeth. "I'm Nychta."

"What're you talkin' about?" Khelya said. "You've been traveling with us this whole time and she's been in this part of the forest. You can't be her."

Dask didn't say anything.

"She used a spell from the Book to separate herself," Matil said in a quiet voice. "I'm the part of Nychta she didn't want. It's why I don't have wings or memories."

"Oh, Matil," Khelya said sadly.

"I think that whatever else the Book does will be dangerous and powerful. And we can't do anything about it."

Everyone settled into a gloomy trudge. The quiet of the dark forest fell over them for only a short time before it was broken.

"The Heilar," Khelya said, sounding excited. "The Heilar can do something about it."

"Haha, right, of course, the stories and legends will save the day." Dask flapped his wings dismissively. "Even if they exist, they're all 'asleep' or whatever."

"All except one."

Matil looked up quickly. "Mr. Korsen?"

"Yep. What do you say we pay him a visit?"

Dask grumbled under his breath but didn't say anything.

"Do we have to go back to Obrigi to find him?" Matil said.

"I've heard he lives next to Eventyr. Northwest of Fainfal, deep in the wilds and beyond the Wall."

There *was* a way to fight Nychta. "I'll go. What about you, Dask?" She twisted her fingers together. "I understand if you don't want to."

"I'm going with you. Despite the fact that it's a fool's errand. And despite the Eletsol. You'll need more than just Khelya on your side."

"What are the Eletsol?"

Khelya made a face. "Crazy alva with a flower obsession."

"Heh, yeah." Dask smirked.

Matil looked between them. "Are they dangerous?"

"Shouldn't be. Well…let's hope not, anyway."

A thought struck her. She took a moment to search her mind for Nychta's pull, and then relaxed, grinning at what she discovered. "It's gone, I don't sense it anymore. We've lost her. She's gone."

The story will continue in

Elders of Eventyr

About the Author

Ellias Quinn is an American storyteller. In her childhood amidst the rain and the woods, she stumbled into Eventyr's border – bruising her head in the process – and through the years has had the great fortune to learn from the bantam residents about its history and cultures. Now, she is humbled by the privilege of relating certain great events from Eventyr's past for the benefit of humankind.

Ellias's favorite time of year are the days just out of Vana, when the sun shines warmly through the cold air, as Thrual creeps in and paints the leaves. On those days she enjoys sitting down with her family to a meal of thick squirrel steaks broiled in the Obrigi tradition.